Barbara Taylor Bradford was born in Leeds, Yorkshire, and by the age of twenty was an editor and columnist on Fleet Street. In 1979, her first novel, *A Woman of Substance*, was published. That enduring bestseller was followed by fourteen others, most recently *A Sudden Change of Heart*. Her novels have sold more than sixty million copies worldwide. She lives in New York City with her husband, film producer Robert Bradford.

By the same author

A WOMAN OF SUBSTANCE
VOICE OF THE HEART
HOLD THE DREAM
ACT OF WILL
TO BE THE BEST
THE WOMEN IN HIS LIFE
REMEMBER
ANGEL
EVERYTHING TO GAIN
DANGEROUS TO KNOW
HER OWN RULES
POWER OF A WOMAN
A SUDDEN CHANGE OF HEART
WHERE YOU BELONG

A Secret Affair

Love in Another Town

BARBARA TAYLOR BRADFORD

HarperCollins*Publishers*

HarperCollins*Publishers*
77–85 Fulham Palace Road,
Hammersmith, London W6 8JB

www.**fire**and**water**.com

This paperback edition 2000
1 3 5 7 9 8 6 4 2

A Secret Affair previously published in paperback by
HarperCollins*Publishers* 1997
Reprinted once
Love in Another Town previously published in paperback by
HarperCollins*Publishers* 1996
Reprinted eleven times
Special overseas edition 1996

A Secret Affair first published in Great Britain by
HarperCollins*Publishers* 1996
Love in Another Town first published in Great Britain by
HarperCollins*Publishers* 1995

ISBN 0 00 651484 7

Set in Postscript Linotype Palatino by
Rowland Phototypesetting Ltd,
Bury St Edmunds, Suffolk

Printed and bound in Great Britain by
Clays Ltd, St Ives plc

A Secret Affair

As always, for Bob,
with all my love

CHAPTER 1

Sarajevo, August 1995

HE WAS CLOSING the small padlock on his duffle bag when a deafening explosion brought his head up swiftly. He listened acutely, with accustomed practice, fully expecting to hear another bomb exploding. But there was nothing. Only silence.

Bill Fitzgerald, chief foreign correspondent for CNS, the American cable news network, put on his flak jacket and rushed out of the room.

Tearing down the stairs and into the large atrium, he crossed it and left the Holiday Inn through a back door. The front entrance, which faced Sniper Alley, as it was called, had not been used since the beginning of the war. It was too dangerous.

Glancing up, Bill's eyes scanned the sky. It was a soft, cerulean blue, filled with recumbent white clouds but otherwise empty. There were no warplanes in sight.

An armoured Land Rover came barrelling down the street where he was standing and skidded to a stop next to him.

The driver was a British journalist, Geoffrey Jackson, an old friend, who worked for the *Daily Mail*. 'The explosion came from over there,' Geoffrey said. 'That direction.' He gestured ahead, and asked, 'Want a lift?'

'Sure do, thanks, Geoff,' Bill replied and hopped into the Land Rover.

As they raced along the street, Bill wondered what had caused the explosion, then said aloud to Geoffrey, 'It was more than likely a bomb lobbed into Sarajevo by the Serbs in the hills, don't you think?'

'Absolutely,' Geoffrey agreed. 'They're well entrenched up there, and let's face it, they never stop attacking the city. The way they are sniping at civilians is getting to me. *I* don't want to die from a stray rifle shot covering this bloody war.'

'Me neither.'

'Where's your crew?' Geoffrey asked as he drove on, peering through the windscreen intently, looking for signs of trouble, praying to avoid it.

'They went out earlier, to reconnoitre, while I was packing my bags. We're supposed to leave Sarajevo today. For a week's relaxation and rest in Italy.'

'Lucky sods!' Geoffrey laughed. 'Can I carry your bags?'

Bill laughed with him. 'Sure, come with us, why don't you?'

'If only, mate, if only.'

A few minutes later Geoffrey was pulling up near an open marketplace. 'This is where the damn thing fell,' the British journalist said, his jolly face suddenly turning grim. 'Bleeding Serbs, won't they ever stop killing Bosnian civilians? They're fucking gangsters, that's all they are.'

'You know. I know. Every journalist in the Balkans knows. But does the Western alliance know?'

'Bunch of idiots, if you ask me,' Geoffrey answered and parked the Land Rover. He and Bill jumped out.

'Thanks for the ride,' Bill said. 'See you later. I've got to find my crew.'

'Yeah. See you, Bill.' Geoffrey disappeared into the melee.

Bill followed him.

Chaos reigned.

Women and children were running amok; fires burned everywhere. He was assaulted by a cacophony of sounds . . . loud rumblings as several buildings disintegrated into piles of rubble; the screams of terrified women and children; the moans of the wounded and the dying; the keening of mothers hunched over their children, who lay dead in the marketplace.

Bill clambered over the half-demolished wall of a house and jumped down into another area of the marketplace. Glancing around, his heart tightened at the human carnage. It was horrific.

He had covered the war in the Balkans for a long time, on and off for almost three years now; it was brutal, a savage war, and still he did not understand why America turned the other cheek, behaved as if it were not happening. That was something quite incomprehensible to him.

A cold chill swept through him, and his step faltered for a moment as he walked past a young woman sobbing and cradling her lifeless child in her arms, the child's blood spilling onto the dark earth.

He closed his eyes for a split second, steadied himself before walking on. He was a foreign correspondent *and* a war correspondent, and it was his job to bring the news to the people. He could not permit emotion to get in the way of his reporting or his judgement; he could never become involved with the events he was covering. He had to be impartial. But sometimes, goddamnit, he couldn't help getting involved. It got to him occasionally . . . the pain, the human suffering. And it was always the innocent who were the most hurt.

As he moved around the perimeter of the marketplace, his eyes took in everything . . . the burning buildings, the destruction, the weary, defeated people, the wounded. He shuddered, then coughed. The air was foul, filled with thick black smoke, the smell of burning rubber, the stench of death. He drew to a halt, and his eyes swept the area yet again, looking for his crew. He was certain they had heard the explosion and were now here. They had to be somewhere in the crowd.

Finally, he spotted them.

His cameraman, Mike Williams, and Joe Alonzo, his soundman, were right in the thick of it, feverishly filming, along with other television crews and photographers who must have arrived on the scene immediately.

Running over to join the CNS crew, Bill shouted above the din, 'What the hell happened here? Another bomb?'

'A mortar shell,' Joe answered, swinging his eyes

to meet Bill's. 'There's must be twenty or thirty dead.'

'Probably more,' Mike added without turning, zooming his lens towards two dazed-looking young children covered in blood and clinging to each other in terror. 'The marketplace was real busy . . .' Mike stopped the camera, grimaced as he looked over at Bill. 'A lot of women and children were here. They got caught. This is a real pisser.'

'Oh, Jesus,' Bill said.

Joe said, 'The mortar shell made one helluva crater.'

Bill looked over at it, and said softly, in a hard voice, 'The Serbs had to know the marketplace would be busy. This is an atrocity.'

'Yes. Another one,' Mike remarked dryly. 'But we've come to expect that, haven't we?'

Bill nodded, and he and Mike exchanged knowing looks.

'Wholesale slaughter of civilians –' Bill began and stopped abruptly, biting his lip. Mike and Joe had heard it all before, so why bother to repeat himself? Still, he knew he would do so later, when he did his telecast to the States. He wouldn't be able to stop himself.

There was a sudden flurry of additional activity at the far side of the marketplace. Ambulances were driving into the area, followed by armoured personnel carriers manned by UN troops, and several official UN cars, all trying to find places to park.

'Here they come, better late than never,' Joe muttered in an acerbic tone. 'There's not much they can do. Except cart off the wounded. Bury the dead.'

Bill made no response. His brain was whirling,

words and phrases racing through his head as he prepared his story in his mind. He wanted his telecast to be graphic, moving, vivid and hard-hitting.

'I guess we're not going to get our R & R after all,' Mike said, a brow lifting. 'We won't be leaving today, will we, Bill?'

Bill roused himself from his concentration. 'No, we can't leave, Mike. We have to cover the aftermath of this, and there's bound to be one . . . of some kind. If Clinton and the other Western leaders don't do something drastic, something especially meaningful, there's bound to be a public outcry.'

'So be it,' Mike said. 'We stay.'

'They'll do nothing,' Joe grumbled. 'They've all been derelict in their duty. They've let the Serbs get away with murder, and right from the beginning.'

Bill nodded in agreement. Joe was only voicing what every journalist and television newsman in Bosnia knew only too well. Turning to Mike, he asked, 'How much footage do we have so far?'

'A lot. Joe and I were practically the first in the marketplace, seconds after the mortar shell went off. We were in the jeep, just around the corner when it happened. I started filming at once. It's pretty bloody, gory stuff, Bill.'

'*Gruesome*,' Joe added emphatically.

Bill said, 'It must be shown.' Then, looking at Mike, he went on quickly, 'I'd like you to find a place where we can film my spot, if possible one that's highly dramatic.'

'You got it, Bill. When do you want to start rolling the tape?'

'In about ten minutes. I'm going to go over there

first, talk to some of those UN people clustered near the ambulances, see what else I can find out.'

'Okay, and I'll do a rekky, look for a good spot,' Mike assured him.

William Patrick Fitzgerald was a renowned newsman, the undoubted star at Cable News Systems, noted for his measured, accurate, but hard-hitting reports from the world's battlefields and troublespots.

His fair colouring and clean-cut, boyish good looks belied his thirty-three years, and his tough demeanour stood him in great stead in front of the television camera.

He had earnest blue eyes and a warm smile that bespoke his sincerity, and integrity was implicit in his nature. These qualities underscored his genuine believability, were part of his huge success on television. Because he had this enormous credibility, people trusted him, had confidence in him. They paid attention to his words, listened to everything he had to say, and took him very seriously.

It was not for nothing that CNS treasured him and other networks coveted him. Offers for his services were always being made to his agent; Bill turned them all down. He was not interested in other networks. Loyalty was another one of his strong suits, and he had no desire to leave CNS, where he had worked for eight years.

Some time later he stood in front of the grim backdrop of burning houses in the marketplace, and his sincerity seemed more pronounced than ever. He spoke sombre words in a well-modulated voice, as always following the old journalistic rule of thumb:

Who, when, where, what, and *how,* which had been taught to him by his father, a respected newspaperman until his death five years ago.

'Thirty-seven civilians were killed and many others wounded today when a mortar shell exploded in a busy marketplace in Sarajevo,' Bill began. 'The mortar was fired by the Serbian army entrenched in the hills surrounding this battle-torn city. It was an obscene act of aggression against innocent, unarmed people, many of them women and children. UN forces, who quickly arrived on the scene immediately after the bombing, are calling it an atrocity, one that cannot be overlooked by President Clinton and the leaders of the Western alliance. UN officials are already saying that the Serbs must be forced to understand that these acts of extreme violence are unwarranted, unconscionable, and unacceptable. One UN official pointed out that the Serbs are endangering the peace talks.'

After giving further details of the bombing, and doing a short commentary to run with the footage of the carnage, Bill brought his daily news report to a close.

Stepping away from the camera after his ten minutes were up, he waited until the equipment was turned off. Then he glanced from Mike to Joe and said quietly, 'What I couldn't say was that that UN major I was talking to earlier says there *has* to be some sort of retaliation, intervention by the West. He says it's inevitable now. Public anger is growing.'

Joe and Mike stared at Bill doubtfully.

It was Joe who spoke, sounding entirely unconvinced.

'I've heard that before,' he said and shook his head

sadly. 'I guess this disgusting war has turned me into a cynic, Billy boy. Nothing's going to happen, you'll see . . . it'll be status quo . . .'

But as it turned out, Joe Alonzo was wrong. The leaders of the Western alliance in Washington, London, and Paris had no choice but to take serious steps to stop the Serbs in their systematic slaughter of Bosnian civilians, or risk being the focus of public outrage and anger in their own countries.

Just two days after the mortar shell exploded in the marketplace, the alliance sent in NATO warplanes to attack the Serbian army in the hills of Sarajevo.

It was August 30, 1995. The bombing began in earnest that day, and it was the biggest attack of the war. There were more than 3,500 sorties in the short space of two weeks, and even Tomahawk Cruise missiles were launched in the assault.

At the end of three weeks, the Serbians had begun to back down, withdrawing their heavy weaponry from the Sarajevo hills at the edge of the city, and making sounds about peace negotiations.

Because of the NATO attack and later developments, Bill Fitzgerald and the CNS crew remained in Bosnia, their week of rest and relaxation in Italy postponed indefinitely.

'But we don't really care, do we?' Bill said one evening when the three of them sat at a large table in the communal dining room of the Holiday Inn.

'No, of course we don't,' Mike answered. 'I mean, who cares about missing a week in Amalfi, relaxing with a couple of beautiful girls. Nobody would *mind* missing that, certainly not I. Or Joe.' He shrugged.

'After all, who gives a damn about sun, sea, and sex. And wonderful pasta.'

Bill chuckled.

So did Joe, who said, 'Me, for one. I give a damn.' He grinned at the cameraman, who was his best buddy, then addressed Bill quietly. 'I was certainly looking forward to our trip. And you were fixated about Venice, Bill, come on, admit it.'

'Yes, it's true, I was. And I plan to make it to Venice soon. Maybe in the next month or two.'

It was late September and relatively quiet out on the streets of Sarajevo; the fighting was less intense, with only sporadic sniping and fewer forays into the city on the part of the bloodthirsty Serbs. The entire foreign press corps were fully aware that the intense NATO retaliation had worked far better in curbing the Serbs than the words of appeasement the West had been uttering thus far.

Bill said, 'I think things *are* going to ease up here, and very soon.'

From their expressions, Mike and Joe were obviously disbelieving, and they did not respond.

Looking at his colleagues intently, Bill added, 'With a little luck, this war should end soon.'

Joe, ever the cynic, ever the pessimist, shot back, 'Want to bet?'

'No, I don't,' Bill replied swiftly. 'You can never really tell what's going to happen with the Serbs. They talk out of both sides of their mouths.'

'And shoot from the hip with both hands. Always fast on the draw, the fucking maniacs,' Joe exclaimed. 'They started this war and they're only going to end it when it suits them. When they get what they want.'

'Which is most of Bosnia, if not, indeed, all of it,' Bill said. 'This war's always been about territorial greed, as well as power, racial bigotry and ethnic cleansing.'

'Greed, power, and hatred, a pretty potent combination,' Mike murmured.

The cameraman glanced at his plate of food, his expression glum. He grimaced and put down his fork; his nose curled in distaste. 'The soup was watery and tasteless, now this meat is greasy and tasteless. Jeez, this damn curfew has been getting to me more than ever lately. I hate having to eat here every night. I wish we could find somewhere else.'

'There's nowhere else to eat in Sarajevo, nowhere that's any better, and you know we can't go out at night anyway,' Bill reminded him. 'Besides, it's difficult driving without any streetlights.' Bill stopped, sat back in his chair, suddenly feeling worried about Mike and Joe. They rarely complained about anything; lately they had done nothing but complain to him. He couldn't say he blamed them. Living conditions in Bosnia never improved, only got worse. He thought of the line he had heard when he first came to the Balkans at the outset of the conflict. It had been told to him by a reporter from a French news magazine and he had never forgotten it: *A day in Bosnia is like a week anywhere else; a week is like a month, a month is like a year*. And it was true. The country was wearing and wearying. It killed the soul, drained the spirit, and damaged the psyche. He was itching to get out himself, just as Mike and Joe were.

'It's not much of a menu, I'll grant you that,' Joe suddenly said, and laughed hollowly. 'It's always the same crummy food every night, that's the problem.'

'Most people are starving in Bosnia,' Bill began and decided not to continue along these lines.

All of a sudden Mike sat up straighter and announced, 'Personally, I aim to be in the good old US of A in November, come hell or high water. I plan to be out on Long Island for Thanksgiving if it's the last thing I ever do. I want to be with my mom and dad, my kid brother and sister. It's been too long since I've seen them. I'm certainly not going to be in this godforsaken place, that's for sure.'

'I know what you mean, old buddy,' Joe said. 'Me . . . I'd like to be in New Jersey for *my* turkey dinner. With my folks. I don't want to spend Thanksgiving in Bosnia either. Screw that!' Joe threw Bill a pointed look, and finished with, 'Let's tell Jack Clayton we want out, Billy boy.'

'Sure, I'll do it tomorrow. No problem. I'm positive our grateful and adoring news editor will understand your feelings, and Mike's, and mine. He'll tell us to hop a plane to Paris, any plane we can get, and to hell with the expense, and then board the first Concorde out of Paris to New York. Pronto, pronto. Sure, he'll tell us to do that.'

'Sarcasm has never been your forte, Bill,' Mike remarked with an engaging grin, then went on: 'But very seriously, talk to Jack tomorrow. Our rest period is long overdue. Originally, we were supposed to have it in July, then it got shifted to August, and finally it was cancelled altogether. We haven't been out of Bosnia, except for a few long weekends in Hungary, for *three months*. I happen to think that we've all reached the end of our individual bits of rope.'

'Could be we have. And you're right, Mike, so is

Joe. Our R & R has been postponed for too long now. We're all edgy. Look, the peace talks are about to start in Dayton in October. That's only a few days away. Things ought to be relatively quiet here during that period, so I can't see that there would be any problems. Jack'll just have to send in another news team, should anything serious erupt when we're gone.'

'There could easily be trouble,' Mike remarked in a thoughtful tone. 'Just because the peace talks are on doesn't mean that the guns will be silent. Not here. Anything goes.'

'Only too true,' Joe agreed. 'Let's not hold our collective breath on that one.'

'I know Jack's a tough news editor, but he is fair. He'll agree to this. Don't forget, *we* elected to stay when the NATO bombs started falling at the end of August. Jack was very appreciative that we did.' Bill paused, thought quickly, and made a sudden decision. 'Let's plan on getting out of here in a week. How does that sound, guys? Okay with you?'

Mike and Joe stared at him, dumbfounded. Then they grinned and exclaimed in unison, *'Okay!'*

CHAPTER 2

Venice, November 1995

THE LIGHT in the piazza was silvery, the sky leaden, frosty. A faint mist rising from the lagoon and the many canals swathed everything in a veil of grey on this cold winter's afternoon.

Bill Fitzgerald walked slowly across St Mark's Square, not caring about the weather in the least. There had been too many abortive attempts on his part to get to Venice, and he was glad he had finally made it.

It was a relief to be here after life in the battlefields of Bosnia; also a relief that the tides and the winds were cooperating and Venice was not flooded, as it frequently was at this time of year. Even if it had been, he wouldn't have cared about that either. The Venetians always managed very well when the city lay under water, so why shouldn't he?

He had been coming here whenever possible for the past few years. It was relatively easy to get to Venice from most cities in Europe, which was where he invariably was, on foreign assignment for his network. And even after only a couple of days here he always felt considerably refreshed, lighter in spirit and uplifted.

La Serenissima, the Venetians called it, this city of churches and palaces floating on water, blazing with colour and liquid light, brimming with treasures of art and architecture. Bill thought it was one of the most intriguing and evocative places in the world, its aspects bound to delight even the most jaundiced eye.

On his first visit twelve years ago, he had spent a great deal of time in many of those churches and palaces, gazing at the breathtaking paintings by Titian, Tintoretto, Veronese, Tiepolo, and Canaletto. These masterpieces touched his soul with their incomparable beauty and, thereafter, the Venetian school of painting was one of his favourites.

He had always wished he could paint, but he was not in the least gifted in that respect. His only talent was with words.

'He's kissed the Blarney Stone, that one,' his maternal grandmother, Bronagh Kelly, used to say when he was growing up. 'True,' his mother would agree. 'That's his gift, a way with words. And he writes like an angel. We must remember that the pen is mightier than the sword.'

Bill was an only child. He had spent a lot of time with adults when he was young, and his lovely Irish grandmother, in particular, was a favourite of his. He had been especially attached to her.

When he was little she had held him spellbound with her stories of leprechauns, lucky shamrocks, and pots of gold at the end of the rainbow. Bronagh had left Ireland with her parents and a younger brother when she was eight, and had grown up in Boston. It was here that she had met and married his grandfather, a lawyer named Kevin Kelly.

'I was born in 1905, and what a birth it was, Billy!' she would exclaim. 'I came into this world at the stroke of midnight on the twelfth of June in the middle of the most violent thunderstorm,' she'd tell him. 'And me darlin' mama said it was a bad omen, that storm.' She always embellished the details of her birth with every retelling, obviously enjoying his rapt expression and widening eyes. 'And indeed it's been a stormy life I've lived ever since, Billy,' she would add, with a huge laugh, which led him to believe she had relished her stormy life.

His wife, Sylvie, had loved Grandma Bronagh as much as he had, and the two had become very close over the years. His grandmother had been a true Celt, spiritual, mystical, and a little fey. Sylvie had shared these traits, been very much like her in many ways.

His only regret, whenever he came back to Venice, was that he had not brought Sylvie here before she died. They had put it off and put it off, and suddenly, unexpectedly, it was too late. Sylvie was gone. Who could have known that she would die like that? In childbirth, of all things in this day and age. 'Eclampsia' it was called; it began with seizures and ended in coma and death.

Losing Sylvie was the worst thing that ever

happened to him. She had been too young to die, only twenty-six. His grief had overwhelmed him; he had been inconsolable for a long time. In the end, he had managed to come to grips with it, throwing himself into work in an effort to keep that grief in check and at bay.

As he went towards the Basilica, his thoughts were still centred on Sylvie. She had died in 1989; the baby, a little girl, had lived. She was called Helena, the name he and Sylvie had chosen. Now six years old, she was the spitting image of her mother, an adorable creature who entranced everyone she met.

Certainly she was a great joy to him. Whenever he felt depressed and disturbed by the rottenness of the world, he had only to conjure up her face and instantly he felt better. She made life worth living, his beautiful child.

A fleeting smile crossed Bill's face, touched his eyes when he thought of her. Because his job as a foreign correspondent took him all over the world, she lived with his mother in New York. Fortunately, he saw her frequently and the time they spent together was genuinely meaningful. She was a good little girl, spirited, intelligent and not too spoiled, although his mother did dote on her only grandchild.

He had just spent two weeks in Manhattan with them, after covering the start of the Bosnia peace talks in Ohio. He would go back again in December, to celebrate Christmas at his mother's apartment in the East Sixties. When he wasn't in the middle of a battlefield or covering a major story in some far-flung corner of the globe, Bill made a point of being with 'my best girls,' as he called them. There was nowhere else he wanted to be, especially on important occasions and holidays.

But this week in Venice was his time for himself. He needed it badly, needed to put himself back together after his three-month stint in Bosnia-Herzegovina. Bill felt diminished by the conflict he had witnessed in the Balkans, and he was depleted, weary of war, of the destruction and the killing.

He wanted to forget. Not that he ever really would forget any of it. Who could? But he might at least be able to diffuse some of those horrifying images, still so vivid, that had left such a terrible scar on his mind.

His best friend, Francis Peterson, a war correspondent for *Time* magazine, believed that none of the newsmen would ever be able to expunge the violent images of Bosnia. 'They're trapped in our minds like flies trapped in amber, there for all time,' Frankie kept saying, and Bill agreed with him. All of them had seen too much savagery; its imprint *was* indelible.

Francis and Bill had met at Columbia University's School of Journalism in 1980, and they had been fast friends ever since. They were often covering the same wars, the same stories, but even when they were not, and were in different parts of the world, they stayed in constant touch.

Francis was currently assigned to Beirut, but he would be arriving in Venice in an hour or two, and they would spend a few days together. Later in the week, Frankie would fly to New York to celebrate his father's seventieth birthday.

Bill was glad his old friend was able to join him. They were exceptionally close, shared the same interests and understood each other well, were usually on the same wavelength.

Suddenly Bill realized he was the only person in St Mark's Square, alone except for flocks of pigeons. The birds flew around him, soaring up above the Basilica. Usually the square was the centre of animation in Venice, teeming with people, mostly tourists from all over the world. Now he was its solitary occupant, and as he glanced about it seemed odd to him, strangely surreal.

As he continued to walk, he became aware for the first time of the unique paving in the piazza. In the past when he had strolled here, there had been hundreds and hundreds of pairs of feet covering it, obviously the reason he had never noticed it before now.

His eyes followed the flow of the pattern: flat grey stones covering most of the square, balanced on either side by narrow white marble bands set in classical motifs. At once he was struck by the way the motifs directed the eye and the feet towards the basilica. No accident, he thought, walking on. When he came to the church, he did not go inside. Instead, he turned right and went down the Piazzetta San Marco, which led to the water's edge.

For a long time Bill stood looking out across the lagoon. Sky and sea merged to become a vast expanse of muted grey, which soon began to take on the look of dull chrome in the lowering afternoon light.

It was so peaceful here it was hard to believe that just across the Adriatic Sea a bloody war still raged. Nothing ever changes really, Bill thought as he turned away from the water at last. The world is the same as it's always been, full of monsters, full of evil. We've learned nothing over the centuries. We're no more civilized now than we were in the Dark Ages. Man's monstrosities boggled his mind.

Hunching deeper into his trench coat, Bill Fitzgerald retraced his steps across the empty square. He began to hurry now as dusk descended, making for the Gritti Palace, where he always stayed. He loved its old-fashioned charm, comfort, and elegance.

The rain started as a drizzle but quickly turned into a steady downpour. Bill, increasing his pace, was almost running as he approached the side street where the front entrance to the Hotel Gritti Palace was located.

He sprinted around the corner of the street at a breakneck pace and collided with another person also moving swiftly. It was a woman. As her large-brimmed cream felt hat and her umbrella went sailing into the air, he reached out and grabbed hold of her shoulders to prevent her from falling.

Steadying himself, and her, he exclaimed, 'Excuse me! I'm so sorry,' and found himself staring into a pair of startled silvery-grey eyes. In Italian, he added, *'Scusa! Scusa!'*

She responded in English. 'It's all right, honestly,' and disentangling herself from his tight grip she ran after her hat, which was blowing down the street.

He followed her, outran her, caught the hat, picked up the umbrella wedged against the gutter, and brought them both back to her. 'I apologize again,' he said.

Nodding, she took the hat and the umbrella from him. 'I'm fine, really.' She glanced at the hat. 'And this isn't any the worse for wear either.' She shook it and grimaced. 'Just a *bit* splattered with mud. Oh well, never mind. Who cares? It was never my favourite hat anyway.'

'I'm a clumsy fool, barrelling around the corner like that. It wasn't very smart of me. Are you sure you're all right?' he asked in concern, unexpectedly loathe to let her go.

She proffered him a faint smile, slapped the hat on top of her dark curls, and sidled away from him, saying, 'Thanks again.'

He stood rooted to the spot as if paralysed, watching her walk off when he wanted desperately to detain her, to talk to her, even invite her for a drink. He opened his mouth. No words came out. Seemingly, he had lost his voice, not to mention his nerve.

Suddenly he galvanized himself. Almost running up the street after her, he shouted, 'Can I buy you a new hat?'

Without pausing, she called over her shoulder, 'It's not necessary, thanks for offering, though.'

'It's the least I can do,' he cried. 'I've ruined that one.'

She stopped for a moment and shook her head. 'No, really, the hat doesn't matter. 'Bye.'

'Please slow down. I'd like to talk to you.'

'Sorry, I can't. I'm late.' She glided on, swung around the corner.

Bill hurried after her.

It was then that he saw the man coming towards her, waving and smiling broadly.

The woman increased her pace, waving back and exclaiming in Italian, 'Giovanni, *come sta*?'

A moment later she was holding her umbrella high over her head so that the man she had called Giovanni could properly embrace her.

Disappointment surged through him. Immediately, Bill turned away, rounded the corner, and went down the street towards the Gritti Palace. He could not help wondering who she was. Certainly she was the most stunning woman he'd seen in a long time. Those luminous silver eyes set in a pale, piquant face, the head of tumbling dark curls, the elegant way she carried herself. She was beautiful, really, in a gamine sort of way. It was just his luck that she was apparently already spoken for. He would have liked to get to know her better.

CHAPTER
3

THEY MET in the bar of the legendary Gritti Palace, which faced the Grand Canal.

'It's great to see you, Francis Xavier!' Bill exclaimed. 'Just great that you could make it.' He enveloped his best friend in a bear hug.

As they drew apart after their rough, masculine embrace, Frank said, 'And likewise, William Patrick. It's been too long this time around. I've missed you.'

'So have I – missed you.'

Still grinning at each other, they both ordered single malt scotch from the hovering waiter and sat down at a small table near the window.

'A lot of wars have been getting in the way,' Frank went on, 'and we seem to have been covering different ones of late.'

'More's the pity we haven't seen the same action.'

They exchanged knowing looks for a long moment, remembering the tough situations they had encountered together and had shared. Genuinely close since journalism school, the two men, who were not only friends but colleagues, understood each other on a very fundamental level. And each worried about the other's well-being. They had a great deal in common, always had had – a love of truth and the need to find it, traits which made them superlative newsmen; diligence, honesty, and a zest for adventure. Yet, despite the latter, both were cautious, fully aware of the dangers involved in their work. Whether together or alone on assignments, they always endeavored to minimize the risks they took in order to get the story.

Their drinks arrived, and after they'd clinked glasses, Frank said, 'There's no way I'll go back to Bosnia, Bill.'

'I know. And I don't blame you. I've sort of had it myself. How is it in Beirut?'

'Fairly quiet. At the moment, anyway. Things are improving, getting more normal, relatively speaking, of course. I don't think it will ever be the Paris of the Middle East again, but the city's perking up. Good shops are opening, and the big hotels are functioning on a more efficient basis.'

'Hezbollah's still lurking, though.'

'You bet! We have to live with the threat of terrorism around the clock. But *you* know that.' Frank lifted his broad shoulders in a light shrug, his dark eyes narrowing. 'Terrorism is more prevalent than ever. Everywhere in the world. The bastards are all over the place.'

Bill nodded, took a sip of his drink, and leaned back in the chair, enjoying being with Francis Peterson.

Frank said, with a wide smile, 'Let's change the subject, get to something more worthwhile. How's my little Helena?'

'Not so little, she's grown a tad. Which reminds me . . .' As he spoke Bill pulled out his wallet, removed a photograph, and handed it to Frank. 'Your goddaughter wanted you to have this. She sends you hugs and kisses.'

Frank stared at the picture Bill had just handed him. He smiled. 'She's the most adorable kid, Billy, you're so lucky. I see she's still got that Botticelli look about her . . . positively angelic.'

'To look at, yes, but she's mischievous, a bit of a scamp, my mother says.' Bill grinned. 'But then who wants a perfect kid?'

'A perfect kid, if there is such a thing, would be insufferable. How's Dru?' he asked, putting the photograph in his own wallet.

'Pretty good, thanks. You know my mother, Frankie, full of piss and vinegar and energy, and as loving of heart as she ever was. She sends you her love, by the way.'

'When you speak to her, give her mine. Better still, I'll call her myself when I get to Manhattan, to say hello. Incidentally, I'm sorry I couldn't get home when you were there. I had a really tough deadline for my piece on Lebanon. There was just no way I could take off at that time.'

'I understood.'

Frank went on, 'I gather you weren't particularly impressed with the peace talks in Dayton.'

Bill shook his head. 'I wasn't. The Serbs are a diabolical bunch. Gangsters. They're never going to agree to a proper and *fair* peace treaty with the Bosnians, you'll see. As for all this UN talk about prosecuting some of the Serbs as war criminals, you can forget it. I assure you it will never happen. They're never going to get those butchers to the Hague to stand trial, for one thing. Just take my word for it. The Serbs are going to get away with their crimes.'

'Tragic though it is, you're probably right, Bill.'

'It's just wishful thinking on the part of the UN.'

'I agree.'

A small silence fell between them.

The two men sipped their drinks quietly, lost for a moment in their own thoughts.

They were a good-looking pair, both of them clean-cut and collegiate in their appearance. Any casual observer would have known immediately that they were Americans.

Frank was as dark as Bill was fair. He prided himself on being third-generation Irish-American, and Black Irish at that. He had a shock of dark hair, black eyes, and a fresh complexion. Like Bill, he was thirty-three, and currently single. His marriage to a television foreign correspondent, Pat Rackwell, one of the rising stars of her network, had foundered on the rocks of her career four years ago.

Fortunately they had had no children, and the divorce had been amicable enough. Whenever they ran into each other on a story, they pooled their information, their resources, and tried to be helpful whenever they could. Very frequently they had dinner together when they were in the same foreign city.

Breaking the silence, Bill said, 'I heard a nasty comment about us the other day.'

'Back in New York?'

'Yes.'

'What was it?'

'That we're war junkies, you and I. That we love danger, love being in the thick of it, and that that's what gives us our jollies. We're characterized as being extremely reckless. A bad example.'

Frank threw back his head and roared. 'Who cares what people think! I bet it was one of your competitors at another network who made *those* lousy comments.'

'As a matter of fact, it wasn't. It was one of the guys at CNS.'

'Aha! He wants your job, William!'

'Yeah, he probably does.' Bill hesitated for a second, then gave Frank a piercing look. 'Do you think the odds *are* against us? That we will get killed one day, when we're covering a war in some godforsaken place?'

Frank was reflective. After a second he murmured, 'So many journalists have lost their lives . . .' He let his voice trail off; his expression remained thoughtful.

'But we won't lose ours. I just feel it in my bones!' Bill asserted, his voice positive all of a sudden.

'You're absolutely right, it's just not in the cards. Anyway, you're bulletproof.'

Bill chuckled.

'Furthermore, you're my lucky charm.'

Bill cut in swiftly, saying, 'Except that I'm not always with you these days, Frankie.'

'True enough, just wish you were. We've had some experiences in the past, shared some highs and lows, haven't we? Remember the Panama Invasion?'

'How could I forget it? December of 1989. Sylvie

had only been dead a few months, and I was so grief-stricken I didn't care what happened to me, didn't give a damn whether I lived or died.'

'But you did care about me,' Frank said in a low voice, staring at his friend with sudden intensity. 'I wouldn't be sitting here tonight if it hadn't been for you, Bill, you saved my life.'

'You'd have done the same for me.'

'Of course I would! But don't ever forget that I've always been very grateful.'

'And so has the female population of . . . whatever city you're living in at the moment.'

Frank grinned at his friend, said facetiously, 'Aw shucks, Billy, don't start that again. I'm not the only newsman who likes a bit of female company occasionally. And what about you? You're not so shy with the girls either.'

'There haven't been many women around lately, I'm afraid, not where I've been.'

Frank nodded. 'Sarajevo's hardly the place for a romantic interlude.'

Bill confided, 'Heard another thing in New York, Francis Xavier.'

'Oh, yeah, and what's that? It obviously has something to do with me, from the tone of your voice.'

'Sure does. Rumour has it you're suffering from a terminal Don Juan complex.'

Frankie chuckled and went on chuckling. He was highly amused.

Bill smiled, feeling comfortable, relaxed, and more at ease with himself than he had been for a long time. He knew that with Frank in Venice, for a few days he would be able to shake his depression, dispel the horrific images of war, and recharge his batteries completely.

Now Bill motioned to the waiter, ordered two more drinks, and said, 'It's not such a bad reputation to have, when you think about it. After all no man can be a Don Juan unless women are interested in him.'

'Only too true. As they say, it takes two to tango. By the way, I ran into Elsa in Beirut a few weeks ago.'

'Elsa?' Bill frowned, looking puzzled.

'Don't tell me you've forgotten Elsa Mastrelli, our guardian angel from Baghdad.'

'*That* Elsa! Oh, my God, how is she?'

'The same. Still covering wars for her Italian news magazine, still playing Florence Nightingale, ministering angel, and earth mother all rolled into one. At least, so I've been told.'

'She was really great. Is she still as attractive?'

'Yes. Well, slight correction necessary here. Elsa has matured, looks more interesting, more experienced, even a bit war-weary, tired. But yes, she's still a knockout, a good-looking woman with a lot of savoir faire. In other words, she's grown up. We had a quick drink at the Commodore and reminisced about Baghdad.'

'That was one hell of a time in our lives, Frankie!' Bill exclaimed animatedly. 'My God, I'll never forget it . . . January of 1991. Only four years ago, but it seems so much longer, don't you think?'

'It sure does. We took some real chances, Billy, in those days.'

'We were only twenty-nine. And very daring.'

'Also very stupid, if you ask me.' Frank threw Bill a pointed look. 'No story's worth dying for.'

'No, it isn't. But we didn't even think about dying,

let's face it. And our Baghdad coverage made both our careers. Weren't we lucky that CNS was the only television network allowed to stay on in Baghdad? And that you and Elsa were the only print journalists given permission to stay on with us to cover the Gulf War?'

'All thanks to you and that enterprising producer of yours, Blain Lovett. What happened to him, is he still with CNS?'

'No, he went to NBC, then moved over to CBS. He's still there, doing very well, but no longer going out on foreign assignments. By choice, I guess.'

'He was great, the way he networked. What a wheeler-dealer he was.'

Bill grinned, remembering his former producer. 'He had his act down pat, making his important contacts before the war started. Long before. And the Iraqis loved his schmoozing. He charmed a lot of them well before the conflict began and so they favoured him. And we were home free when holy hell finally did break loose.'

'I'll never forget the day he told you that our Iraqi minders were letting CNS bring in all that television equipment from Jordan,' Frank said. 'Including that satellite phone. I, for one, was flabbergasted.'

'So was I, Frankie, and where would we have been without it? That phone was our only link to the outside world, and CNS was the only network getting coverage out for the world to hear and see.'

'It did wonders for CNS, pushed them to the top of the pile in live news coverage in particular. And actually, Billy, we were fortunate to come out of that debacle alive, all things considered, and all those direct hits the hotel took. And there was Elsa, what a terrific little trooper she was . . .'

Frank paused as he realized that he had lost Bill's attention. 'What's wrong?' he asked.

'Nothing.'

'Something's wrong. You're not listening to me. And you have the strangest expression on your face.'

Bill turned to Frank. 'I don't want you to look now, but it's that woman over there. At the other side of the bar. Did you see her come in?'

'How could I fail to miss her? She's the only other person here except us. So, what about her?'

'I almost knocked her over earlier today. Collided with her this afternoon as I barrelled around the corner, on my way back to the hotel. I chased her hat.'

'Chased her hat?'

'Oh never mind, and don't look at me like that.'

'Like what?'

'As if I'm nutty.'

'Well, you are a bit crazy, Billy, and so am I, thank God. Life's too damned hard not to be slightly crazy from time to time. How else are we going to deal with all the stress and tension? Anyway, what about this woman?'

'I was very taken with her this afternoon. I wanted to get to know her better.'

'I can't say I blame you. She's interesting-looking. Is she Italian?'

'I don't think so, even though she looks as if she might be. I'm pretty sure she's an American, certainly she sounds it. Anyway, her hat flew off as we collided, so I ran after it. I also ran after her as she thanked me and walked off. I wanted to invite her to have a drink with me. It's funny, Frankie, but I didn't want her to go.'

'Why didn't you ask her to have a drink?'

'I tried to, but she was hurrying, almost running. I was right behind her, and so naturally I saw her with the man she was meeting. Just my luck that she's involved with someone. For all I know he might even have been her husband. I watched them embrace. Still, I must admit I've thought about her for the past few hours, off and on.'

'There's only one thing to do.'

'What's that?'

'Go over and invite her to have a drink with us,' Frank suggested. 'You'll get the lay of the land pretty quickly.'

'I guess you're right.' As he spoke, Bill pushed himself to his feet and strode across the bar, walking in a direct line towards the young woman.

She looked up from a notebook she was holding and smiled when she saw him. 'Hi!' she said, sounding friendly.

'Since you wouldn't let me buy you a new hat, could I at least buy you a drink?' Bill began. 'My friend and I would love you to join us for . . . drinks *and* dinner.'

'That's really nice of you both, but I can't. I'm waiting for a friend. I have a previous engagement,' she explained.

Bill looked crestfallen. 'Just my luck, er, er, our luck. Well . . .' His voice trailed off and he half turned to go, and then he swung around to face her again. 'You're an American, aren't you?'

'Yes, I am. From New York.'

'So am I.'

'I know.'

'My name's Bill –'

'Fitzgerald,' she supplied, eyeing him, looking suddenly amused. 'I know who you are; in fact, I watch your newscasts all the time, Mr Fitzgerald.'

'Call me Bill.'

'All right.'

'And you are?'

'Vanessa Stewart.' She thrust out her hand.

Leaning forward, Bill took hold of it, and shook it. He discovered he did not want to let it go. 'I have a great idea,' he said and finally released her hand.

'You do?' She raised a dark brow and her large silver-grey eyes were quizzical as they focused on him intently.

Bracing his hands against the back of the chair and leaning forward, drawing closer to her, Bill said, 'We must be the only three Americans in Venice at the moment, so we *must* spend tomorrow together.'

'*Tomorrow?*' Her brows drew together. 'Why tomorrow?'

'It's Thanksgiving.'

'Oh, my God, I'd forgotten.'

'Well, it is. Thursday, November the twenty-third. And it would be a crime if the only three Yanks in Venice didn't celebrate this most American of all holidays together. Join me and my friend, Francis Peterson of *Time*. Come on, what do you say?'

'Very well, I'll join you, but only on one condition.'

'What's the condition? Shoot.'

'That we have a proper Thanksgiving dinner with turkey and all the traditional trimmings.'

Bill's face lit up in the most engaging way, and he

grinned boyishly. 'You've got a deal!' he declared.

She smiled up at him. 'Then I'll be happy to come, thank you very much. Shall we meet here in the bar?'

'Good idea. Champagne first, and then on to our turkey dinner with all the trimmings. What time?'

'Seven. Is that all right?'

'Perfect.' From the corner of his eye Bill saw the Italian, Giovanni, entering the bar. He inclined his head and politely took his leave. Moving away from her table swiftly, he retraced his steps across the room.

Frank had been watching Bill alertly, and now he said, 'What happened?'

'She can't join us tonight. For obvious reasons. The Italian is on the scene again.'

'Is that him over there now? The guy she met this afternoon?'

'Yes. Giovanni. However, she has agreed to have dinner with us tomorrow night.'

Frank looked impressed. 'That *is* an accomplishment, old buddy. How did you do it?'

'I reminded her that it's Thanksgiving, pointed out that we were more than likely the only three Americans in Venice, and added that it would be a crime if we didn't celebrate the holiday together.'

'And she agreed?'

'On one condition.'

'And what's that?'

'A turkey dinner. She wants a traditional Thanksgiving meal with all the usual trimmings.'

'You didn't promise it, did you?'

'Sure I did. Why are you looking sceptical, Francis?'

'Where the hell do you think you're going to find a

turkey? In Venice, of all places, for God's sake! This is a pasta land, Billy.'

'I know, and don't worry. Just trust me.'

'But Bill, a *turkey* –'

'Did I ever let you down in Baghdad? Who's the one who always managed to find the most delectable stuff in that war-torn city . . . from Johnnie Walker to cans of corned beef.'

'Well, you were pretty good,' Frank admitted, grinning.

'I know what I'm doing,' Bill remarked. 'I booked us a table at Harry's Bar tonight. And we'll go there again tomorrow. Everyone from Arrigo Cipriani, the owner, and the maitre d' to the youngest busboy knows me well. Please believe me, Harry's Bar will make us a real American Thanksgiving dinner. They'll get a turkey, no matter what. After all, the mainland's not far away.'

'I know better than to argue with *you*, Billy. And what's the lady's name?'

'Vanessa Stewart. She's from New York. She knew who I was.'

Frank threw him an amused look. 'Good God, don't sound so surprised, Bill. The whole of America knows who you are. Your face is in their living rooms every day of the week.'

CHAPTER 4

DO YOU THINK she's stood us up?' Frank said the following evening. He and Bill were sitting in the bar of the Gritti Palace, waiting for Vanessa Stewart to arrive. He glanced at his watch. 'It's twenty past seven.'

'Stood *us* up! *Never,*' Bill answered in a jocular tone, with a quick laugh. 'Two dashing war correspondents like us. Good Lord, Frankie, don't you know by now that we're irresistible?'

When Frank merely threw him a sharp look and made an exasperated noise, Bill added in a more sober tone, 'But seriously, I don't think she's the type to do that.'

'What makes you so sure?'

'I just am, trust me on this,' Bill replied firmly. 'I thought she seemed like a serious person yesterday, and although we spoke only briefly, I detected something in her, an air of breeding. I know she would have phoned us here by now if she weren't coming, to make some sort of polite excuse. I sensed that she was not flaky, not the flighty kind at all.'

'If you say so. And I guess it's a woman's prerogative to be late,' Frank responded. Then he and Bill exchanged swift looks and promptly sprang to their feet as Vanessa Stewart appeared in the doorway of the bar. She hurried in, gliding forward at a rapid pace.

The young woman, who was of medium height and slender, wore a burgundy-coloured outfit made of crushed velvet and carried a matching wool coat. The narrow velvet pants were paired with a loose, tunic top, which, with its square neckline and long sleeves cut wide at the cuffs, had a medieval look about it. Strands of amethyst-and-ruby-coloured glass beads were twisted into a choker around her neck, and small gold medallions gleamed at her ears.

Both men wore admiring expressions as she drew to a standstill in front of them, a look of concern on her face.

'Sorry I'm so late,' she said in an apologetic voice, shaking her head. 'So rude of me, but it was unavoidable. I was delayed at a meeting this afternoon. When I got back to the hotel it was late and I had to change. I didn't want to lose any more time by calling you in the bar. I thought it best just to dress and hurry down.'

'Are you staying here?' Frank said.

'Yes, I am.'

'It's not a problem,' Bill exclaimed, wanting to put her at ease. Smiling warmly, he went on, 'Vanessa, I'd like to introduce you to my friend Francis Peterson of *Time* magazine. And Frankie, this is Vanessa Stewart.'

'It's very nice to meet you,' Vanessa said, shaking Frank's outstretched hand.

'And I you,' the journalist answered, offering her a welcoming smile, thinking how personable she was and how attractive, in an offbeat way. Bill had described her to him as being gamine, and it was true, she did have a roguish, saucy kind of charm. With her huge grey eyes in that small, piquant face and her short, curly, dark hair she looked very young and vulnerable. She reminded him of someone, someone he couldn't quite place.

Vanessa put her coat on a chair and sat down.

Bill said, 'Would you like a glass of champagne or do you prefer something else?'

'Oh, champagne's lovely, thank you.' She settled back in the chair and crossed her long legs.

Champagne was poured, and after they had all clinked glasses Bill said, with unconcealed curiosity, 'You mentioned you were delayed in a meeting. So are you here on business?'

'Yes, I am.' Vanessa cleared her throat, and went on, 'I'm a designer. Of glass. I get most of it blown here. On Murano, to be exact. So I'm coming and going all the time.'

'Are you a New Yorker?' Frank asked.

'Yes. I was born there.'

'Do you live in Manhattan?'

She nodded. 'In the East Fifties.'

'Good old New York,' Frank murmured. 'There's nowhere else like it in the whole world.'

Bill said, 'What kind of glass do you design?'

'Vases, fancy bottles, big plaques and plates, decorative objects mostly, things to put on display. But I also make jewellery, like these beads.' She touched the choker on her neck and explained, 'But mostly I create objects for the home. Last year Neiman Marcus launched a line of mine, which I designed exclusively for them, and it's been a big success. That's why I'm here right now, to supervise the new collection.'

'Oh, so it's currently being made, is it?' Bill said.

'Yes, at one of the oldest glass foundries on Murano. There's nothing like Venetian glass, in my opinion anyway. I think it's the best in the world.'

'Where did you study in the States?' Frank probed.

'The Rhode Island School of Design, but also here in Venice. I did a graduate course for a year.'

'So you lived in Venice!' Bill exclaimed. 'How I envy you. I love this city.'

'So do I.' Vanessa's face took on a glow; she smiled at him. 'La Serenissima . . . the Serene Republic, and it's so aptly named, isn't it? I always feel truly content here, peaceful, yet very alive. Venice is a state of being, I think.'

Bill looked at her closely. He knew exactly what she meant about Venice. Struck by her openness, he nodded, returned her smile, and found himself staring into her luminous grey eyes. He averted his face, picked up his drink, and took a quick swallow. He felt suddenly self-conscious of his awareness of her, of his sexual attraction to her.

Frank, conscious of Bill's sudden discomfort, said, 'And tell me, Vanessa, where do you normally spend Thanksgiving?'

'With my mother, if we happen to be in the same place. And sometimes with my father, if Mom's away. It depends on the circumstances.'

'You make it sound as if your mother travels a lot,' Frank remarked, raising a brow questioningly.

'She does.'

'For pleasure or business?' he asked, still probing.

'Her work.'

'And what does your mother do?'

'She's an actress.'

'In the theatre?'

Bill sipped his champagne, leaning back in the chair, listening, thinking that Frankie was asking too many questions. But at the same time he wanted to hear her answers. She intrigued him in a way no woman had for the longest time.

'Oh, yes, my mother works in the theatre, and in films,' Vanessa said.

'Would we know her?' Bill leaned forward, focused his attention on her.

Vanessa laughed. 'I think so. My mother is Valentina Maddox.'

'Is she really!' Bill cried. 'Well, now that I know who she is I must admit you have the look of her, a very strong resemblance, in fact.'

Frank said, 'And Audrey Hepburn many years ago, when she was in *Sabrina*. That's who you reminded *me* of when you first walked in. Hasn't anybody ever told you that you look like her?'

Vanessa was still laughing. She nodded.

Frank now asked, 'Aren't your parents divorced?'

'Yes. But they're still friends, and they see each other from time to time. They both live in New York.

Well, Dad does. My mother's really a gypsy, flitting around the world, going wherever her work takes her.'

'Do you have any brothers or sisters?' Bill inquired.

'No.' Vanessa sat up straighter and looked from Bill to Frank, then began to laugh again. 'What a lot of questions you both ask!'

'We're journalists. It's our job to ask questions,' Frank replied.

They walked to the Calle Vallaresso, just off San Marco, where Harry's Bar was located.

It was a cold night. Frost hung in the air and ringed the moon, a clear silver sphere in an ink-dark sky. Cloudless and clear, it was littered with a thousand tiny pinpoints of brilliant light.

The streets were relatively deserted. Only a few people were about. As the three of them walked along, they could hear the clatter of their own shoes on the cobblestones.

'Hollywood couldn't have done it better,' Bill remarked at one moment, glancing at the sky. 'Hung that moon up there like that. What a fantastic film set Venice is, actually.'

Vanessa exclaimed, 'That's what my mother used to say when she came to visit me! She has always thought Venice to be the most theatrical of places in the whole world.'

'She's right,' Bill said, taking hold of Vanessa's arm, guiding her as they went down the narrower streets in the direction of the famous restaurant. He loved the closeness of her, the scent of her perfume. It was light, floral. Enticing. Just as she herself was enticing. He was very drawn to her, just as he had been yesterday, but tonight the feeling was more powerful.

They walked on in silence for a few seconds until Bill said, 'I suppose you know all about Harry's Bar.'

'Not really,' she responded. 'I went there with my parents, but only once. Didn't Ernest Hemingway make it his hangout?'

'He did, yes, along with a lot of other writers and journalists and celebrities. It was founded in the nineteen thirties, when an American, Harry Pickering, the now famous Harry, borrowed money from a hotel barman. The bartender was Giuseppe Cipriani, and when Harry paid him back he gave him additional money to open a bar. And *voila*! The restaurant was born.'

'I love stories like that,' Vanessa said, and then shivered slightly, drew further into her coat.

'Are you cold?' Bill asked solicitously.

'No, no, I'm fine.'

Frank, who had been silent during the walk to the restaurant, announced, 'There's Harry's Bar, straight ahead. We'll be inside in a minute.'

They were given a royal welcome when they walked into Harry's Bar. Once they had shed their coats, they were escorted to one of the best tables at the back of the room. 'Welcome, Signore Fitzgerald,' Arrigo Cipriani said. 'And 'appy Thanksgiving.'

'Thanks, Arrigo. Now, how about some Bellinis to celebrate the holiday?'

'Good idea,' Frank said.

'That'd be lovely,' Vanessa agreed, and once they were alone she turned to Bill, and said, 'I've forgotten what a Bellini is. I mean, I know it's champagne but what's in it besides that?'

'Fresh peach juice.'

'Now I remember! They're fabulous.'

A great deal of camaraderie had developed between them in the short time they had known each other. Vanessa had taken their probing questions at face value, had not been offended, and they in turn had been struck by her attitude, realizing what a good sport she was. And so the gaiety and banter continued at Harry's, only to be interrupted when a waiter arrived at their table, presenting the menus with a flourish.

'I ordered a special main course for us all last night,' Bill explained.

'Si, Signore Fitzgerald, I know. But you didn't order a first course.'

'True, I didn't. What do you suggest?'

'What about *risi e bisi*, I know you like it.' Looking at Vanessa and then at Frank, the waiter continued, 'It's a wonderful risotto. Mmm.' He kissed his finger-tips. 'Rice with peas, ham, and Parmesan cheese. Delicious.'

'Sounds good enough to eat,' Frank joked.

Bill grinned at Vanessa. 'It is good. I think I'll have it. How about you?'

'All right. Thank you.'

'We'll all have it,' Frank added. 'And let's take a look at the wine list, please, Antonio.'

'Si, Signore Peterson.' The waiter nodded and departed.

Vanessa pushed back her chair and said, 'Excuse me for a moment,' and left the table, heading for the ladies' room.

Bill leaned over and said to Frank, 'So, what do you think of her?'

'She's lovely, and you were right, she's not a bit flaky. In fact, I think she's a very nice young woman, one who's rather serious by nature.'

Bill said, 'I like her.'

'It's more than *like*, Bill, that's too soft a word.'

'What do you mean?'

'You're bowled over by her, and you're going to get involved with her. She with you.'

'I'm not so sure.'

'About yourself? Or her?'

'Both of us.'

Frank smiled broadly, and a knowing glint entered his black Irish eyes. 'Oh Bill, my boy, take my word for it, you are heading for the big one here. She's irresistible to you, has all the things you love in a woman. As for her, she can't take her eyes off you. She's intrigued, flattered by your interest in her, and she hangs onto every word you say.'

'I think you exaggerate.'

'Trust me, I don't. I've got eyes in my head, and I've been watching you both for almost two hours now. You're both trying to hide it, but you're falling for each other.'

'I wonder who that Italian is? Giovanni?' Bill muttered.

'We can't very well ask her. Anyway, she's not wearing any rings, at least not a wedding ring, only that crested signet on her little finger.'

'But that doesn't mean anything these days. And she does spend a lot of time here, she said so.'

'That doesn't mean anything either, Billy. I'm telling

you, that young woman –' Frank stopped as Vanessa glided up to the table.

The two men rose, and Bill helped Vanessa into her chair.

Once she was seated, she smiled across at him, and said, 'You reminded the waiter you'd ordered a main course last night. Not a turkey?'

'Of course it's a turkey. I ordered a traditional Thanksgiving dinner for us, and fortunately they were able to oblige. After all, that was your condition, Vanessa.'

She stared at him for a long moment, and shook her head slowly. Her eyes twinkled mischievously when she finally murmured, 'But I was only teasing. I never thought for one moment that you'd find a turkey in Venice . . .'

Bill stared at her.

Vanessa's touch was featherlight as she rested her hand on his arm. 'You see, I *wanted* to spend Thanksgiving with you . . . with or without a turkey.'

CHAPTER
5

WHAT FRANCIS PETERSON had predicted finally came to be.

Bill and Vanessa fell in love.

As Bill said much later, they probably did so on Thanksgiving night at Harry's Bar, although it took them several days to acknowledge their feelings.

During the Thanksgiving weekend they got to know each other better. In fact, they were a threesome, since they spent Friday and Saturday with Frank.

For these two days Vanessa became their guide, showing them places in Venice that not even Bill, the Venice aficionado, knew about. These were small, unique art galleries, museums and churches off the beaten track, bars and cafes known only to the Venetians themselves, shops where the best bargains were to be had.

At Bill's insistence, she took them out to Murano, where she did much of her work. They went to the island by *vaporetto*, a water taxi that took only seven minutes to get there.

Bill and Frank both wanted to see her designs, and so they visited the ancient glass foundry where her glass pieces were handblown. Both men were impressed by her stunning designs, her talent and creativity, and they realized she was a true artist.

That evening, at her request, they escorted her to a cocktail party given by an old friend of hers from her student days, who owned a palazzo on the Grand Canal situated diagonally across from the Gritti Palace. They needed a gondola to get there.

The two newsmen found the slightly ramshackle palace an amazing place, and were fascinated by its many treasures. Carlo Metzanno, their host, was an interior designer, and he had given the massive, centuries-old palace a great deal of style and elegance. As he showed them around, he explained the provenance of many of the art objects, paintings, and antiques. Prominently displayed were several extraordinary pieces by Vanessa. These were fluid, sinuous, and impressive.

The three of them stayed at the cocktail party for an hour, mixing with a colourful group of people including a couple of local artists, a famous French movie star, a playwright from London, and an American architect.

When they left the palazzo, the same gondola that they had hired for the evening took them to the Giudecca, the narrow sliver of an island across the Canale della Giudecca. Vanessa had invited them to dinner, and she had booked a table at Harry's Dolci, the charming and intimate 'little sister' of Harry's Bar. After their meal they strolled over to the Hotel Cipriani for espressos and stregas before going back to Venice in the gondola. 'We've become the three musketeers,' Frank said as they took their seats, settling back to enjoy the ride to the Gritti Palace. 'We're now old pals.' Bill and Vanessa laughed, and Bill said, 'I think that's swell.'

Bill had planned what he termed 'an adventure' for Saturday night. Once again, a gondola was hired for the evening, and this carried them down the narrow winding backwaters of Venice until they arrived at an old house that looked like a hole in the wall. It turned out to be a marvellous family restaurant, one Bill knew well, which was a popular eating place favoured by Venetians in the know.

It was a gay evening filled with bonhommie. They laughed and joked, exchanging a lot of amusing banter. A considerable amount of genuine affection flowed between them. The two men had grown quite close to Vanessa, and she to them.

'Here's a toast, then,' Frank said as the dinner drew to a close. 'To dear friends – old and *new*.' He clinked his glass of red wine to Bill's glass and then Vanessa's. Smiling at her genially, he added, 'You're a good sport, kid, the way you've put up with us. Especially *me*, with all my questions. I've enjoyed being with you for the last couple of days. You've been like . . . a breath of fresh air.'

Vanessa coloured slightly, the flush rising from her neck to touch her face. Frank had teased her a lot, and now she was touched by his compliments, his unexpected courtliness.

'What a nice thing to say, Frank, thanks, and I've enjoyed *your* company.'

'I'm going to miss you both,' Frank went on, looking from Vanessa to Bill. 'Most especially you, William Patrick. Battlefields are not the same without you.'

'I know,' Bill replied, his eyes focused on his best friend. 'I'll miss you, too, but who knows, we may well be covering the same story in the next few months.'

'Could be,' Frank said. 'I hope so.'

As they left the restaurant a short while later, Vanessa shivered and moved nearer to Bill, who put his arm around her protectively and drew her close against him.

Venice in winter, and especially in the evening, was mysterious, even frightening. The gondola glided down many dark waterways, heading for the Gritti Palace. Mist rose up from the murky canals, and there was no noise except for the slap of the oars as they hit the water. Everything was shadowy, eerie in the dim light.

On either side of the narrow waterways, buildings loomed up like strange inchoate monsters under the threatening sky. At times the mist was more like fog, thick and almost impenetrable. The dampness clung to them, seemed to penetrate their clothes.

The three friends stayed huddled in the gondola, shivering, fighting the cold, talking quietly until they reached the hotel.

'I'm glad we're back,' Vanessa said with another shiver as Bill helped her to alight at the small dock in front of the Gritti Palace. 'There are times when Venice at night frightens me, fills me with foreboding –' She cut herself off, feeling suddenly foolish. After all, she had two men to protect her, not to mention the muscular gondolier who looked like a prizefighter.

Since they each had their rooms on different floors, they said good night in the lobby.

Frank, who was leaving the following morning for Milan and then a direct flight to New York, kissed Vanessa on both cheeks. He gave Bill one of their customary bear hugs.

'See you, William,' he said nonchalantly, walking to the elevator. Suddenly, he paused, turned around, and looked at them both for a split second, the expression on his face unexpectedly serious.

'Take care of each other,' he said and disappeared behind the sliding doors of the elevator.

Bill and Vanessa remained standing in the lobby, staring at each other.

Vanessa's eyes were full of questions as she murmured, 'What an odd thing for him to say –' She stopped, her gaze still riveted on Bill.

'Not really,' Bill answered quickly. Then, after the merest hesitation, he went on, 'You see, he knows how I feel about you.'

'How is that?'

'I'm very . . . *drawn* to you, Vanessa.'

She was staring up at him; she nodded. 'I guess he knows I feel the same way.'

'You do?'

'Oh, yes, Bill.'

Bill inclined his head slightly. 'So, Frankie *was* right.

He sensed it from the beginning. He was quite positive he knew exactly how we *both* were feeling.'

'He's very astute.' She spoke in the softest of voices.

'He is. Do you want a nightcap? Or something hot, maybe? Hot lemon tea?'

'Not here, though,' Vanessa said.

'Your room or mine?'

'Oh yours, please,' Vanessa answered with a small, shy smile. 'You have a suite, mine is nothing so grand.'

Putting an arm around her shoulder, Bill led her to the other elevator at the far end of the lobby. The minute the door closed, he did what he had been wanting to do for the past three days. He took her in his arms and kissed her.

Vanessa kissed him back, and with such intensity he was momentarily startled. When the elevator came to a halt, they quickly pulled apart. As they stepped out, he noticed her flushed face. She was usually so pale.

Drawing a finger down one side of her cheek, he leaned into her and whispered, 'You're burning up. Hot to the touch.'

She looked at him swiftly but said nothing.

With their arms wrapped around each other, they walked along the corridor to his suite. After letting them in, Bill closed the door with his foot. Shooting the bolt with one hand, he pulled her into his arms with the other. Once more they clung together, kissing with growing fervour.

Suddenly Bill held her away from him and said, 'Let's take off our coats.' So saying, he helped her out of hers, struggled to shrug off his trench coat, and threw both on a nearby chair.

Silently Bill took hold of her hand tightly, led her into the adjoining bedroom and over to the bed. Vanessa seated herself on the edge of it, all the time watching him as he bent down and took off her shoes, first one and then the other.

After kissing each foot, he slid his hand under her wide, flared skirt, stroking her leg, moving up until his fingers caressed her inner thigh.

'Bill?'

'Yes?'

'Let's get undressed.'

A half smile touched his mouth. With swiftness he rose, took her hands in his and pulled her to her feet, so that they were facing each other. Vanessa moved closer, placed her arms around his neck, kissed him on the mouth passionately. As she did so, he reached behind her and unzipped her wool skirt.

The skirt fell to the floor, lay in a swirl of purple at her feet. She stepped away from it, then swung back to him, her eyes focused on him with intensity.

Bill looked at her closely. What he saw surprised and pleased him. Her face was flushed, full of desire, and her silvery eyes brimmed with longing. For him.

Roughly Bill pulled her to him, bent his face to hers, and kissed her deeply. He slid his tongue into her mouth, let it graze hers, and she did the same, exciting him more than ever with her fervour and unabashed desire. He felt the blood rush to his face; he was aroused as he had not been aroused for years. He wanted her so much, had wanted her for days, and now he felt as though he would explode. He had an enormous erection. He pressed himself against her; she bent to his will, letting her whole body flow against his.

Leaning away from her slightly, he looked down at her breast, touched it gently. How taut it was under the thin silk blouse. Fumbling, he undid the first few buttons, put his hand inside her blouse. He kissed her breast, then sucked on the hardening nipple.

'Please, let's lie down, Bill.'

Clinging to each other they staggered to the bed. She began to take off her blouse, but he stopped her.

'Let me do it,' he said in a low voice. 'I want to undress you. Please, darling.'

She nodded. Her eyes never left his face as he opened her blouse. After slipping it over her shoulders, he began to kiss her neck, her arms, and brought his mouth back to her breast. As his tongue tantalized the nipple, he undid her bra. At last both of her small, rounded breasts were free and he buried his head between them.

Bill could feel Vanessa's strong hands in his hair, smoothing and stroking, massaging his neck and shoulders. He heard her soft moans as he moved from one breast to the other, tenderly kissing and touching them, inflaming himself as well as her.

After a moment he sat up, looked down at her stretched out on the bed. How exciting she was to him, so vulnerable in her delicate beauty. She wore a lacy, black garter belt and sheer, black stockings. Carefully he undid the suspenders and rolled down each stocking, took off one, then the other. His eyes ravished her body, so trim and lean, yet shapely. Unfastening the garter belt, he slipped it off.

She stared up at him, her eyes wide and unblinking. 'I want you,' she said in a husky voice.

He nodded, stood up, threw off his clothes haphazardly, lay down next to her. Taking her in his arms, he kissed her eyes, her lips, her ears. 'I want to kiss every part of you,' he whispered against her hair.

'I'd like that,' she murmured.

He slid down the bed, brought his mouth to the core of her. She responded wildly, crying his name. Her body suddenly convulsed in a spasm, and she grasped his shoulders hard, gasping as she did so.

Before he could stop himself, Bill was astride her, lying on top of her. Both his hands reached up into her dark curls, and he covered her mouth with his, touching his tongue to hers. He needed to take her to him. Now. Without further delay. Bracing his hands on either side of her he raised himself up, stared down into her eyes.

'Yes,' she cried. 'Oh, yes, Bill.'

His hands left her hair, moved on to fondle those taut breasts with their erect nipples. He pushed his hands under her back, then her buttocks, lifting her closer to him, fitting her body to his. He was harder than ever and slid inside her easily.

And she welcomed him with her warm and pliant body, cleaving to him, thrusting up to him. She became welded to him. She moved her legs, threw them around his back, as high as they would go, so that he could shaft deeper and deeper into the warm, soft core of her. And they found their own rhythm, moving faster and faster until they were frenzied.

Bill thought his heart was going to burst. He sank deeper and deeper into her until he was entirely enveloped by her. 'Vanessa,' he gasped. 'Vanessa.'

'Yes, Bill!' she cried. 'Don't stop.'

He brought his mouth to hers again, and holding her tightly in his arms, they came to a climax together, sharing their ecstasy. And their joy in each other was unparalleled.

CHAPTER
6

'THAT WAS all too quick,' Bill said, encircling her with his arms, pulling her closer to him. 'I'm afraid I was overanxious.'

'No, you were wonderful.'

'I've wanted us to be together like this since the other afternoon, when I almost knocked you over.'

'So have I.'

'Really and truly, Vanessa?'

'Yes, honestly.'

He felt her smile against his chest. Before he could stop himself, Bill asked, 'Who's Giovanni?'

She swivelled her eyes to look up at him. 'How do you know his name?'

'I heard you greet him the other afternoon, just after I'd chased your hat.'

'I see. He's an old friend ... we met when I was

doing my graduate course here. We became close, he helped me in lots of ways.'

'Are you lovers?'

'No.' Vanessa hesitated, then added, 'Giovanni lives with someone, has for several years . . . another man.'

'Oh.' Bill cleared his throat, and after a moment he said, 'We asked you lots of questions, Frankie and I, but we didn't ask your age, being the gentlemen that we are. But how old are you, actually?'

'Twenty-seven. Soon to be twenty-eight. And you're about thirty-five, aren't you?'

He laughed. 'Thanks a lot! And no, I'm thirty-three,' he replied and kissed the top of her head. 'You said you were staying another four days. That means you're leaving on Wednesday. Correct?'

'Yes, I have to work at the glass foundry on Monday and Tuesday.'

'Can I see you in the evenings? Can we be together until you leave?'

'Of course, I want that too, Bill.'

'Listen, I'm coming to New York in December. For the Christmas holidays, in fact. Are you going to be around?'

'Yes.' There was a small pause before she continued, 'Bill, there's something I must tell you.'

He heard an edge in her voice all of a sudden and he frowned. 'Go ahead.'

Vanessa took a deep breath and plunged. 'I'm married.'

For a moment Bill did not respond, and then he moved up on the pillows.

Vanessa struggled free of his embrace, turned to face him.

They stared at each other intently.

Vanessa saw surprise mingled with hurt on his face.

'Don't be angry with me. Don't look at me like that,' she cried.

'How do you expect me to look, for God's sake? I'm disappointed, Vanessa. You lied to me.'

'No I didn't, we never mentioned my marital status.'

'You lied by omission.'

'What about your private life, Bill? Is there a woman in *your* life? You don't need a piece of paper to make a commitment to someone. Making it legal doesn't necessarily make the bonds any stronger, the attachment greater. Do you live with a woman?'

'No.'

She sighed.

He said, 'Do you live with him?'

'Sort of . . .'

'What does that mean?'

'He's away a lot. And I go to my studio in the Hamptons a great deal of the time. I have a barn and a cottage in Southampton. So we're not together often.'

'And when you are? Is it a proper marriage?'

She shrugged.

'Do you sleep with him?' he pressed.

Vanessa did not respond.

'Your silence is golden . . . it means that you do.'

'It's not a good marriage –'

His hard laugh stopped her short. 'Ah, the misunderstood married woman!' he exclaimed.

'No, it's not like that!' She leapt off the bed, ran into the bathroom, and came back a moment later wrapped in a terry cloth robe. Seating herself on the edge of the bed, she took hold of his hand.

Bill looked at her, his face taut. He was trying to come to grips with his emotions. After making such passionate love he had been euphoric, a feeling he had long forgotten existed. And he had felt at ease with this young woman who had come so unexpectedly into his life. He knew he wanted to get to know her better, to spend time with her. Her announcement that she was not free had been a bombshell.

Vanessa exclaimed, 'Please, Bill, don't be angry. Let me explain.'

'I'm not angry, and go ahead, be my guest. *Explain,*' he said and there was a sarcastic note in his voice.

Ignoring this, Vanessa said, 'Peter's a lawyer, a show-business lawyer and very successful. He's away a lot, mostly in Hollywood. It wasn't like that at first, but his business has grown. And I'm travelling, too. I suppose, in a way, we've grown apart a bit. But he's a good man, and he's been very supportive of me, as I have of him. So we sort of . . . muddle through. It's not a great marriage, but it's not a bad one either.'

'Have you never thought of leaving him?'

She shook her head. 'He's a good man, as I just said. I wouldn't want to hurt him.'

'What about you, Vanessa? Aren't you entitled to have a happy relationship with a man?'

'I don't think it's possible to build one's happiness on someone else's unhappiness.'

'I know what you mean.'

'In any case, Peter would fall apart if I left him. I just couldn't have his pain on my conscience.'

'Do you have children?'

'No, sadly we don't.'

'How long have you been married?'

'Four years.'

'Do you still love him?'

'I care about him –' She came to a halt, looked thoughtful, finally confided, 'Peter's been in my life for such a long time. We're good friends, and we have a lot in common. He's always encouraged me in my work, my career, never stood in my way. He's a nice person. I like him. I respect him, and I love him. But –'

'You're not in love with him, is that what you're trying to say?'

'Yes.' Vanessa bit her lip and shook her head. 'I mean, how could I be here with you like this if I were?'

Bill laid his head back against the pillows and closed his eyes. A small sigh escaped, and without opening his eyes, he said softly, 'I just wish you'd told me you were married, that's all.'

'I wanted to,' Vanessa said. 'I intended to, and then we started to have such a good time together. I liked you so much. I wanted to be with you, and I just thought you'd lose interest if you knew I had a husband.'

He said slowly, 'You should have been straightforward with me.'

'Have *you* been with me?'

He sat up swiftly and stared at her. 'Yes, I have. There isn't a woman in my life. You know I'm widowed. My God, the whole world knows I'm widowed. And I haven't had a really good relationship since Sylvie died. Oh, yes, there've been a few women, but I've never fallen in love, or had a meaningful relationship since my wife died six years ago. To tell you the truth, I thought that you and I might have something going for us, that this was the beginning of something special. I want a good relationship, Vanessa, I want to have another chance at happiness.' He shrugged. 'I guess I was wrong to think it might be with you.'

Vanessa said nothing, looked down at her hands twisting nervously in her lap.

The awkward silence grew.

At last she said, 'How do you *really* feel about me, Bill? Be scrupulously honest.'

He gave her a hard penetrating stare. 'We've just made passionate love, and you ask me that?' He gave a short laugh, pursed his lips. 'Obviously I'm overwhelmingly attracted to you, turned on by you. I enjoyed making love with you. Let's face it, we've just had wonderful sex. I like being with you. I admire your talent. As I told you in the lobby a short while ago, I'm very taken with you, Vanessa.'

'And I am with you, Bill. So much so I haven't really been able to think straight for the last couple of days. All I know is that I just want to be with you. Whenever we can. You're a foreign correspondent, you're obviously going to go back to Bosnia or somewhere else, and I have my own career . . .' She shook her head, and tears brimmed in her eyes. 'I thought we would see each other whenever we could, be together as often as possible and . . . see what happens.'

'Let things work themselves out in their own time, is that what you mean?'

'Yes. Whenever my mother was facing difficulties, she would always say to me, "Vanny, life takes care of itself and a lot of other things as well. And usually it's for the best." That's still her philosophy, I think.'

Bill looked at her thoughtfully. 'So, what you're

saying is that you want to have an affair with me? A secret affair. Because you don't want your husband to be hurt. Am I correct?'

'It sounds terrible when you put it that way.'

'But it *is* the truth. And as a newsman, I *am* a seeker of truth.'

Vanessa shook her head, biting her lip again. Slowly, tears trickled down her cheeks.

'Oh, for God's sake, don't start crying!' he said, and reached for her, pulled her into his arms. He flicked her tears away with his fingertips, then tilted her face to his. Softly, he kissed her on the mouth.

When he stopped, she said, 'Please tell me you're not angry with me, Bill.'

'I'm not angry. Only selfish. I always want things my way, like most men. And listen, you haven't committed a crime. Anyway, why should you stick your neck out for me?' He laughed. 'I'm always in harm's way . . . a bad risk.'

'Don't say that!' she cried, her eyes flaring.

Tightening his grip on her, he brought his face closer to hers and whispered, 'I *want* to be your lover. Now why don't you take off that robe so that I can start practising.'

CHAPTER 7

It was an extraordinary day, clear, light-filled. A shimmering day. The sky dazzled. It was a perfect blue, unmarred by cloud, and the sun was brilliant above the rippling waters of the lagoon. The air was cool, but not as cold as it had been over the past few days, and the mist had dissipated.

On this bright Sunday afternoon, Bill and Vanessa walked through the streets and squares for several hours, holding hands, hardly speaking but comfortable in their mutual silence. Both were swept up in the beauty of Venice. They walked on past the Accademia, down the Calle Gambara into the Calle Contarini Corfu, until they came at last to the Fondamenta Priuli-Nani.

'Of course I remember this area now,' Vanessa said, turning to Bill, smiling up at him as they headed down the street. 'That's the old boatyard of San Trovaso, where gondolas are repaired,' she continued, gesturing to the decrepit-looking buildings ahead of them. 'I came here once with my father. He wanted to see the Church of San Trovaso. It's very old, if I remember correctly.'

'Yes, it is,' Bill replied. 'It was built in the tenth century, and that's where I'm taking you now, actually. To the church. I want to show you one of my very favourite paintings. It's by Tintoretto. And incidentally, gondolas are also *made* at the San Trovaso boatyard, it's one of the last of the building yards left in Venice.'

'They've all more or less disappeared. So many of the old crafts have become defunct,' she murmured, sounding regretful. 'But, thank goodness, glassblowing hasn't!' she finished with a light laugh, grinning at him.

They continued on past the boatyard, and walked up over the Ponte delle Meravegie, the bridge of marvels. Within seconds they were approaching the Church of San Trovaso, its cream-coloured stone walls and slender bell tower rising up above the trees, a sentinel silhouetted against the cerulean sky.

After they had entered the church, Vanessa and Bill stood quietly for a moment, adjusting their eyes to the dim light and the overwhelming silence. They both genuflected, and Bill threw Vanessa a swift glance but made no comment, realizing that she also must be a Catholic. They slowly moved forward, walking down the nave towards the altar.

Immediately, Bill brought Vanessa's attention to the two paintings hanging on either side of the choir. 'Both are by Tintoretto,' he explained. 'The last two pictures he ever painted. In 1594. Come on, let me show you the one I love the most.' A moment later they were in front of *The Adoration of the Magi*, Tintoretto's great masterpiece.

'I've always liked this particular Tintoretto myself,' Vanessa volunteered. 'It's absolute perfection. The colours, the images, the incredible brushwork.'

'Wasn't he marvellous,' Bill said, 'A towering genius.' He fell silent, simply stood staring at the picture, rooted to the spot, unable to tear his eyes away.

At this moment it struck Vanessa that Bill was mesmerized by the painting. Several times she threw him a surreptitious look, but she made no comment, not wanting to break the spell for him; she understood how moved he was by this great work of art.

Finally dragging his eyes away from the painting, he said, 'When I look at this Tintoretto, and the other treasures in Venice, and consider man's incredible talent, his ability to create incomparable beauty, I can't help wondering how man can also be the perpetrator of an evil so stupendous it boggles the mind. It's hard to reconcile the two.'

'But the two have always coexisted,' Vanessa answered, putting her hand on his arm. 'Venice *is* the total personification of visual beauty. It's there for us to *see*, to take pleasure from, wherever we look. The art, the architecture, the many different treasures that have been accumulated here over the centuries, the very design and layout of Venice itself – ' She paused for a split second before she added softly, 'You have just come out of Bosnia, where you witnessed inhumanity and savagery, cruelty beyond belief. And those images must still be in your mind, Bill. How can you not make comparisons?'

'You're right, yes, I know that,' he said, and turning away from the painting at last, he took hold of her arm and led her down the nave, back to the front door of the ancient church. 'I suppose the beauty of paintings and music help to make the hard realities of life . . . bearable.'

'I think so.'

Once they were outside in the sunlight, Bill blinked and shook off the images of the Balkans war that had momentarily overtaken him. He exclaimed, 'It's such a long time since I've taken a gondola up the Grand Canal. Shall we do it, Vanessa? It's still the most spectacular trip, isn't it?'

'Absolutely. And I'd love it. It's ages since I've done it myself, and I guess the Grand Canal personifies Venice, doesn't it? Besides, I find gondolas a very relaxing way to travel.'

Bill felt a sudden rush of happiness surging up in him. He knew it was because of Vanessa, her presence by his side. He put his arm around her, hugged her to him. 'I'm glad we met, I'm glad we're here today in Venice. I'm glad we made love last night. I'm glad we have a few more days together.' He stopped, tilted her face to his and looked at her, a faint smile briefly touching his mouth. 'Whatever your circumstances are, Vanessa, you're the best thing that's happened to me in a long time.' He kissed the tip of her nose. 'Clandestine though it must be, I want our affair to continue.' His eyes searched hers questioningly.

She nodded. 'So do I. Whenever we can, wherever we can,' she answered, and reached up, threw her arms around his neck, pulled his face to hers, and put her mouth on his. 'There,' she added, 'sealed with a kiss.'

He laughed, and so did she, and with their arms wrapped around each other they walked back the way they had come. Retracing their steps past the old boatyard, they went down the narrow streets until they came again to the Campo dell' Accademia, where Bill hired a gondola to take them back to the Gritti.

Immediately they were seated, Bill put his arm around Vanessa again and pulled her closer to him, realizing as he did that in only a few days this woman had come to mean so much to him. It didn't seem possible that he could care so deeply for someone other than Helena or his mother, but he did now. And it was all very sudden at that.

For her part, Vanessa was thinking similar things, and wondering how her life would ever be the same again. It wouldn't, she was positive. Not ever again. Because of Bill.

The two of them sat with their backs to the gondolier, who was in the prow. They were facing St Mark's Basin, the vast expanse of water that rolled up to the quay.

Directly in front of them were the island of San Giorgio, the Church of the Salute, and the Dogana, the beautiful domed customs building. These buildings, known as the three pearls to the entrance of Venice, were turning golden in the late afternoon sunlight.

'The light of Turner,' Bill said, leaning forward intently, looking at the sky. 'Vanessa, do you see the changing light? It's gone a peculiar yellow, the yellow

Turner captured so perfectly on canvas. I've always loved the paintings he did of Venice.'

'So have I. And this view is the very best,' she replied. 'The entire city floating on water, the water changing with the light. The whole scene is . . . dreamlike . . .' Vanessa paused, thinking how truly lovely it was. Magical, almost otherworldly. It moved her; she felt the unexpected prick of tears in her throat, touched as she was by the beauty of this city.

Sky and shifting water merged, golden, then iridescent in the lowering light of the afternoon. All the colours of Venice were reflected now in the Grand Canal as they floated along it, heading for the hotel.

Fading sunlight caught the cupolas of the basilica, streaking them to silver, touching the pale colours of the palazzos, giving the pink, terra-cotta, ochre, and powdery yellow a dusky, golden cast. All these colours of La Serenissima blended in a delicate mix, with just the hint of green here and there. And everywhere the sense of blue . . . blues bleeding into watery greys.

The gondola slid slowly up the Grand Canal, past the ancient palazzos jammed close together, almost higgeldy-piggeldy, tall and narrow. The houses were built on stilts, just as Venice itself was built on pilings pounded into the sand, silt, and rock centuries ago.

Sinking, she thought, they say it's sinking. And it was, very slowly, even though some of the rot had been stopped.

Vanessa stared at the palazzos, all of them full of priceless treasures, works of art by the great masters, paintings, sculptures, silver and gold objects, tapestries, furniture. How terrible if it all sinks, she thought with a shudder. What a tragedy that would be.

Bill increased the pressure of his arms around her, and she leaned back against him. She was falling in love with him. She shouldn't, but she was, and she didn't know how to stop herself.

They sat in the bar of the Gritti Palace and had hot chocolate, tiny tea sandwiches, and small, delicious cakes. It was growing dark outside, the bright sunlight of earlier had dulled to leaden grey, and a wind had blown up, but it was warm inside, comfortable in the bar. They were enjoying being together, getting to know each other better.

At one moment Vanessa murmured, 'You haven't really said where you're going from here, Bill. Is it Bosnia again?'

He was silent for a moment and then he nodded, his face suddenly grim. 'But only to do a wrap-up. I won't be there longer than three or four days, thank God.'

'The war must have been awfully hard to cover . . . I saw such horrors whenever I turned on the television. I can't imagine what it was like to actually be there.'

'It was hell.'

'It affected you . . . I know from the way you spoke with Frank.'

'Yes, the war did affect me, change me. I've been a witness to genocide . . . the first war and genocide since the last war and genocide in Europe. That was in the thirties when the Nazis started persecuting the Jews, exterminating them, along with the gypsies and anyone else they thought needed killing off. I never imagined it could happen again, or if it did, that the world would permit it.' He shook his head and shrugged. 'But the world *has* permitted it, and the civilized world, at that. Excuse me, Vanessa, I shouldn't use that term. Nobody's civilized as far as I'm concerned. All any of us have is a thin veneer; scratch that in the right place and a monster will appear.' He gave her a hard look, and went on, 'As a newsman I have to be dispassionate, objective and balanced. Like a bystander, *watching*, in a sense.'

Vanessa nodded. 'Yes, I understand, but that must be very hard for you.'

'It is now. At one time I could move around at will, from battlefield to battlefield, without being upset or disturbed. Bosnia has altered all that. The savagery, the butchering of innocent, unarmed civilians. My God, it was horrific at times . . . what we all witnessed. There are no words strong enough or *bad* enough to describe it.'

Vanessa was silent.

After a moment she reached out and took hold of his hand, held it tightly in hers, knowing better than to say a word.

Bill was quiet for some time. He finally said, 'I'm going to be doing a special on terrorism. I have two months to put it together. We'll start filming in January through February, so that we can air it in March.'

'That's why you're not going to be based in Sarajevo?'

'Correct. I'll be travelling through the Middle East.'

'Will . . .' She tightened her grip on his hand and leaned into him. 'Will we be able to meet?'

'I hope so, darling. I'm counting on it.'

'Shall we make Venice our place of rendezvous?'

He squeezed her hand. 'I think that's a brilliant idea.'

'When are you coming to New York in December?'

'About the fifteenth. I have two weeks' vacation due.' He searched her face. 'That won't present a problem will it, meeting in New York?'

'No, of course not. And I've a favour to ask,' she said, smiling.

'Then ask it.'

'Can I meet your daughter?'

'Do you want to *really*?'

'Yes, Bill, I do.'

'Then you've got a date. I'll take you all to lunch. Helena, my mother, and you. It'll be great, having my three best girls out on the town with me.'

CHAPTER 8

New York, December 1995

VANESSA STEWART had always prided herself on her honesty. It was not only an honesty with those people who occupied her life, but with herself. For as long as she could remember, she had despised prevaricators and even those who merely half-fudged the truth.

But now on this icy December day she had to admit to herself that she had not been honest for a long time. At least, not as far as her private life was concerned.

There was no longer any question in her mind that she had lied to herself about the state of her marriage. And lied to Peter, too, by not forcing him to admit that their marriage was floundering, not working on so many different levels.

I've lied by omission, she thought, remembering the line Bill had used in Venice some ten days ago now.

By not being open with Peter, I've only compounded our basic problem. I'm as much at fault as he is. And there was a problem. More than one, in fact.

Face the truth, Vanessa suddenly admonished herself. Be a big girl, accept things the way they are now. They're not the same as they once were; they haven't been for a long time.

A distracted look settled on her face as she focused on her marriage, the drawings spread out in front of her now forgotten. She and Peter no longer communicated very well, hardly at all, really. The shared confidences of their courtship and the early days of their marriage had long since been abandoned. Their sex life was practically nonexistent. And whenever they did make love these days it was usually because they had quarrelled. Peter had always believed that this was the best way of making up. Certainly the easiest for him, she now thought.

But quite aside from this, they spent a great deal of their time apart. They were always in different places, or so it seemed to her.

And their interests were very different. They had grown apart . . . as they had grown in different ways.

It's no marriage at all, Vanessa thought. It's just a sham, truly it is. We stay together out of . . . *what*? Suddenly she did not know why they stayed together. Unless it was out of habit. Or loyalty. Or lack of a better place to go. Or someone else to go to. Or laziness. Which one of these reasons it was, she had no idea. Perhaps it was all of them in combination.

Placing the pencil on top of her drawing board, Vanessa leaned back in the tall chair where she sat and stared out of the huge window in front of her. Her mind was racing.

Her design studio was in a building downtown in Soho, on the corner of Mercer and Grand. It was a fifth-floor loft looking south, and she had fallen in love with it at first sight because of its spaciousness and extraordinary natural light.

The view from her window was familiar to her, but it never failed to please her. She had not grown tired of looking out at her own special corner of Manhattan. The splendid nineteenth-century buildings were lined up before her eyes, while behind them the pristine twin towers of the World Trade Center, all black glass and steel, pierced the afternoon sky.

Two centuries juxtaposed, she thought, as she did every so often. The past. The present. The future.

The future. Those words danced in her head.

What was *her* future?

Was it to continue to live this lie with Peter? This lie that was their marriage . . . no, the remnants of their marriage.

Or was she going to leave him?

Is that what the future held? A life without Peter Smart, the only man she had ever known, except for Bill Fitzgerald? Well, that wasn't quite the truth either, if she were scrupulously honest. There had been one other man in her life. Steven Ellis. Her college beau. Her first lover, her only lover until she had met Peter. And then married him.

And now Bill Fitzgerald was her lover. Her clandestine lover. Was it because of Bill that she was suddenly looking truth in the face? Had her relationship with him forced her to be honest for the first time in several years? More than likely. Yes, it's because of Bill and the way you feel about him, a small voice in her head whispered.

A deep sigh escaped her. She did not know what to do. Should she make Peter see their marriage for what it was, a sham? If she did, what would happen? And what did *she* want to happen? Peter might say they should start all over again, try to make a go of it. And where would she be then? Was that what she wanted? A future with Peter Smart?

What she had said about him to Bill was true. Peter was a good man, a decent human being. And he did love her in his own way. Furthermore, he looked after her well, and he had been extremely supportive about her work, had encouraged her career. Peter was a caring man in a variety of ways, and reliable, dependable, loyal.

And she was absolutely convinced he would be hurt and unhappy if she left him. He depended on *her* in so many ways.

Why would she leave Peter anyway?

Because of Bill?

Yes.

But Bill hasn't asked you to leave Peter. He hasn't made any kind of commitment to you, that insidious voice whispered. In fact, he rapidly agreed to an affair, a secret affair. He accepted the idea of being your clandestine lover. Actually, he suggested it, the voice added.

But Bill or no Bill, her life with Peter had grown . . . empty? *Yes.* Stale? *Yes.* Lonely? In many ways, *yes.* They didn't share anything anymore, at least that was the way she saw it, the way she felt. There was so much lacking in their relationship. For her, anyway. Maybe Peter felt differently. Maybe he expected less of marriage than she did.

And what did she want in a marriage?

Emotion. Love. Warmth. Companionship. True feelings shared. Sexual love. Understanding. Was that too much to ask of a man? Surely not. Certainly it was not too much for her to give.

Peter had not offered her many of these things lately, quite the contrary. And wasn't that one of the reasons she had ended up in bed with Bill in Venice? Yes, the little voice answered. But it had also happened because she was overwhelmingly attracted to Bill. Falling in love with him? Yes, it was happening. Hadn't she known that days ago in Venice?

Falling in love, Vanessa thought. More like falling into madness.

It was dusk when Vanessa left her studio and got into the waiting radio cab that she had ordered earlier. As the driver headed uptown, her thoughts again turned to the problems in her life. Wrestling with them was not proving to be very fruitful; certainly she wasn't coming up with any answers for herself. The only thing she knew for sure was that her Venetian interlude with Bill, the feelings they had shared, had only served to point up the unsatisfactory relationship she had with Peter.

Comparisons, she thought, I hate comparisons. They're odious. But, of course, how could she not compare the emotional closeness she and Bill had enjoyed with the aridness of her life with Peter?

It suddenly struck her that Peter was denying her

his love, himself, just as he had denied her a child. Instantly, she crushed that thought, not wanting to confront it, or deal with it now.

On the spur of the moment, she leaned forward and said to the driver, 'I need to make a stop on the way uptown. I'd like to go to Lord & Taylor, please.'

'Okay, miss,' the driver said, and turned left off Madison when they reached East Thirty-ninth Street. He headed west to Fifth Avenue, where the famous old store was located.

The driver parked the cab on the side street, but Vanessa walked around to Fifth Avenue and stood looking at the Christmas windows. They were always the best, she knew that from her childhood. The windows were full of wondrous mechanical toys, breathtaking scenes from famous fairy tales and the classics, magical to every child.

Pressing her nose against the window, as she had done when she was a child, she smiled inwardly, watching an exquisitely made toy ballerina, dressed in a pink tutu, pirouetting to the strains of 'The Sugar Plum Fairy.' The music was being piped out into the street, and it brought back such a rush of forgotten memories that Vanessa's throat tightened unexpectedly.

Her mother and father had always taken her to see *The Nutcracker* if they were in New York over Christmas, just as they had brought her here to see the store's windows before going inside to meet Santa Claus and confide her Christmas wish.

Sometimes they had not been in Manhattan at Christmas, but in California or Paris or London, depending on her mother's current movie or play. Or what her father, Terence Stewart, was directing at the time. She was an only child, and they had always taken her with them on location or wherever they went. She had never suffered because of their theatrical careers; she had had a lovely, and very loving, childhood and had remained extremely close to her parents.

Eventually Vanessa turned away from the window, suddenly overcome by feelings of immense sadness and loneliness. An aching emptiness filled her, as it so often did. It was a feeling that threatened at times to overcome her. Somehow, she always managed to throw it off. She knew what it was – the longing for a child. But Peter did not want the responsibility of a child, and so she had buried the longing deep inside herself, sublimated the desire for a baby in her work. But, occasionally that terrible yearning gripped her, as it was doing now. She tried to still it, wishing it away.

Pushing through the swinging doors, Vanessa went into the store, her mind focusing on Helena, Bill's little girl. She was looking for something truly special. Helena was six, and there were so many things to buy for a child that age. Taking the escalator, she rode up to the children's department, spent ten minutes looking around and left empty-handed. Nothing had caught her eye.

As she hurried across the main floor, Vanessa stopped to buy tights and winter boot socks, then picked up eye makeup she needed before returning to the cab.

When she arrived at their apartment on East Fifty-seventh Street, Vanessa was surprised to find her husband at home. He usually never got in from his law office before seven in the evening at the earliest.

She shrugged out of her topcoat in the foyer and was hanging it up in the closet when he came out of their bedroom.

He was holding a couple of silk ties in his hand, and his face lit up at the sight of her. Smiling hugely, Peter said, 'Hi, sweetie.'

'You're home early,' she answered, walking forward.

He nodded, kissed her on the cheek as she drew to a standstill. 'I wanted to get my packing done before dinner.'

'Packing?' A frown marred the smoothness of her wide brow. 'Where are you going?'

'To London. Tomorrow morning. I have to see Alex Lawson. As you know, he's filming there at the moment. Anyway, his contract for his next two movies is finally ready, and I've got to go over it with him, walk him through it. It's a bit more complicated than usual.'

'Oh, I see.'

'Don't look so glum, Vanessa. I'll be back in ten days, certainly in time for Christmas.'

'Does it take ten days to walk an actor through a contract? Or is he particularly dumb?'

'Vanessa! How can you talk like that about Hollywood's biggest heartthrob,' he said and laughed a deep-throated laugh, amused by her comment. 'You, of all people! Coming from a show business family as you do.'

When she made no response and moved away, Peter took hold of her arm and gently turned her to face him. 'I thought we'd go somewhere special for Christmas.

Mexico . . . Bali . . . Thailand. Anywhere you want.'

'But my mother will be in New York for Christmas . . .' Her voice trailed off. Suddenly she felt depressed.

'All right, then we'll stay here; it was just an idea. But no problem, no problem at all, sweetie.' He went back into the bedroom.

Vanessa followed him, placed her Lord & Taylor shopping bag on the bed, and sat down next to it.

Peter spent a moment or two sorting ties, then he turned around and gave her a puzzled look when he saw the expression on her face. 'What's the matter?' he asked, walking over to the bed, looming up in front of her.

She met his steady gaze with one equally as steady, but the expression on her face was thoughtful. Her husband was thirty-eight years old. Slim, attractive, a man in his prime. He had a genial personality, natural charm, and was popular both with his friends and clients. A brilliant lawyer, he had become highly successful in the past few years, and the success sat well on him. Peter Smart had everything going for him. And yet his personal life was abysmal. She ought to know; she shared it with him. It was empty, arid, pointless. As was hers. Didn't he notice this? Or didn't he care? Then it suddenly hit her like a ton of bricks: Was there another woman in his life? Is that why he had nothing to give *her* anymore?

'You're looking odd,' Peter remarked in a quiet voice.

She cleared her throat. 'I'm sorry you're going away; I'd hoped we could spend a quiet weekend together. I want to talk to you, Peter.'

He frowned. 'What about?'

'*Us*.'

'You sound serious.'

'I feel serious. Look, you and I . . . things are just not right between us these days.'

He gaped at her. 'I don't know what you mean, Vanessa.'

'What's our life about?' She gave him a penetrating stare. 'We seem to be . . . drifting apart.'

'Don't be so silly!' he exclaimed with one of his light, genial laughs. 'Our life is very much on track. You're a doer and an achiever, and you have a career you love. You're doing extremely well, and you've accomplished so much with the design studio. I'm going great guns at the law firm. Things couldn't be better on that score. So why do you ask what our life is all about? I don't understand what you mean.'

All of a sudden she knew that he didn't, that he was genuinely puzzled. She exclaimed, 'But we're never together. We're always in different places, and when we are in the same city, you constantly work late. And when we're at home you haven't got a lot to say to me anymore, Peter; and there's another thing, we don't seem to be as close physically as we were.' It was on the tip of her tongue to ask him if he was having an affair, and then she changed her mind. He might well ask her the same question, and then what would she say?

Peter was shaking his head, looking miserable, the laughter of earlier wiped out of his eyes. He threw the ties onto a chair and sat down on the bed next to her, took hold of her hand. 'But, Vanessa, I love you, you know that. Nothing's changed. Well, I guess it has.

I'm successful, very successful, and in a way I never dreamed I could be. This is the big one for me, the big chance, and I don't want to screw it up. I can't, because what I do now, how I handle everything now, is for our future. Yours and mine. Our old age, you might say.'

'Old age!' she exploded. 'But I don't care about that! I want to live now, while I'm still young.'

'We are living, and living very well. And doing well. That's what counts, sweetie.' He gazed into her eyes, and said more softly, 'I guess I've been neglecting you lately. I'm sorry.' He put his arms around her, tried to kiss her, but Vanessa drew away from him.

'You always think you can solve our problems, our disagreements, by making love to me,' she said.

'But you know we always *do* solve what ails us when we're in bed together. We work it out that way.'

'Just for once it would be nice to make love with you because we *want* to make love, not to get us over one of our quarrels.'

'Then let's do it right now.'

'I don't want to, Peter. I'm not in the mood. Sorry, but this little girl doesn't want to play tonight.'

He recoiled slightly, startled by her sarcastic tone, and said slowly, 'Is this about the baby? Is this what all this talk of drifting apart is about? Is that it, Vanessa?'

'No, it's not.'

'I know I've been tough on you about having a baby –' he began and stopped abruptly.

'Yes, you have. You made it perfectly clear that you didn't want children.'

'I don't. Well, what I mean is, I don't right now. But

listen, sweetie, maybe later on, a few years down the line; maybe we can have a child then.'

She shook her head and before she could stop herself she said, 'Perhaps we ought to separate, Peter. Get a divorce.'

His expression changed immediately and he sat up straighter on the bed. 'Absolutely not! I don't want a divorce and neither do you. This is silly talk. You're just tired after all the work you did in Venice, and the schedule you've set for yourself with the new collection.'

Vanessa was regarding him intently, and she realized that he was afraid of losing her. She could see the fear in his eyes.

When she remained totally silent, Peter went on swiftly, 'I promise you things are going to be different, Vanessa. To be honest, I thought you were happy, excited about your design career. I hadn't realized . . . realized that things weren't right between *us*. You do believe me, don't you?'

'Yes,' she murmured wearily. 'I believe you, Peter.' She got up off the bed, and walked towards the bedroom door. Dismay lodged in her chest. 'There's not much for dinner. Shall I make pasta and a salad?'

'Certainly not. I'm going to take you out, sweetie. Shall we go next door to Mr Chow's?'

Vanessa shook her head. 'I don't feel like Chinese food.'

'Then we'll go to Neary's pub. Jimmy always gives us such a great welcome, and I know you love it there.'

CHAPTER 9

Southampton, Long Island, December 1995

VANESSA SURVEYED the living room of the cottage through newly objective and critical eyes. There were no two ways about it, the room looked shabby and decidedly neglected.

She did not care about the shabbiness; the faded wallpaper, the well-washed chintz and worn antique rug were all part of its intrinsic charm. It was the feeling of neglect that bothered her. She knew that the entire cottage was scrupulously clean, since it was maintained by a local woman. But the living room, in particular, had a lackluster air to it.

Bill would be arriving in a few hours to spend the day and part of the next with her, and she wanted the cottage to look nice. Since he spent so much of his time roughing it in battle zones and second-rate hotels, she felt the need to make it comfortable, warm and welcoming for him.

When her parents had divorced several years ago, they had not known what to do with Bedelia Cottage. Neither of them had wanted it and yet they had been reluctant to sell it, oddly enough because of sentimental reasons. They both had a soft spot for it.

And so they had ended up giving it to their daughter. Vanessa had been thrilled.

It was located at the far end of Southampton and stood on three acres of land that ran all the way up to the sand dunes and the Atlantic Ocean.

The cottage was not in the chic part of town, nor was it very special, just a simple, stone-and-clapboard house, about forty years old. It had four bedrooms, a large kitchen, a living room, and a library. There was a long, covered veranda at the back of the cottage which fronted onto the sea.

Once the house was hers, she had turned the old red barn into a design studio and office and converted the stone stables into a small foundry with a kiln. It was here in the studio and foundry that she spent most of her time designing and executing the handblown glass prototypes she took to Venice to be copied and produced in Murano.

Being as preoccupied as she was with work, Vanessa did not give the cottage much attention. Piles of old newspapers and magazines, which she had saved for some reason, were stacked here and there; current books, which she hoped one day to read, were piled on a chest and the floor; and several large vases of dried flowers, which had looked so spectacular in the summer, had lost their colour and were falling apart.

Glancing at her watch, she saw that it was just eight o'clock. Bill was arriving at one. Mavis Glover, who had looked after the cottage for years, usually came at nine.

Suddenly deciding not to wait for her to appear, Vanessa made a beeline for the piles of books, carried them to the library next door and found a place for them all on the bookshelves. For the next hour she worked hard in the living room, discarding newspapers, magazines, and the bedraggled dried flowers.

Finally, standing in the middle of the room and glancing around appraisingly, Vanessa decided she had made a vast improvement. Because the room was no longer cluttered, the furniture was suddenly shown off to advantage. The French country antique pieces stood out. Their dark wood tones were mellow against the white walls and the blue chintz patterned with pink and red tulips, which hung at the windows and covered the sofas and chairs.

Not bad, not bad at all, Vanessa thought, and hurried out to the large family-style kitchen. Last night, when she had arrived, she had put the flowers she had brought from the city into vases; now she carried one of these back to the sitting room. The second one she took upstairs to her bedroom.

This had once been her parents' private sanctuary, and to Vanessa it was the nicest room in the cottage. Certainly it was the largest. It had many windows overlooking the sand dunes and the ocean beyond, and a big stone fireplace was set in one of the end walls.

Entirely decorated in yellow and blue, the room had

a cheerful, sunny feeling even on the dullest of days. It was comfortable to the point of luxury.

Hurrying forward, Vanessa put the vase of yellow roses on the coffee table in front of the fire, and then went into the bathroom to take a shower. Once she was made up and dressed she would start on lunch while Mavis cleaned the rest of the cottage.

As she stood under the shower, letting the hot water sluice down over her, Vanessa luxuriated for a moment or two in thoughts of Bill. He had arrived in New York last Friday, December the fifteenth, as he had said he would. That was five days ago now. They had managed to snatch several quick drinks together on Sunday and Monday. He was busy with CNS most of the time; but when he was not, she did not want to intrude on hours he had set aside for his daughter.

'I'll drive out to the Hamptons on Wednesday morning,' he had told her over their last drink at the Carlyle. 'I can stay over until Thursday, if that's all right with you. How does it sound?'

It had sounded wonderful to her, and her beaming face had been her answer to him.

She could hardly wait to see him, have his arms around her, his mouth on hers. At the mere thought of making love with him, her body started to tingle. She snapped her eyes open and turned off the shower.

No time for fantasizing, she chastised herself, reaching for a towel. Anyway, within the space of a few hours she would have the real thing. They would be together.

Once she was dry, Vanessa dressed quickly, choosing a heavy red sweater to go with her well-washed blue jeans. Since it was a cold day, she put on thick white wool socks and brown penny loafers. Her only jewellery was a pair of gold earrings.

Once she had applied a little makeup and sprayed on perfume, she ran downstairs to prepare lunch for Bill.

He was late.

Vanessa sat in the small library, leafing through *Time* and *Newsweek*, wondering where he was, hoping he was not trapped in traffic.

Foolish idea that is, she thought. It was a Wednesday morning in the middle of December, and the traffic had to be light from Manhattan. It was only in the summer that it became a nightmare. She was quite certain Bill would find it straight sailing today; she had given him explicit driving instructions, and, anyway, the cottage was easy to find, just off the main road.

By one forty-five, when he had still not arrived, her anxiety was growing more acute by the minute. She was just deciding whether or not to call the network when she heard a car drawing up outside and she rushed to the front door.

When she saw Bill alighting, then taking his bag out of the trunk, she felt weak with relief. A moment later he was walking into the house, his face wreathed in smiles.

He took hold of her at once, pulled her into his arms. She clung to him tightly.

'Sorry, darling,' he said against her hair. 'I was delayed at the network and then it was tough getting out of New York this morning. A lot of traffic. Christmas shoppers, I guess.'

'It's all right . . . I thought something had happened to you.'

'Nothing's going to happen to me,' he said, tilting her face to his in that special way he had.

'Let's go into the living room. It's warmer,' Vanessa murmured, taking his arm. 'I've got white wine on ice, or would you prefer Scotch?'

'White wine's fine, thanks.'

They stood together in front of the roaring fire, sipping their wine and staring at each other over the rims of their glasses.

'I've missed you, Vanessa.'

'I've missed you too.'

'You know something . . . I think about you all the time.'

'So do I – I think of you, I mean.'

'It's funny,' he said softly, looking at her closely. 'I feel as if you've been in my life always, as if I've known you always.'

'Yes. It's the same for me, Bill.'

He shook his head, smiled faintly. 'I didn't dare touch you when we were in the bar of the Carlyle . . . you're very inflammatory to me.'

She stared at him, saying nothing.

He stared back.

Putting his glass on the mantelpiece, he then did the same with hers, moved closer to her, and brought her into the circle of his arms. He kissed her hard, pressing her even closer to him, wanting her to know how much she excited him.

Vanessa tightened her embrace, responding to him

with ardour, and this further inflamed him. Bill said in a low, hoarse voice, 'I want you so much, want to be close to you.'

Pulling away from him, she nodded, took hold of his hand, and led him upstairs to her bedroom.

There was tremendous tension between them. They undressed with great speed, sharing an urgent need to be intimate and closely joined. As they fell on the bed, his hands were all over her body. Loving hands that touched, stroked, explored, and brought her to a fever pitch of excitement.

They could not get enough of each other. He continued to kiss her, and she returned his kisses with the same intense passion she had felt in Venice. And Bill luxuriated in the nearness of her, in the knowledge that she longed for him, needed him so desperately. He felt the same need for her. It was a deep, insatiable need.

Stretching his body alongside hers, he took her suddenly, moving into her so swiftly he heard her gasp with surprise and pleasure. As she clasped him tightly in her arms, her legs wrapped around him, they shared a mounting joy.

Vanessa lay quietly in his arms.

The wintry afternoon sunshine cast its pale light across the yellow walls, turning them to bosky gold.

The only sound was the light rise and fall of Bill's breath as he drowsed and, far beyond the windows, the faint, distant roar of the Atlantic Ocean.

She found the stillness soothing.

Their lovemaking had been passionate, almost frantic, and even more feverish than in Venice. Their need for each other had been so overwhelming, it had stunned them both; afterwards they had stared at each other in astonishment. Now this tranquillity was like a balm.

Stretching her body slightly, trying not to disturb him, Vanessa took pleasure from her sense of satisfaction and fulfilment. How different she was with Bill; she even surprised herself. Each time they made love, they seemed to soar higher and higher, reach a greater pitch of ecstasy. It always left her reeling.

In some ways, Vanessa no longer recognized herself. She knew she had undergone a vast change since meeting Bill Fitzgerald. He brought out something erotic and sensual in her, made her feel whole, very feminine, very much a woman.

Pushing herself up onto one elbow, Vanessa looked down at him. The tense, worried expression he invariably wore had disappeared. In repose, his face was smooth, free of pain and concern. He looked so young, very vulnerable. And he touched her deeply.

Vanessa was aware that they had an intimacy of heart and mind as well as body, and it pleased her. They genuinely understood each other, and this compatibility gave them a special kind of closeness that few people shared.

She knew she was in love with him. She knew she wanted to be with him. For always. But was that possible? How could it be? She was not free. She had a husband who loved her, who was terrified of losing her. And for her part, she owed him loyalty and consideration.

Troubling thoughts of Peter insinuated themselves into her mind. She pushed them to one side. Too soon to think of the future . . . Later. She would think about it later.

In the meantime, she was absolutely certain of one thing. With Bill Fitzgerald she was her true self, without pretence or artifice. She was the real Vanessa Stewart.

She brought a tray of food and a bottle of white wine upstairs to the bedroom, where they had a picnic in front of the fire. And after they had devoured smoked salmon sandwiches, Brie cheese and apples, and downed a glass of wine each, they dressed and went out.

The thin sun still shone in the pale azure sky and the Atlantic had the gleam of silver on it. It was a blustery day with a high wind whipping the waves to turbulence.

Bundled up in overcoats and scarves, their arms wrapped around each other, they walked along the dunes, oblivious to the world, to everything except themselves and their intense feelings for each other.

At one moment Bill stopped and spun her to face him, looked down into her expressive grey eyes. 'I'm so happy!' he exclaimed. 'Happier than I've been for years.'

'What did you say?' she shouted back, also competing with the roar of the ocean.

'. . . happier than I've been for years,' he repeated, grinning at her, catching her around her waist, pulling her to him. 'I love you,' he said, his mouth on her ear. 'I love you, Vanessa Stewart.'

'And I love you, Bill Fitzgerald.'

'I didn't hear you,' he teased.

'I LOVE YOU, BILL FITZGERALD!' she screamed at the top of her lungs.

His joyous laughter filled the air.

She joined in his laughter, hugging him to her.

And then, holding hands, they ran along the sand dunes, buffeted forward by the wind, euphoric in their love, happy to be alive, to be together.

Later that evening they sat in front of the fire in her bedroom, listening to Mozart's violin concertos.

Vanessa, suddenly looking across at Bill, saw how preoccupied he was as he stared into the flames, noted how tensely set his shoulders were.

'Are you all right?' she asked in a soft voice. When he did not respond, she pressed, 'Bill, is something wrong?'

He lifted his head, looking directly at her. But still he said nothing. Disturbed by the sadness on his face, she went on, 'Darling, what is it? You look so . . . unhappy . . . even troubled.'

He took a moment, averting his eyes, focusing again on the fire. Finally he said, 'This is not a game for me.'

Frowning, she gaped at him. 'It isn't a game for me either.'

Bill said, 'This afternoon I told you I loved you. It's the truth.'

There was such a questioning look on his face she couldn't help but exclaim, 'And I love you. I *meant* what I said, Bill. I don't lie. Do you doubt me?'

He was silent.

'How could you possibly doubt me?' she cried, her voice rising. 'It's not possible to simulate the kind of emotions you and I have been sharing since we met.'

'I know that, and don't misunderstand my silence,' he was quick to answer. 'I know you have deep feelings for me.' Leaning forward, he took hold of her hand, gripped it in his. 'I just want you to know that I'm serious about you –' He paused, pinned his eyes on her. 'I'm playing for keeps.'

Vanessa nodded.

'Just so long as you know,' he said.

'Yes, I do, Bill.'

'I'll never let you go, Vanessa.'

'You might change your mind,' she began, but halted when she saw the stern expression on his face.

'I won't.'

Vanessa sat back on the sofa, gazed abstractedly at the painting above the fireplace.

He asked in a low voice, 'What are you going to do?'

'I'll tell Peter I want a divorce.'

'Are you sure?'

'Yes, I'm sure.'

'So am I. I've never been more sure of anything in my life.' Moving closer to her on the sofa, he put his arms around her and held her against him. And he knew he had the world in his arms. She was the only woman for him, the only woman he wanted.

CHAPTER 10

New York, December 1995

BILL HAD ASKED VANESSA to meet him at Tavern On The Green at twelve-thirty on Saturday, and as she walked into the famous restaurant in Central Park she realized what a good choice it had been.

Always festive at any time of year, it was spectacular during the Christmas season. Beautifully decorated Christmas trees were strategically placed, strings of tiny fairy lights were hung in festoons throughout while branches of holly berries in vases and pink and red poinsettias in wooden tubs added an extra fillip to the seasonal setting.

The magnificent Venetian glass chandeliers, which were permanent fixtures in the main dining room, seemed more appropriate than ever at this time of year.

Bill spotted her immediately. Rising, he left the table and hurried forward to meet her.

As he came towards her, she thought how handsome he looked, and he was extremely well-dressed today. He wore a navy blue blazer, blue shirt, navy tie, and grey pants. He was bandbox perfect, right down to his well-polished brown loafers.

Grabbing her hands, he leaned into her, murmured, 'You look great, darling,' and gave her a perfunctory kiss on the cheek. 'Come and meet the other two women I love,' he added as he led her to the table, the proud smile still in place.

Vanessa saw at once how attractive and elegant his mother was, and she seemed much younger than sixty-two. Dressed in a dark red wool suit that set off her beautifully coiffed auburn hair, she looked more like Bill's older sister than his mother.

Sitting next to his mother was undoubtedly the most exquisite child Vanessa had ever seen. She had delicate, perfectly sculpted features, wide-set cornflower blue eyes that mirrored Bill's, and glossy dark blonde hair that fell in waves and curls to her shoulders.

'I've never seen a child who looks like that,' Vanessa exclaimed softly, turning to Bill. 'Helena's . . . why she's positively breathtaking.'

He squeezed her arm. 'Thank you, and yes, she is lovely looking, even though I say so myself.'

They came to a standstill at the table, and Bill said, 'Mom, I'd like to introduce Vanessa Stewart. And Vanessa, this is my mother, Drucilla.'

'I'm so glad to meet you, Mrs Fitzgerald,' Vanessa said, taking his mother's outstretched hand.

'Hello, Miss Stewart.' Drucilla smiled at her warmly.

'Oh, Mrs Fitzgerald, please call me Vanessa.'

'Only if you call me Dru, everyone does.'

'All right, I will. Thank you.' Vanessa looked down at the little girl dressed in a blue wool dress, who was observing her with enormous curiosity. 'And you must be Helena,' she said, offering the six-year-old her hand.

'Yes, I am,' Helena said solemnly, taking her hand.

'This is Vanessa,' Bill said.

'I'm delighted to meet you, Helena,' Vanessa murmured, and seated herself in the chair Bill had pulled out for her.

'Now, what shall we have to drink?' Bill asked, looking at all of them. 'How about champagne?'

'That would be nice,' Vanessa said.

'Yes, it would, Bill,' his mother agreed.

'Is this a celebration?' Helena asked, gazing up at Bill, her head on one side.

'Why do you ask that, Pumpkin?'

'Gran says champagne is only for celebrations.'

'Then it's a celebration,' Bill responded, his love for his child spilling out of his eyes.

'And what's this celebration?' Helena probed.

Bill thought for a moment, looked at his mother, and answered, 'Being here together, the four of us. Yes, that's what we're celebrating, and Christmas, too, of course.'

'But I'm not allowed champagne,' Helena remarked, staring at him, then swivelling her eyes to Dru. 'Am I, Gran?'

'Certainly not,' her grandmother responded firmly. 'Not until you're grown up.'

Bill said, 'But you are allowed a Shirley Temple, and that's what I'm going to order for you right now.' As he was speaking, Bill signalled to a hovering waiter, who promptly came over to the table and took the order.

Vanessa said to Dru, 'It was a great idea of Bill's to suggest coming here for lunch; it's such a festive place.'

Dru nodded. 'You're right, it's fabulous. Bill tells me you met in Venice. When he was there with Frank Peterson.'

'Yes . . .' Vanessa hesitated and then, noticing Bill's beaming face, she went on more confidently, 'We spent Thanksgiving together.'

'The only three Americans in Venice on that particular day,' Bill interjected. 'So we had no alternative but to celebrate together. And a good time was had by all.'

'I'd like to go to Venice,' Helena announced, looking from her father to her grandmother. 'Can I?'

'One day, sweetheart,' Bill said. 'We'll take you when you're a bit older.'

'Do you work with my daddy?' Helena asked, zeroing in on Vanessa.

'No, I don't,' Vanessa answered. 'I'm not in television, Helena. I'm a glass designer.'

The child's smooth brow furrowed. 'What's that?'

'I design objects, lovely things for the home, which are made in glass. In Venice.'

'Oh.'

Vanessa had been carrying a small shopping bag when she arrived, and this she had placed with her handbag on the floor. Now she reached for it, took out a gift tied with a large pink bow, and announced, 'This is for you, Helena.'

The child took it, held it in her hands, staring at the prettily wrapped present. 'What is it?'

'Something I made for you.'

'Can I open it now, Daddy?'

'Yes, but what do you say first?'

'Thank you, Vanessa.' Helena untied the ribbon, took off the paper, and then lifted the lid off the box.

'It's quite fragile,' Vanessa warned. 'Lift it out of the tissue paper gently.'

Helena did as she was bidden, held the glass object in her hands carefully, her eyes wide. It was a twisted, tubular prism that narrowed to a point. Its facets caught and held the light, reflecting the colours of the rainbow. 'Oh, it's beautiful,' the child gasped in delight.

'It's an icicle. An icicle of many colours, and I made it specially for you, Helena.'

'Thank you,' Helena repeated, continuing to hold the icicle, moving it so that the glass caught the light.

'It is very beautiful,' Dru murmured, turning to Vanessa. 'You're a very talented artist.'

'Thank you.'

Bill said, 'May I look at it, Helena?'

'Yes, Dad. Be careful. Vanessa says it's fragile.'

'I will,' he murmured, his eyes smiling at Vanessa as he took the icicle. 'This is quite wonderful,' he said, and then nodded when the waiter brought the champagne in a bucket of ice. 'You can open it now, please,' he said.

After the glass icicle was returned to its box and put on the floor next to Helena's chair, and the wine had been poured, Bill lifted his flute. 'Happy Christmas, everyone.'

'Happy Christmas,' they all responded.

Helena took a sip of her Shirley Temple and put it down on the table. Turning, she stared hard at Vanessa, and, with undisguised inquisitiveness, she asked, 'Are you Daddy's girlfriend?'

Taken aback by the child's candour, Vanessa was speechless for a moment.

Bill answered for her. 'Yes, she is, Helena.' He smiled at his little daughter, then looked over her head at his mother, raising a brow eloquently.

Drucilla Fitzgerald nodded her approval. And she did approve of this pretty young woman whom she had known for only twenty minutes. There was something about Vanessa that was special; she could tell that, being the good judge of character that she was. Vanessa was to be encouraged, Dru decided. Anyone who could bring this look of happiness to her son's face had her vote of confidence. He had been so lonely after Sylvie's death. And morose for years. She had not seen him so buoyant, spirited, and full of good cheer for the longest time. Suddenly, she felt as if a weight had been lifted off her shoulders.

'Let's order lunch,' Bill said. 'Do you know what you want, Pumpkin?'

'Yes, Daddy. I'd like to have eggs with the muffin, like we did last time.'

'Eggs Benedict,' Dru clarified. 'I'd love it too, but I don't think I'd better. Not with my cholesterol. I suppose I'll have to settle for crab cakes.'

Bill looked at Vanessa. 'Do you know what you want?'

'I'll have the same as your mother, Bill, thank you.'

'And I'll keep Helena company, go for the Eggs Benedict,' he said.

Helena touched Vanessa's arm. 'Are you going to marry Daddy?'

Vanessa was further startled by the child's outspoken question, and by her precocity. She glanced swiftly at Bill.

Dru sat back in her chair, observing the three of them.

Bill grinned at Helena and said, 'You ask too many questions, Pumpkin, just like Uncle Frank does sometimes. And we don't know yet whether we're going to get married or not . . . we need to spend more time together, get to know each other better.'

Helena nodded.

Bill went on, 'But you and Gran will be the first to know if we do. I promise you.'

Later, as Bill helped Vanessa into a cab, he whispered, 'Not a bad idea my kid had, eh?'

'Not a bad idea at all,' Vanessa replied.

'Take this, darling,' he said, pressing something into her hand.

'What is it?' she asked, looking down at it, realizing that it was a key. 'What's this for?'

'The suite I booked at the Plaza. For us. Suite 902. Can we meet for a drink later tonight? Say around nine?'

'But of course,' she said and slipped the key into her bag.

CHAPTER 11

Venice, January 1996

IT HAD BEEN RAINING all afternoon, hard, driving rain that was still coming down in an endless stream. The sky was the colour of anthracite, pitted here and there with threatening black clouds, and below her the Grand Canal was swollen, looked as if it might overflow at any moment.

Vanessa turned away from the window and moved into the room, shivering slightly. Although Bill had turned up the heat earlier, when she had first arrived from the airport there had been a chill in the air. It was a dampness that seemed to permeate her bones. She tightened the belt on the bathrobe she was wearing and shrugged further into it as she huddled in a chair near the radiator.

Vanessa was glad to be back in Venice with Bill. It was the first time they had seen each other since

Christmas. He had left New York at the end of December, to travel through the Middle East and Europe. Tel Aviv, Jerusalem, Amman, Beirut, Ankara, and Athens were some of the cities on his list. He was busy preparing his special on international terrorism for CNS; time was of the essence since it had been scheduled to air early in March.

Bill had arrived at the Gritti Palace a day earlier than Vanessa, flying in from Athens the night before just as she was leaving New York. They would have five days together in their favourite city. She had work to do out at the glass foundry on Murano. Bill was going to polish his script for the show, and they would be together in the afternoons and evenings.

A smile touched her mouth as she thought of Bill and her love for him. He meant more to her than she had ever imagined possible. He was the man of her life. For the rest of her life. They were meant to be together, and there was nothing that could keep them apart. She knew that now.

A small sigh escaped as she thought of the past few weeks. Apart from seeing Bill, meeting his mother and Helena, December had been a ghastly month for her. Peter had stayed in London longer than he had intended, and after his return to Manhattan he had left almost immediately for Los Angeles. He had been away so much she had barely had a chance to discuss their private life, and Christmas had been miserable for the most part.

Finally, early in January, she had cornered him one evening when he returned from the office earlier than usual. Endeavoring to be as gentle as possible, while displaying no weakness whatsoever, Vanessa had told him she wanted a divorce.

Peter had reacted badly, overreacted really, and had been adamant that they remain married. Even though he had agreed, in the end, that their relationship was no longer what it had once been, he nonetheless refused even to consider divorcing. Very simply, he balked at the idea and wouldn't listen to her. At least not that particular evening.

Vanessa had come to realize that there was only one thing to do, and that was to get on with her life, lead it as she saw fit, and be independent. Ten days before leaving on this trip to Venice, she had taken her courage in both hands and left Peter, moving all of her clothes and possessions into the loft in Soho.

The loft had once been an apartment before she had turned it into a studio-office, and it had a good-sized working kitchen, a full bathroom, plus a guest toilet. Once she had purchased a sofa bed and installed it in the back storage room, turning this into a bedroom, the loft had become a comfortable place to live. Most important, it had made Peter realize just how determined she was to end their marriage. Her departure had a tremendous impact on him; he at last understood how serious she was about a divorce.

As her mother had said to her, 'Actions make more of a statement than words ever could, Vanny, and it's best to end this now, while you're both still young enough to start all over again, find new partners.' Both of her parents had been very supportive of her decision to leave Peter. However, she had not told them about Bill, deeming it wiser to keep her own counsel at this moment.

Vanessa heard Bill's key in the lock and glanced at the door as he came in. Getting up, she went to him, her face full of smiles.

He had gone downstairs a few minutes earlier to pick up a fax which had arrived from New York. Now he waved it and said, 'Neil Gooden and Jack Clayton *love* the footage so far. Neil says he can't wait to see the rest of it.' Bill handed her the fax. 'Here, read it yourself, darling.'

She scanned the two pages, digested everything, and handed it back to him. 'Congratulations, Bill. From what Neil says, you've worked miracles and in less than three weeks. Aren't you thrilled he thinks it's going to be a smash?'

'From his mouth to God's ears,' Bill said with a huge grin, and putting his arm around her shoulders he walked her over to the sofa.

'I do think it's coming together, though. I just need to cover two more cities and then it's a wrap, as far as the field reporting is concerned. When you go back to New York, I'll head for Paris, work there a couple of days with my crew and the producer. Then we'll all go on to Northern Ireland, make Belfast our last stop. Incidentally, I've finally come up with a good title.'

'What is it?'

'I'm thinking of calling the special *Terrorism: The Face of Evil*. What's your feeling about it?'

'I think it sounds good. And it says exactly what you mean.'

He nodded. 'Yes, I guess it does. What I've managed to do is cover terrorism around the world. I've been filming interviews with experts, and some terrorists who are in jail in Israel. I'm backing up the new stuff with footage of past acts of terrorism, from the 1972 killing of the Olympic athletes and Lord Mountbatten's murder by the IRA to the Lockerbie crash, the World Trade Center bombing, and the Oklahoma City explosion. I've endeavored to make it very personal, very intimate. I want it to hit home, touch the average American. I'll be using some interviews I did with survivors of terrorism, and relatives of victims of terrorists. I'm quite gratified by the way it's come together.' Bill got up, walked across to the mini bar, and took a bottle of mineral water from it. 'Do you want anything, Vanessa?'

She shook her head.

Bill strode back to the sofa, sat down next to her. After taking a sip of water, he placed the bottle on the coffee table and placed his arm around her. 'Moving into the loft was a very good idea, Vanessa. It's shown Peter how serious you are about a divorce.'

'Yes, it has. He phoned me yesterday, just as I was leaving for Kennedy. And while he didn't actually *agree* to a divorce, he did sound more amenable, if a little crushed. I have the feeling he's beginning to accept the idea.'

'That's a relief.' Bill looked at her intently. 'Did you tell him about me? About us?'

'No, I didn't, Bill. I didn't think it was necessary. And anyway, it would be like a red flag to a bull. Very inflammatory.'

'I don't care if he knows, you know. I'm a big boy. I can look after myself.'

'Yes, but why rub salt in the wound? Anyway, Peter really has come to accept how bad our relationship has been for the last few years . . . I prefer to leave it at that.'

'Whatever you say, sweetheart, you're the boss.'

She gave him the benefit of a loving smile.

He leaned closer, kissed her on the mouth. 'The concierge just told me Venice will be flooded by seven o'clock. No Harry's Bar tonight, I'm afraid. We'll have to eat here.'

'That's fine, Bill. The restaurant downstairs is good.'

'Oh, but I thought we would have room service, eat here in the suite.'

'Yes, if you want, I think it's more comfortable anyway, and I don't have to get dressed.'

He nodded and reached for her. 'My thought precisely.'

'You once suggested that we make Venice our point of rendezvous,' Bill said to her much later that evening, after they had made love, eaten dinner, and made love again. 'And I think that's a great idea. It's going to be very convenient for me.'

They were in bed and Vanessa lay within the circle of his arms. She swivelled her eyes to meet his. 'What do you mean?'

'When I've finished the special on terrorism, I'm being assigned to the Middle East. I'll be based either in Israel or Lebanon, that's up to me. But whichever it is, I can fly straight up to Venice. It's an easy trip. I'll try to be here whenever you're working at the foundry in Murano, if only for a couple of days, or a long weekend.'

Her face lit up. 'Oh, Bill, that'll be wonderful, being

able to see you every month. Well, more or less. Why the Middle East, though?'

'I didn't want to go back to Bosnia, as you know, even though there's trouble there again. There always will be, too, if you ask me. And the peace accords are very fragile, not likely to last, especially if the UN troops leave. Still, I wanted out, and Jack Clayton was aware of that ages ago. So he asked me if I'd like to go back to the Middle East to cover the whole area. I know it well, and Frankie's in Lebanon. So it'll be like old home week.' He grinned at her. 'As I'm telling you this, I'm beginning to realize that I will base myself in Beirut, set up camp with Frankie at the Commodore Hotel.'

'When will that be, darling?'

'In March sometime. I'll be cutting and editing at CNS in New York in the middle of February, preparing the special. And then I'll go.'

'I thought everything was quiet in the Middle East right now.'

'As quiet as that area will ever be. There are always rumblings of some kind, somewhere, be it Iran, Libya, Saudi Arabia, Syria, Israel, or Iraq. You name it. Flare-ups happen all the time,' Bill explained.

'If your assignment starts in March, when do you think we can meet here again?'

Bill held her closer, smiling at her, his blue eyes crinkling at the corners. 'In March, of course. The end of March.'

CHAPTER 12

Venice, March 1996

'ARE YOU SURE there are no messages for me?' Vanessa said, her eyes focused intently on the concierge standing behind the desk at the Gritti Palace.

'No, Signora Stewart, no messages.' His faint smile seemed almost apologetic as he added, 'No, nothing at all. No faxes, nothing, signora.'

'Thank you.' Vanessa turned away from the desk and walked rapidly towards the elevator.

Once she was back in her room, she sat down at the writing table in front of the window and gazed absently out at the Grand Canal.

It was a cool, breezy Saturday in late March, but the sun had come out and given a certain radiance to the afternoon. Yet she was hardly aware of the weather; her thoughts were focused on Bill. She opened her appointment book and stared at the date.

It was March the thirtieth, and she had been in Venice for four days, working at the foundry on Murano. Bill was supposed to have arrived on Thursday afternoon, the twenty-eighth, to join her for a long weekend.

But he was forty-eight hours late, and she did not understand why. After all, it was not as if he were in a war zone and in any danger. Beirut was quiet at the moment; he had told her that himself. She dismissed the idea that something might have happened to him.

It struck her then that he could have gone somewhere else in the Middle East to cover a story. He had talked about Egypt and the Sudan to her when he had been in New York in February. They had been able to meet only once at that time because he had been busy editing his special on terrorism, and then he had had to leave for Beirut.

Yes, that was most likely the reason he was late. Right now he was probably on a plane, flying to Venice from some distant spot. This thought cheered her, but an instant later she was worrying again. If he had been delayed because he was caught up on a story, why hadn't he phoned her?

Frowning to herself, Vanessa reached for her address book and quickly found the number of the Commodore Hotel in Beirut. Glancing at the hotel's chart for direct dialling to foreign cities, she picked up the phone and punched in the numbers for Beirut and the hotel.

It was only a second or two before she heard the hotel operator saying, 'Hotel Commodore.'

'Mr Bill Fitzgerald, please.'

'Just a moment, please.'

She heard the ringing tone. It seemed to her to be interminable. He did not pick up. He was not in his room.

'There's no answer,' the operator said. 'Do you wish to leave a message?'

'Yes. Please say Vanessa Stewart called. He can reach me at the Gritti Palace in Venice.' She then gave the operator the number and hung up, sat staring at the phone.

After a few moments, she rose and walked over to the coffee table. Picking up the remote control, she turned up the volume on the television set. The CNS weatherman was giving the weekend forecast for the States. She sat down on the bed and watched CNS for the next couple of hours.

World news. American news. Business news. Sports news. But no news of Bill Fitzgerald, chief foreign correspondent for CNS.

Later in the evening, for the umpteenth time that day, Vanessa checked her answering machines at the Manhattan loft and the cottage in Southampton. There was no message from Bill.

At one point she ordered sandwiches, fruit, and a pot of hot tea. She had not eaten anything since breakfast, and suddenly she was feeling hungry. After her light supper she watched CNS until the early hours, although she did so with only half an eye. It was mostly repeats of everything she had seen earlier, and her mind was elsewhere anyway.

On Sunday morning, after she had drunk a quick cup of coffee, Vanessa dialled the Commodore Hotel in Beirut and asked for Bill Fitzgerald.

Once again, there was no answer in his room.

This time, Vanessa asked to be put through to Frank Peterson. She clutched the phone tightly, listening to the ring, hoping that at least Frank would pick up. He did not.

After a split second the hotel operator was back on the line. 'I'm sorry, both of them seem to be out, miss. Would you like to leave a message?'

'Yes, for Mr Fitzgerald. Please ask him to call Vanessa Stewart at the Gritti Palace in Venice.'

Vanessa spent a miserable Sunday, waiting for the phone to ring and watching CNS and CNN on television, alternating between the two cable networks. At one point she checked her answering machines in the States, but there were no messages. Not a whisper from anyone. She even phoned the international news desk at CNS headquarters in New York. But they wouldn't give her any information about Bill's whereabouts.

By late afternoon she had given up hope of Bill arriving. In any case, she was due to leave for New York on Monday morning, and so she got out her suitcase and began to pack. She did so in a flurry of emotions – frustration, anger, disappointment, worry, and dismay.

That night, when she went to bed, Vanessa was unable to sleep. She turned restlessly for hours, praying for morning to come.

Eventually she must have dozed off because she awakened with a start as dawn was breaking. As she lay there in the dim, grey light Vanessa finally acknowledged what she had been denying all weekend: The real reason Bill had not shown up was because he was no longer interested in her. Their affair was over for him. Finished. Dead.

No, she thought, he cared too much. I'm wrong.

And yet deep down she knew she was right. There was no other possible reason for his absence.

She closed her eyes, remembering all the things he had said to her . . . that he loved her . . . that he was playing for keeps . . . that he was serious about her . . . that this wasn't a game for him. He'd even encouraged her to divorce Peter. Why did he do that, if he hadn't meant what he said?

Well, of course he meant those things when he said them, that niggling voice at the back of her head muttered. He was glib, slick, smooth. A wordsmith. Clever with all those wonderful words that tripped off his tongue so lightly. Wasn't that all part of his talent? Hadn't he told her that his grandmother had always said, when he was growing up, that he'd kissed the Blarney Stone?

There was another thing, too. He was back in the close company of Frank Peterson, his best friend, his alter ego. Frank was a man Bill had characterized as a womanizer with a terminal Don Juan complex. Those had been his exact words. Maybe they were off somewhere together for the weekend. Bill was very close to Frank, and impressed by him. And perhaps some of Frank's habits were contagious.

Suddenly she felt like a fool. She had been sitting here waiting for Bill for four days and there hadn't been the slightest word from him. As chief foreign correspondent for CNS he had access to phones wherever he was. He could have called her from anywhere.

But he had not, and that was a fact she could not ignore.

Dismay lodged in the pit of her stomach and she found herself trembling. Tears sprang into her eyes and she sat up, brushing them aside as she turned on the light, looked at her travel clock. It was five o'clock. She sat on the side of the bed for a moment, endeavoring to pull herself together. As painful as it was, she had to admit that she had been dumped. Why, she would never know. She began to cry again, and she discovered that she could not stop.

CHAPTER 13

Southampton, Long Island, April 1996

'OVER THE YEARS, I've discovered that the more you love a person, the more they're bound to disappoint you in the end,' her mother had once said to her, adding: 'And, in my opinion, men understand this better than we do. That's why they rather cleverly spread their bets. Always remember that, Vanny. Don't give all for love. And don't be duped.'

But she had given all for love. And she had been duped. And she had remembered her mother's wise words far too late for them to matter.

Was it true? Did men spread their bets when it came to women? Was that what Bill had done?

Certainly she had loved him a lot, put all of her trust in him. And in the end he *had* bitterly disappointed her. But no, wait, it was so much more than disappointment, wasn't it? He had humiliated her, made her feel foolish, even ridiculous, and he had hurt her so badly she thought she would never recover from that hurt. It cut deep . . . deep into her very soul.

She had been so open with him, so honest, baring her soul, her innermost secret self. She had given him everything she had to give, far more than she had given any other man, even her husband.

Seemingly, her gifts of love and adoration had meant nothing to him. He had discarded her as easily as he had picked her up in the bar of the Hotel Gritti Palace.

Unexpectedly, and quite suddenly, she remembered something he had said to her about Frank, something about Frank hedging his bets as far as women were concerned. Perhaps all men did that.

Vanessa let out a long sigh and walked on across the sand dunes, her heart heavy, her mind still fogged by the pain of Bill's defection.

It was a fine, clear day in the middle of April – cold, with a pale sun in a pale sky. The Atlantic Ocean was calmer than it had been for days despite the wind that was blowing up.

She lifted her eyes and stared up into the sky when she heard the *cawk-cawk* of seagulls. She watched them as they wheeled and turned against the clouds.

The wind buffeted her, driving her towards the beach. She hunched down farther into her heavy duffle coat and stuck her gloved hands into her pockets. She felt dispirited to the point of depression.

She was well aware that her depressed emotional state was because of Bill Fitzgerald and what he had done to her. She found it hard to believe that he had disappeared from her life in the way that he had, but it was true. At times she even tried to tell herself she didn't care. But of course she did.

Their love affair had been so intense, so sexual, so passionate in every way and so . . . *fierce*. He had swept her off her feet and into his bed and then out of his life when he had grown tired of her. Just like that. *Puff*! She was gone. Had their affair been too hot? Had it burned out too fast for him? She was not sure. How could she be sure . . . of anything . . . ever again?

Vanessa felt the splatter of raindrops on her face and immediately looked up. Thunderheads were darkening that etiolated sky, turning it to leaden grey, and there was the sudden bright flourish of lightning, then the crack of thunder.

Turning swiftly, she walked back to the cottage at the edge of the dunes. She made it just in time. It was a cloudburst. The heavens opened and the rain poured down.

She locked the door behind her, took off her duffle, and went into the library. Here she turned on lamps, struck a match, and brought the flame to the paper and logs Mavis had stacked in the grate.

Since she had returned, Mavis Glover had taken to coming almost every day, fussing over her, bringing her fruit and vegetables and other groceries. Once Mavis had even offered to pick up newspapers and magazines, but Vanessa had told her not to bother. She was not interested in the outside world; she had cut herself off from it.

She had returned from Venice and moved out to Southampton permanently. She had turned herself into a virtual hermit. She had unplugged her telephone and pulled the plugs on the radio and the television. In fact, she vowed she would never look at television again as long as she lived.

She was out of contact with everyone. Out of action. The only person she saw or spoke to was Mavis.

Licking my wounds, she thought now as she sank onto the sofa in front of the fire. Licking my wounds like a sick animal.

The truth was, she did not want to see anyone, not even her mother. The world was well lost for her.

Peter had sent the divorce papers; they had arrived yesterday by special delivery. She had laughed loudly and hollowly when she had seen them. As if they mattered now. She had pushed for the divorce when Bill was a part of her life, and now seemingly he had discarded her.

The anger flared again in her and with it came the hot, endless tears. Pushing her face down into the cushions, she cried until she thought there were no tears left in her.

She sat up with a start. The fire had almost gone out. Glancing at the mantelpiece, she focused on the clock. It was just five. Time to go to work.

Pushing herself up off the sofa, Vanessa looked out of the window and saw that the rain had ceased. The late afternoon sky, washed clean of the dark clouds, was clear again.

After putting on her duffle coat, she walked slowly across the lawn to the red barn, then stopped for a brief moment as she passed the small copse of trees to the left of the house. Years ago her mother had planted hundreds of daffodils, and she had added to them since she had owned the cottage.

Many of them were pushing their golden heads upward, fluttering in the breeze, pale yellow beacons in the soft light. How fresh and springlike they looked. So pretty under the trees. Her eyes filled. She brushed her damp cheeks with her fingertips and walked on.

Once she was inside her studio, Vanessa focused on her work. Going to the drawing board, she switched on the light above it and was soon sketching rapidly, drawing spheres and globes, until she found her way through the many shapes springing into her mind. She settled, at last, on kidney and oval shapes.

Her work had become her salvation. She found it hard to sleep at night, and so she had reversed her routine. From five o'clock until eleven she created her designs in the barn. She had a drink and ate dinner at midnight, and then read half the night, until fatigue finally overcame her.

And once the designs on paper were finished, she worked in the foundry, hand-blowing the glass pieces. As she did she would ask herself how she would ever be able to go to Venice again. She would have to because of her work. But she knew she must find another hotel. She would never again set foot in the Gritti Palace.

CHAPTER 14

Beirut, April 1996

'YOU WERE THERE, JOE! What really happened?' Frank Peterson exclaimed, his voice rising slightly. His face was pale, and he looked strained and anxious.

Leaning over the table, he pinned his eyes on Joe Alonzo. 'What the hell happened to Bill?' he demanded again.

Joe shook his head. He looked as if he were about to burst into tears. 'I'm telling you, Frank, it was over before I could blink. We were in West Beirut, not too far from here, near the mosque. We all got out of the car, Mike, Bill, and me. Bill started to walk towards the mosque; Mike and I went to the trunk, to take out our equipment. Suddenly this big Mercedes slid to a stop. Three young men jumped out, grabbed Bill, and hustled him into the car. Then the Mercedes sped off.'

'And you didn't follow it!' Frank said in a hard, tight voice, staring at the CNS soundman. 'Jesus, Joe!'

'I know, I know, Frank, I can guess what you're thinking. But the point is, Mike and I were stunned for a second. We couldn't believe it.'

'And so you didn't react.'

'We did, but not fast enough! Within a few seconds we ran to our car, raced after the Mercedes, but we couldn't find it. The damned thing had just disappeared. Literally, into thin air.'

'These local terrorists know all the side streets and back alleys,' Frank said, and eyed Joe thoughtfully. 'And if you and Mike hadn't been taking your equipment out of the trunk, you would've probably been grabbed as well,' he asserted in a quieter tone.

'Damn right we would!' Mike Williams said, coming to a halt at the table where Frank and Joe were sitting in the bar of the Marriott in the Hamra district of Beirut.

Frank jumped up at the sight of Mike, grabbed his hand and shook it. 'Join us, Mike, I've just been talking to Joe about Bill's kidnapping.'

'It's a hell of a thing . . . we're at our wits' end . . .' Mike sat down heavily. He looked tired and worried. 'When did you get back to Beirut, Frank?'

'Last night. From Egypt. I was covering a story there when the new trouble between the Israelis and Hezbollah erupted. The civil war is over, everything's on the mend, and then they start skirmishing again. But did they ever *really* stop?'

'I doubt it,' Mike replied. 'Still, it's the first time the Israelis have attacked Beirut directly in fourteen years. And with laser-homing Hellfire missiles, no less, shot from four helicopter gunships off the coast. My jaw practically dropped when it happened two days ago.'

'Yeah, but the Israelis were actually responding to Hezbollah's bombing of Israel,' Joe pointed out quickly.

Frank nodded. 'And after Israel's attack on Beirut, Hezbollah retaliated yesterday by sending another forty rockets into Israel. The war of attrition continues.'

'Nothing changes much,' Mike murmured and motioned to a waiter, ordered Scotch on the rocks.

Frank said, 'I couldn't believe it when I saw the story on CNS about Bill's kidnapping. My God, I'd just left him when he was taken. I flew out of Beirut on March twenty-seventh and he was grabbed the next day. And for most of the time I was away I thought he was having a good time in Venice.'

'He never made it to Venice,' Mike responded. 'I'm sure you realize the network sat on the story for a few days, hoping he would be released quickly. When he wasn't, they got it on the air at once.'

'Who's behind it? Have you heard anything?' Frank probed.

'No, we haven't,' Joe answered.

'I was just on the phone to Jack Clayton,' Mike explained. 'The network still doesn't have any information. Nobody's claiming this, the way the bastards usually do. It's a bit of a mystery. Total silence from all terrorist groups, according to New York.'

'It's got to be Hezbollah,' Frank said in a knowing tone. He turned from Mike to Joe, raising a brow. 'Who else but them?'

'You're right,' Joe agreed. 'That's what Mike and I

think, too. At least, we believe that the Islamic Jihad is behind it. You know better than anybody, Frank, that the terrorist arm of Hezbollah is full of wackos. They're the ones who took Terry Anderson and William Buckley, and they're not known for fast releases.'

'Terry Anderson was a hostage for seven years,' Frank muttered.

'Don't remind me,' Mike said dourly. 'By the way, we've been in touch with Bill's mother.'

'I spoke with her myself from Egypt,' Frank answered. 'As soon as I knew what had happened. It's remarkable the way she's holding up.'

Joe volunteered, 'We try to call her every few days. Unfortunately, there's not much we can tell her.'

'Hearing from you helps her a great deal, I'm sure of that.' Frank lifted his glass, downed the last of his Scotch. Leaning back in his chair, he thought for a moment about Vanessa. He had tried to reach her for days, but there was no answer at her loft or the cottage in the Hamptons. 'What's the network doing about trying to find Bill?' he asked.

'There's not a lot they can do,' Mike said. 'Bill's picture has been circulated throughout Beirut, the whole of Lebanon, in fact. And a great deal of pressure has been put on the Lebanese and Syrian governments, and right from the beginning. Even though the story wasn't released immediately, the CNS top brass were on top of the situation at once, the same day Bill was snatched.

'And pressure was put on the White House as well. Let's face it, Frank, there's nothing anyone can do until an organization claims the kidnapping as theirs. Only then can the US Government and the network start pushing for Bill's release.'

'I always kidded him, said he was bulletproof,' Frank began and stopped when Allan Brent, the Middle East correspondent for CNN, stopped at their table.

'We've just had a news flash,' he said. 'Hezbollah is claiming they have Bill Fitzgerald.'

'Oh, Jesus!' Frank cried.

'How long ago was the flash?' Joe asked.

Allan Brent glanced at his watch. 'It's now seven, about six-thirty, thereabouts.'

Mark Lawrence, who was covering Bill's kidnapping for CNS, appeared in the doorway of the bar. When he spotted the CNS crew with Frank and Allan Brent, he hurried over. He said to Mike, 'I guess you've heard that the Islamic Jihad has Bill.'

'Yes,' Mike said. 'Allan just told us.'

'I hope to God Bill's all right,' Frank cried. 'I *pray* to God he's all right. That group is fanatical, unstable, and unpredictable.'

It was always dark in the cramped, airless room.

They had nailed old wood boards over the windows and only thin slivers of light crept in through the cracks.

Bill Fitzgerald turned awkwardly on the narrow cot; his movements were restricted by handcuffs and leg chains. Managing at last to get onto his back, he lay staring up at the ceiling, trying to assess what day it was.

All along he had attempted to keep track of time; he figured he had been a hostage for almost two weeks. When he asked his various guards, they wouldn't tell him. All they ever said was, 'Shut up, American pig!'

He felt dirty, and wished they would allow him to have another shower. He had only been permitted two since his capture. His clothes had become so filthy he had begged them to give him something clean, which one of his guards had done yesterday. *Finally*. Cotton undershorts, a T-shirt, and a pair of cotton pants had been thrown at him, and he had been unchained in order to change into them. The clothes were cheap, but it was a relief to have them.

He had no idea where he was, whether he was still somewhere in Beirut or in the Bekaa Valley, that hot-bed of Hezbollah activities where the Iran-backed militia was in control. So many hostages had been held there.

Bill didn't even know why he had been taken, except that he was an American and a journalist. But he *was* certain of one thing – the identity of his kidnappers. They were young men of the Islamic Jihad, the terrorist arm of Hezbollah, and dangerous. Some of them were slightly crazed, on the edge, capable of anything.

They kept him chained up, shouted abuse at him, beat him every day, and gave him little food or water. And what food they did provide was stale, almost inedible. Yet despite their continuing mistreatment of him, he was not going to let them break his spirit.

Bill kept his mind fully occupied as best he could.

He thought mostly of his child, his mother, and of Vanessa, the woman he loved. He worried about them, worried about how they were reacting to his kidnapping, how they were handling it. He had faith in them, knew they would be strong; even his child would be strong.

As he lay staring at the dirty ceiling, he envisioned Vanessa's face in his mind's eye, projected her image onto the ceiling.

How lovely she was, so special, and so very dear to him. And how lucky he was to have found her. He knew they would have a wonderful life together. The first thing he was going to do when he was free was make a child with her. She wanted one so badly; she had confided that to him the last time they had been together.

He had worried about her for the first few days he was in captivity, knowing she was alone in Venice, waiting for him. And with no idea why he had not shown up.

Bill heard the key turning in the lock. He focused his eyes on the door and steeled himself for his daily beating. In the dim light he saw one of his captors entering the cell.

'Put on blindfold,' the young man said, walking across the room, showing the grimy rag to Bill.

'Why?' Bill asked, endeavoring to sit up.

'No speak, American pig! American spy!' the young man shouted and tied the blindfold around Bill's eyes roughly, pulled him to his feet, and led him across the cell.

'Where are you taking me?' Bill demanded.

'No speak!' the terrorist yelled, pushing Bill out of the room.

CHAPTER 15

Southampton, Long Island, April 1996

VANESSA SAT UP with a jerk, feeling disoriented, blinking as she looked around the library. Dimly, in the distance, the thudding noise that had awakened her continued.

She pushed herself to her feet, hurried across the room and out into the hall. Instantly the thudding sounded louder, and she realized that someone was hammering on the front door of the cottage.

She ran across the hall, shouting, 'I'm coming,' and flung open the door. Much to her surprise and consternation she found herself staring into the face of Bill's mother.

'Dru!' she exclaimed, completely taken aback. 'Hello! Have you been knocking long?'

When his mother did not answer, but simply stared at her blankly, Vanessa went on, 'Why have you come to see me? What are you doing here?' Her brows knitted together in a frown when suddenly she became aware of Dru Fitzgerald's troubled face and bloodshot eyes. She also noticed that she looked painfully thin. 'Dru, what's the matter?' she asked, urgency echoing in her voice.

Dru leaned against the door jamb, unexpectedly breathing hard, as if she was experiencing some sort of difficulty. She managed to say, 'May I come inside, Vanessa?'

'How rude of me to keep you standing here. Of course, please come in. Can I get you anything?'

'A glass of water, please. I must take a pill.'

Vanessa took hold of Drucilla's arm and escorted her into the cottage. After leading her to the sitting room, and settling her in a chair, she went to the kitchen for the water.

A moment later Vanessa returned. She handed the glass to Dru, waited for her to take the pill, then said, 'I can tell you're distressed about something. What's the matter?'

Drucilla Fitzgerald, staring intently at her, realized with a small jolt that Vanessa did not know what had happened to Bill. How that was possible she wasn't sure, but, nonetheless, she was quite certain it was true. Dru wondered how to tell her. Tears flooded her eyes, and she clasped her hands together to stop them from trembling.

Vanessa was about to ask her again what was causing her upset when Dru cleared her throat, reached out and took hold of Vanessa's hand.

Dru said slowly, almost in a whisper, 'I've been trying to reach you on the phone for days.' No longer able to control herself, she began to weep. She groped in her wool jacket for her handkerchief.

'I've had my phone turned off,' Vanessa explained, and as she said these words she had a terrible sense of foreboding. 'It's Bill! Something's happened to Bill, hasn't it?'

Dru continued to cry, her sobs almost uncontrollable, her pain even more apparent now.

Vanessa went and sat next to her on the sofa, put her arm around Dru's shoulders. 'I'm totally in the dark, Dru. I've had not only the phone turned off but the television as well. I've cut myself off from the world for the past two weeks.'

Dru turned to look at her, the tears streaming down her pale face. Her mouth began to tremble. 'He's dead,' she said in a voice that was barely audible. 'My son is dead. My only child has been taken from me in the most cruel way. Oh Vanessa . . . Vanessa . . . Why did they kill him? They shot him. He's never coming back. He's gone. Oh, whatever shall we do without him?' She continued to weep, gasping, holding her arms around her body. Her sorrow was unendurable.

Vanessa was gaping at Dru. She had gone cold all over, and she was stunned, reeling from shock, unable to respond for a moment. Her eyes welled, and she began to shake. At last, she said, 'I don't understand . . . *who* killed Bill?' Choking on these words, she was unable to continue, just held onto Dru tightly. The two women clung together, sobbing.

Eventually, through her tears, Dru said, 'It was Hezbollah. The Islamic Jihad. They kidnapped Bill, Vanessa. I realize now that you didn't know, otherwise you would have come to Helena and me, to be with us.'

'When?' Vanessa gasped. 'When was he taken?' Her voice shook and fresh tears flowed; she knew the answer even before Dru spoke.

'March the twenty-eighth,' Dru answered. 'It was a Thursday. They took him that morning in Beirut. He was out with the crew, Joe and Mike –'

'Oh, my God! My God!' Vanessa cried out, pressing both of her hands to her face, trying to stem the tears. They slid through her fingers, fell down onto her cotton shirt, leaving damp splotches. 'I was waiting for him in Venice, and he didn't come! I thought he'd lost interest in me, that it was over between us. But he couldn't come, could he? Oh, Dru, Dru . . .'

'No, he couldn't. He loved you, Vanessa, he wanted to marry you. He told me that. He also told me that you were married, that you were getting a divorce.'

Vanessa swallowed hard. 'Bill was mine and I was his and that was the way it was. How could I have forgotten that?'

Drucilla sighed and looked into Vanessa's face sadly. 'When we're in love, things are always very extreme, intense . . .'

'I love him with all my heart. I shouldn't ever have doubted him in Venice. I should have known something terrible had happened, something beyond his control.'

Dru was silent for a second, and then she said softly, 'You were feeling hurt.'

Vanessa suddenly lost control again and started to weep bitterly. 'When was he shot?' she asked through her tears.

'We're not sure.' Dru found it hard to continue. She brought her hand to her trembling mouth, and took a few moments to regain her composure.

Slowly, she went on, 'Andrew Bryce, the president of CNS, and Jack Clayton, Bill's news editor, came to see me yesterday.' Pausing, she took a deep breath before saying, 'To tell me themselves that the Islamic Jihad had just announced they had executed Bill. They left his body at the French Embassy in Beirut, who have given it to the American Hospital to send home.'

'But why did they kill him?' Vanessa cried. '*Why*, Dru?'

'Andrew and Jack don't know. No one knows. The Islamic Jihad haven't said anything. They've given no explanation.'

The two women who loved Bill Fitzgerald sat together on the sofa, not speaking, lost in their own troubled thoughts, silently sharing their heartbreak and sorrow.

After a while, Vanessa spoke. Looking at Dru, she said, 'Where is Helena?'

Dru covered her mouth with her hand once more, the tears starting afresh. After a moment she said, 'I brought her with me. I hadn't the heart to leave her. She's walking the dunes with Alice, the nanny. The child's heartbroken, she worshiped him so.'

Vanessa nodded. Rising, she walked across the room to the window, stood looking out at the dunes, her mind full of Bill and the love they had shared. She thought of his child. And she came to a sudden decision.

Turning to look at Bill's mother, Vanessa said, 'I

think you and Helena should stay here with me for a few days, Dru. Bill would want us to be together.'

Much later that night, when she was alone in her bedroom, Vanessa wept for Bill once more. She wept for the loss of the man she loved, the life they would never share, and the children they would never have.

It was a long night of tears and anguish. There was a moment when guilt reared up, but she crushed it before it took hold. It was a ridiculous waste of time to feel guilty because she had doubted him briefly. He would be the first to say that, just as his mother had.

As dawn broke over the dunes, Vanessa came to understand that her grief would last for a long time, and that she must let it run its course. Bill Fitzgerald had been the love of her life, and she had lost him in the blink of an eye. Lost him because of some insanity on the other side of the world. It was wrong, all wrong. He had been far too young a man to die.

It should not have happened, but it had, and she was alone. Just as his child and his mother were alone, bereft and lost without him. They were her main concern now. She would do what Bill would want her to do . . . console and comfort them.

They needed her. And she needed them.

CHAPTER 16

'I'M GLAD Alice listened to you, Dru, and took her vacation,' Vanessa said, stirring the chicken soup she was making, peering into the pot on the stove. 'It would have been foolish of her to cancel it, when she had it all planned. But you know, she never did say where she was going.'

Dru did not respond.

Vanessa said, 'Where has she gone, actually?'

Still Dru did not answer and Vanessa swung around, exclaimed, 'My God, what's wrong,' threw down the wooden spoon, and rushed across the kitchen.

Drucilla was leaning back in the chair, her face drained of all colour, starkly white against her red hair. She was clutching herself and wincing.

Vanessa bent over her. 'Dru, what is it?'

'Pain. In my chest. My left arm hurts. I think I'm having a heart attack.'

'Don't move! I'll get the car. Southampton Hospital's not far away. On Meeting House Lane. I'll have us there in a few minutes. Just don't move, Dru. Okay?'

Dru nodded.

Vanessa ran to the garage, backed the car out, parked it near the cottage, and leapt across the lawn to her studio. She had left Helena drawing there earlier. Pulling open the door, she called, 'Helena, come on, we have to go!'

'Where?'

'To the hospital. Your grandmother's not well.'

'I'm coming,' the child shouted fiercely, jumped off the stool, and flew across the floor. 'Is it her heart?'

'She thinks so, yes,' Vanessa said, took hold of Helena's hand, and ran with her to the cottage. 'Get in the car, honey, and I'll be out in a minute with Gran.' As she spoke, Vanessa helped Helena into the backseat and fastened the safety belt.

Inside the house, Vanessa grabbed her handbag from the hall closet, and dashed back to the kitchen; Dru was slumped in the chair with her arms still wrapped around herself.

Bending towards her, Vanessa asked, 'Dru, do you feel any worse?'

'No. Just the same.'

'Can you make it to the car?'

'Yes, Vanessa. If you help me,' Dru murmured in a weak voice.

Together the two women walked slowly across the kitchen and outside to the car. 'Try not to worry. You're going to be all right,' Vanessa said as she fastened the seat belt around Dru, praying that she would be.

And she kept on praying all the way to the hospital.

'Mrs Fitzgerald *has* had a heart attack, fortunately not too severe,' Dr Paula Matthews said, drawing Vanessa to one side of the waiting room. 'She's going to be all right, but she will have to watch herself, take care of herself.'

'Yes, I understand, Dr Matthews, I'll see that she does. In the meantime, how long does she have to be in the hospital?'

'A few days. Five at the most. She's in our cardiac care unit, more for observation and a rest than anything else.' The doctor smiled at Vanessa, then glanced at Helena, who was sitting on a chair near the window. 'I've never seen such a beautiful child,' she said. 'You're very lucky.'

'Yes,' Vanessa murmured, not knowing what else to say.

'Anyway, I know Mrs Fitzgerald's anxious to see you both, so let me take you to her room.'

A moment or two later Vanessa and Helena were sitting by the bed where Drucilla lay looking pale and weak. 'I'm so sorry, Vanessa, to put you to all this trouble,' Dru said in a low voice. 'What a nuisance I am.'

'Don't be so silly,' Vanessa exclaimed. 'You're not any trouble to me at all. And Helena and I are going to come and see you every day.'

Helena said, 'And Vanessa says we'll bring you things. Like books and magazines.' She smiled at her grandmother. 'And flowers, Gran.'

'Thank you, darling,' Dru murmured.

'Please don't worry about Helena,' Vanessa went on, taking hold of Drucilla's hand, squeezing it. 'She's no trouble, we'll be fine together.'

'But your work . . .' Dru began, looking worried.

'I can do my work and take care of Helena,' Vanessa reassured her. 'Just think about yourself and getting better.'

'I don't know how to thank you.'

'Thanks are not necessary, Dru, you know that. And I'm here for you, whenever you need me.'

'Bill told me you were a loving woman, and he was right,' Dru said. She averted her face for a moment, blinking back tears. Then, turning to look at them both again, she forced a smile. 'A hospital's no place for you two. Go and have lunch, and I'll see you tomorrow.'

'"Half a pound of tuppeny rice, half a pound of treacle. Mix it up and make it nice. Pop goes the weasel!"' Vanessa sang, leading the child around the room in a circle, holding both her hands.

Helena laughed, much to Vanessa's relief. She had been in floods of tears all morning, suddenly reacting to her grandmother's departure for the hospital the day before. Drucilla's heart attack, coming so quickly after Bill's death, had been too much for the little girl to handle.

Vanessa understood Helena's concern for her grandmother, but she had not been able to stem her tears, or comfort her. At least not until now. The little game they were playing seemed to have helped. It had brought a sparkle to the child's eyes.

'What a funny song,' Helena said. 'What's a weasel?'

'A little furry animal with a bushy tail that lives in the woods.'

'How do you know this song?'

'When *I* was six, I was living in London for a while with my parents. I had a nanny who was English. She taught me the song.'

'Can you teach me?'

'Of course. Sing along with me, Helena. Here we go. "Half a pound of tuppeny rice, half a pound of treacle. Mix it up and make it nice. Pop goes the weasel." '

Helena sang with her, and they went round and round in circles, holding hands. After half a dozen times Helena knew the words, had committed them to memory.

She laughed merrily and clapped her hands. 'I'll sing it for Gran when we go to the hospital this afternoon.'

'What a good idea, Pumpkin.'

The smile slid off Helena's face and she recoiled, gaping at Vanessa.

'What is it? What's wrong?'

'Don't call me Pumpkin. Only Daddy calls me that. It's his name,' she cried fiercely, and burst into tears.

Vanessa went to her, put her arms around her, held her close. 'I'm sorry, Helena, I didn't know. Don't cry, honey. Please.'

But Helena could not stop sobbing, and she clutched Vanessa as if never to let her go.

Vanessa smoothed her hand down the child's back, endeavoring to comfort her, to soothe her, making hushing noises.

After a while the sobs lessened, and Helena grew

calmer. Vanessa led her across the studio to the sofa, lifted her up onto it, and sat down next to her. Taking a tissue from the box on the coffee table, she wiped Helena's eyes, then drew her into the circle of her arms. 'In a little while we'll go into town and have a hamburger for lunch. How does that sound?'

'Can I have french fries?'

'Of course.'

'And an ice cream?'

Vanessa smiled at her. 'Yes, if you want.'

Helena nodded; then she bit her lip, suddenly looking tearful again.

'What's wrong, honey?'

'Is Gran . . .' Her bottom lip trembled and tears shimmered on her long lashes. 'Is Gran going to die?'

'No, of course not! Don't be silly!'

'People die of heart attacks, Vanessa. Jennifer's grandmother did.'

'Who's Jennifer?'

'My friend.'

'Well, *your* gran isn't going to die, I promise you that.'

'But she's in the hospital.'

'I know, and she's getting better. I explained to you yesterday, the reason Gran is in the hospital until Friday is because she needs a rest. That's all. Her heart attack wasn't a bad one, honey. Trust me, she'll be all right.'

'They're mending her heart at the hospital.'

'Yes,' Vanessa murmured, giving the child a reassuring smile.

'Gran's heart is broken. It broke the other day. When the men came.'

'Men?' Vanessa repeated, momentarily puzzled.

'Daddy's men. From the network.'

'Oh, yes, of course.'

'They told her my daddy is dead and it broke her heart.'

'Yes, darling . . .'

Helena gave Vanessa a piercing look. 'Is Daddy in Heaven?'

Vanessa swallowed. 'Yes,' was all she could manage.

The child continued to look at her closely. 'With my mommy?'

'That's right. They're together now,' Vanessa said, striving hard for control.

'When is he coming back, Vanessa?'

'Well . . . well . . . you see . . . he won't be able to come back, Helena. He's going to stay with your mother . . . he's going to look after her.' Vanessa averted her face, brushed away the tears.

Helena seemed confused. She frowned hard. 'I want him to look after me.'

'I know, I know, but he can't, honey, not right now. Gran's going to look after you.'

'But what if she dies too?'

'She won't.'

'How do you know?'

'I just do, Helena.'

'Why did the men kill my daddy?'

'Because they're bad men, darling.'

Helena stared at Vanessa and started to weep again. 'I want my daddy to come back. Make him come back, Vanessa.'

'Hush, hush, honey, don't cry like this,' Vanessa

murmured, endeavoring to soothe her. 'I'm here. I'll look after you.'

Helena pulled away, looked up into Vanessa's face. 'Can we live with you?'

For a moment Vanessa was taken aback, and then she replied, 'We'll have to talk to Gran about that.'

Helena nodded.

'By the way, where has Alice gone on vacation?' Vanessa continued, wanting to change the subject, distract Helena.

'To Minnesota. To see her mom and her brothers and sisters. Alice has a great-grandmother and she comes from Sweden.'

'Tell me some more about Alice.'

'Well, she takes me to school and picks me up from school, and she takes me to Central Park and she plays with me.'

Vanessa leaned back against the sofa, relieved that the six-year-old was now chattering normally, that she had managed to divert her.

CHAPTER 17

ON FRIDAY MORNING, Drucilla Fitzgerald was released from Southampton Hospital.

Vanessa and Helena were there to pick her up and take her back to Bedelia Cottage on the dunes. After the three of them had lunch together, Vanessa sent Helena to draw and paint in the studio. She needed to be alone with Dru for a short while in order to talk to her.

'Helena's a lovely little girl, she's a real credit to you,' Vanessa said as she and Drucilla relaxed over a cup of herb tea in the sitting room. 'We've become very good friends.'

Dru smiled and nodded. 'I know. She told me, and she sang "Pop Goes the Weasel" for me. She enjoyed herself with you, Vanessa, and I'm so glad she wasn't a problem.'

'No, not at all, Dru,' Vanessa began, and paused, then said, 'But I think . . .' She shook her head. 'I was going to say I think there's a problem, but I don't mean that at all.'

Dru was frowning, looking perplexed. 'What are you getting at, Vanessa dear?'

'I remember that when I was little I worried about a lot of things. All children worry; Helena worries.'

'About my health, is that what you mean?'

'Yes. Children can easily feel insecure, and threatened, when a parent is sick or in the hospital. And I believe Helena feels very vulnerable.'

'Yes, I'm sure she does, but she'll be all right, now that I'm out of the hospital. However, it'll take her a long time to . . . get over her father's death.' Drucilla choked up. It was a moment before she finished softly, 'It'll take us all a long time.'

'Yes, it will . . .' Vanessa's voice trailed off as she stood, walked to the window, and gazed out at the sea. It was a deep blue on this mild afternoon in early May, streaked with sunlight and no longer bleak and uninviting. In her mind's eye she saw Bill's face; he was never out of her thoughts. She focused on his little daughter, and she knew exactly what she must say to Drucilla.

Turning swiftly, Vanessa came back to the sofa and sat down next to Bill's mother. She gave her a thoughtful look, and said, 'Before your heart attack, you told me you had no relatives, and I was wondering if you had ever appointed a legal guardian for Helena?'

Drucilla did not seem at all startled by this question, and she answered evenly, 'No, I never have. We never have. It didn't seem necessary. But I know what you're getting at, Vanessa. You're wondering what would become of Helena if I were to die. Isn't that so?'

'Yes, it is. You're a young woman, Dru, and this heart attack has been a . . . well, a sort of warning, I think. I know you'll look after yourself from now on, and you're not likely to die until she's grown. But –'

'You're only voicing what I was thinking as I lay in that hospital bed this week,' Dru cut in. 'I've worried a lot about Helena, worried about her future. I'm sixty-two, as you know, and I aim to live for a long time. Still, you never know what might happen. Life is full of surprises and shocks . . .'

'Would you consider me? Could I become Helena's legal guardian, Dru?'

'Oh, Vanessa, that's lovely of you to volunteer, but would you want that kind of responsibility? I mean, what if I did die while she's still little? Would you want to care for a child . . . you're young, only twenty-seven, and one day you're bound to meet someone else. To be the guardian of another man's child could be a burden . . . a stumbling block to a relationship.'

'I don't see it that way, Dru, I really don't. If I were Helena's legal guardian. I would fulfil my obligations to her, no matter what the circumstances of my life. I realize you don't know me very well, but I am sincere and very trustworthy.'

'Oh, darling, I know that. Bill loved you so very much, and certainly I trust *his* judgement. Besides, I'm a good judge of character myself, and the day I met you, at Christmas at Tavern On The Green, I knew the sort of person you are. I felt then that a weight had been lifted from my shoulders because I could see how changed Bill was because of you. He was so happy. And I suddenly feel as if a weight has been lifted from me again.' Dru took hold of Vanessa's hand and held it tightly; suddenly her eyes welled. She said, 'I can think of no one I would like more to be Helena's legal guardian. I know that with you she would always be safe.'

Vanessa's eyes were also moist. 'Thank you, Dru. As soon as you're up to going to New York, I'd like to make an appointment with my lawyer. Or yours, whichever you prefer. We will set all this in motion. Is that all right with you?'

Dru nodded. 'I hope to live to a ripe old age, but it's good to know you're there in the background.'

'I'd like us to be together, Dru; I'd like to get to know Helena better, and you too. I was wondering, would you consider spending the summers here with me?'

If Drucilla was startled she did not show it. Without hesitation, she said, 'I'd like that, Vanessa, I really would. And I know Helena will be happy. She loves it here.'

'Then it's settled.' Vanessa leaned closer, kissing Dru on the cheek. 'There's something else I have to tell you.'

'Yes, what is that?'

'Frank called very early this morning. He's come to New York . . . with Bill's things . . . from his hotel room in Beirut. He wants to come and see us tomorrow. Is that all right?'

Drucilla found it hard to speak. She simply nodded her head and held Vanessa's hand all that much tighter.

* * *

'He was my best friend, I loved him,' Frank said quietly, looking at Bill's mother. 'Everybody loved Bill. He was such a special man.'

'He's dead and our lives will never be the same,' Dru murmured, her face ringed with sorrow. 'But we must go on, and bravely so. That's what he would want.'

'Only that,' Frank agreed. 'He was the bravest man I ever knew. He saved my life. Did you know that, Dru?'

'No, I didn't,' she replied. 'He never told me that, Frank.'

'He wouldn't, he was very modest in his own way –'

'Uncle Frankie!' Helena cried as she appeared in the doorway with Vanessa and rushed forward into his arms.

Frank held her tightly. She was part of Bill, and she looked so much like him, he thought. His throat tightened and for a moment he couldn't speak, so choked up was he.

Frank looked over Helena's head, his eyes meeting Vanessa's, and he nodded slightly. Then, releasing his godchild, he went to greet Vanessa, embracing her. 'I'm so sorry, so very sorry,' he said.

'So am I,' she whispered. 'I loved him, Frank.'

'I know. He loved you . . . I have something for you.' Drawing away from her, Frank reached inside his jacket, took out an envelope. 'I found this in Bill's room at the Commodore in Beirut.' He handed her the envelope.

She stared down at it. *Vanessa* Bill had written across the front. She bit her inner lip, pushing back the tears when she saw his handwriting. She stared at it for a long moment, afraid to open it.

Dru, watching her carefully, said softly, 'Perhaps you'd like to be alone when you read it, Vanessa. We'll leave you.'

'No,' Vanessa said. 'It's all right . . . I'll go . . . outside.' She left them in the sitting room and went across the back lawn and down to the dunes, clutching the letter tightly in her hand.

There was a sheltered spot where she often read, and she sat down there for a while, staring out at the sea, thinking of Bill, her heart aching.

Finally she opened the envelope and took out the letter.

Beirut
Monday, March 25th, 1996

My very dearest Vanessa:

I know I'll be seeing you in a few days, holding you in my arms, but I have such a need to talk to you, to reach out to you tonight, I decided to write to you. Of course you'll be reading this letter when I'm there with you in Venice, since I'll be bringing it with me.

The next few lines blurred as her eyes filled with tears, but after a few moments she managed to recover, and went on reading.

I don't think I've ever really told you how much I love you, Vanessa – with all my heart and soul and mind. You're rarely out of my thoughts and all I want is to make you happy. You've brought me back to life, given new meaning to my life. And now I want to share that life with you. You will, won't you, darling? You will be my wife and as soon as that's possible?

In my heart I can hear you say yes, yes, yes in that excited way you have. And I promise you I'll love and cherish you always. You know what, let's make a baby in Venice. I know how much you want a child. And I want it to be mine. I want to know that part of me is growing inside you. So let's do it this weekend, let's make a baby.

I've never told you this before, but in the last six years my life has been hellish. Three people I loved very much died on me. First Sylvie, then my father, and finally my grandmother. Their deaths broke my heart.

But over the past few months I've come to understand that the heart broken is the strongest heart.

Bill

Vanessa sat there for a long time, holding the letter. And then she folded it carefully, put it back in the envelope, and rising, she walked slowly across the dunes and into the cottage.

Love in Another Town

For my dearest husband Bob,
to whom I owe so much

CHAPTER 1

JAKE CANTRELL SLOWED his pick-up truck as he approached Lake Waramaug near the Boulders Inn, came to a standstill and gazed out of the window.

The lake was still; it held a glassy sheen, looked almost silver in the late afternoon light of this cool April day. He lifted his eyes to the etiolated sky, so bleached out that it, too, seemed as pale and as unmoving as the water. In stark contrast were the rolling hills rising up around the lake, darkly green and lush with trees.

Jake could not help thinking once again how beautiful the view was from this angle: a dreamy landscape of water and sky. To Jake, it was somehow evocative, reminded him of another place, yet he was not sure of where . . . some place somewhere he had never been, except in his imagination perhaps . . . England, France,

Italy or Germany, maybe even Africa. Some place he would like to go one day. If he ever got the chance. He had always wanted to travel, dreamed about going to exotic lands, but thus far in his twenty-eight years of life on this planet he had only been to New York City a few times, and twice to Atlanta where his sister Patty was now living.

Shading his eyes with one hand, Jake scanned the vistas of land, water and sky once more, then nodded. How incredible the light is today, almost otherworldly, he thought, as he stared ahead.

He had always been fascinated by light, both natural and artificial. The latter he worked with on a daily basis, the former he frequently endeavoured to capture on canvas, when he had time to pick up a paintbrush and indulge himself. He loved to paint whenever he could, even though he wasn't very good at it. But it gave him a great sense of satisfaction, just as did creating special lighting effects. He was working on a big lighting job now, one that was tough, tested his talent and imagination and fired his creativity. He loved the challenge.

The car behind him honked him forward, and, rousing himself from his thoughts, he pushed his foot down on the accelerator and drove on.

Jake headed along Route 45 North which would take him up to Route 341 and all the way to Kent. As he drove he kept noticing the unusual clarity of the light today; it echoed the light over the lake and seemed to get even brighter the farther north he drove.

Lately he had come to realize that this clear bright light was endemic to this part of the state, called the northwestern highlands by some, the Litchfield Hills by others. He did not care what people called the area. All he knew was that it was beautiful, so breathtaking he thought of it as God's own country. And the extraordinary, incandescent skies, almost uncanny at times, inspired awe in him.

This particular area was relatively new to him, even though he had been born in Hartford, had grown up there, and had lived in Connecticut all his life. For the past four-and-a-half years he had been a resident of New Milford, but he had rarely ventured beyond the town's boundaries. That is until a year ago, just after he had finally separated from his wife Amy.

He had stayed on in New Milford, living alone in a small studio on Bank Street for almost a year. It was around then that he had started driving into the countryside, going farther afield, looking for a new place to live, something a bit better than the studio, an apartment or, preferably, a small house.

It was on Route 341 near Kent that he had found the little white clapboard three months ago. It had taken him a few weeks to get it cleaned up, painted and made reasonably habitable, then he had scoured the local junk shops and sales looking for furniture. He was surprised at the things he managed to find, at prices which he considered reasonable. In no time at all he had managed to make the little clapboard fresh-looking and comfortable. His final purchases were a brand new bed, a good rug and a television set, all bought in one of the big stores in Danbury. Finally, he had moved in three weeks ago and had felt like a king in his castle ever since.

Jake drove on at a steady speed, not thinking about anything in particular except getting home. *Home.* He found himself contemplating that word all of a sudden.

It hovered there in his mind. 'Home,' he said out loud. And yes, he *was* going home. Home to his house. He savoured this thought, liking it. A smile lingered on his sensitive mouth. *Home. Home. Home.* The word suddenly had a very special meaning to him. It signified so much.

It struck him then that never in nine years of marriage to Amy had he ever called their various apartments home; usually, whenever he referred to them, he would say *our place*, or *back at the ranch*, or some such thing.

Now he realized that until today the word *home* had always meant the house in Hartford where he had been raised by his parents, John and Annie Cantrell, both dead for several years.

But the little white clapboard on Route 341, with its picket fence and neat garden, was indeed home, and it had become his haven, his place of refuge. There were several adjoining fields with a large barn standing in one of them, and this he had turned into a workshop and studio. Currently, he was renting the property, but he liked it so much he was seriously thinking of buying it. *If* he could get a mortgage from the bank in New Milford. *If* the owner would sell. Jake wasn't sure about either possibility at this moment. He could only hope.

Apart from being the right size, the house was close enough to Northville, where he had moved his electrical business a few weeks ago. He had wanted to be out of New Milford altogether because Amy still lived and worked there. Not that there was any animosity between them; in fact, they were quite good friends in spite of their break-up.

Their separation had been reasonably amicable, although initially she had not wanted to let him go. Eventually she had agreed. What option did she have? He had been long gone from her emotionally and physically, even when they still shared the same apartment in New Milford. The day he had finally packed his bags and made his intentions clear for the last time, she had exclaimed, 'Okay, Jake, I agree to a separation. But let's stay friends. *Please.*'

Long absent in spirit, and with one foot already out of the door, he had willingly agreed. What harm could it do? And, anyway, if it mollified her so much the better. Anything to make his escape easier, to get away from her at long last, in a peaceful way and without another row.

Jake's thoughts centred entirely on Amy for a moment or two. In many ways he felt sorry for her. She wasn't a bad person. Just dull, unimaginative and something of a killjoy. Over the years she had become an albatross around his neck, dragging him down, and inducing in him an unfamiliar state of depression.

He knew that he was bright and quick and clever. He always had been, even as a child. And he was good at his job. His former boss at Bolton Electric had constantly told him he was a genius with lighting and special effects. And because of his drive, hard work and talent he had moved up in life; he had wanted to move even farther, but she had held him back.

Amy was always afraid – afraid things would go wrong if they did anything out of the ordinary, or if he made a move to better himself and them and their existence. She had fought him two years ago when he had left Bolton Electric and started his own business.

'It's not going to work, it'll fail and then where will we be?' she had wailed. 'Anyway, what do you know about being a contractor?' she had gone on nervously, her face pinched and white and tight-lipped. When he hadn't answered her, she had added, 'You're a good electrician, Jake, I know that. But you're not good at business.'

He had been infuriated by her remark. Glaring at her, he had shot back, 'How do you know what I'm good at? You haven't been interested in me or anything I do for years.'

She had gaped at him, obviously shocked, but he was speaking the truth. It seemed to him now, as he remembered those words, that Amy had lost interest in him during the second year of their marriage.

Jake sighed. It had all become so sad and discouraging, and he wondered, for the umpteenth time, how it could have gone so wrong. They had grown up together in Hartford, had been childhood sweethearts, and had married right out of school. Well, almost. In those days the future had glittered brightly for him, had been full of promise.

He had his dreams and ambitions. Unfortunately Amy had neither. Within a few years he had come to realize that she not only fought change with great tenacity but actually feared it.

Whatever he wanted to do to grow, to make things better for them, she threw cold water on it. Five years into the marriage he had begun to feel that he was drowning in all that cold water of hers.

The future with Amy had started to look so bleak, so

without promise or happiness, that he had eventually begun to drift away from her.

Content to plod along, following her usual routine, she had never even noticed when he was gone from her in body and spirit. He might live in the same apartment but he was no longer really there.

Inevitably, he strayed and had a couple of affairs with other women and discovered he didn't even feel guilty. He had also realized at the time – over two years ago now – that the game was up between them. Jake was not a promiscuous man, and the very act of infidelity told him that there was nothing left of their relationship, nothing left to salvage. At least for him.

Through her apathy and fear, her lack of trust in him and in his ability, Amy had killed their marriage. She had taken hope away from him.

Everyone needed hope . . . everyone needed dreams. What did a man have, for God's sake, if not his dreams? Amy had trampled on his.

And yet he did not blame her; he felt sorry for her, perhaps because he had known her for so long, nearly all of his life. Then again, he was aware that she had never meant to hurt him in any way. Amy gave so little of herself she therefore had so little. She was missing out on life.

Amy was still pretty in a pale blonde way, but she did nothing to help her delicate colouring, so she appeared faded and drab these days. And she had put on weight. Not a lot, only a few pounds, but because she was small that bit of extra weight made her look dumpy.

She'll never get married again, Jake thought with a sudden flash of insight, and groaned inwardly. He would probably end up paying her alimony forever, until the day she died. Or he did. But what the hell, he didn't care. He knew he could always make money. He had an unfailing self-confidence.

Jake slowed the pick-up when he came to his white clapboard house, pulled into the yard and parked in front of the garage. Walking around to the back, he let himself into the kitchen.

Home, he thought, and glanced around the room. Then he grinned. He *was* home. He *was* free. He had his own business now, and it was doing well. He had a bright future again. His dreams were intact after all. Nobody could take them away. He was at peace with himself. And with the world at large. He was even at peace with Amy, in his own way. Eventually they would divorce and truly go their separate ways.

And if he was lucky he would meet another woman one day and fall in love. He would get married again. And hopefully there would be a child. Maybe even children. A wife, a home, a family, and his own business. Those were the things he wanted and it seemed to him that they were simple, fundamental things. Certainly there was nothing complicated about them. Yet Amy had made them seem unattainable because she had not wanted them. She hadn't even wanted to have a child. She'd been afraid of that too.

'What if there's something wrong with the baby?' she had said to him once, just after he had told her he wanted to have a child. 'What if the baby's born defective in some way? What would we do, Jake? I wouldn't want a defective baby.'

Startled, he had stared at her in complete bafflement, frowning, not understanding how she could mouth such things. It was then that he had felt a spurt of anger inside, and that anger had stayed with him for a very long time.

Just over a year ago he had realized that Amy had cheated him of life for the entire time they had been married. To him that was a crime. But then he had allowed her to do it, hadn't he? You were only a victim if you permitted yourself to be one, his mother had told him once. He reminded himself not to forget that.

Amy was so negative she was a genuine loser. He had tried to help her to change but she had looked at him blankly, obviously not understanding what he was getting at.

Suddenly impatient with himself, he pushed away thoughts of Amy. After all, she was on her own now. As was he.

Opening the fridge door, Jake took out a beer, prised off the cap with the opener on the counter, then stood leaning against the sink, drinking from the bottle, enjoying it; beer always tasted better from the bottle.

The phone began to ring. He reached for it. 'Hello?'

'Jake, is that you?'

He straightened slightly on hearing the voice. 'Yes, it is. How're you, Samantha?'

'I'm fine, Jake, thanks. You haven't forgotten the meeting tonight, have you?'

'No, I haven't. But I'm running late. Just got in from work. I'll be there soon. Real soon.'

'Don't kill yourself. I'm late myself today. I'll see you at the theatre.'

'Okay.' He glanced at the kitchen clock. It was just turning five-thirty. 'In about an hour?'

'That's good for me. 'Bye.'

'See you later,' Jake said, and hung up.

He finished the beer and went through into the bedroom. After pulling off his boots and jeans he stripped off his heavy sweater, T-shirt and underpants, then strode into the bathroom to take a shower.

Five minutes later he was towelling himself dry, and after putting on a terry-cloth robe he padded through into the small living room.

Standing in front of his CD player, his eyes scanned the shelf of discs next to it. He had inherited his love of music from his mother, especially classical music and opera. She had had a beautiful voice, and he had been reared on Verdi and Puccini, as well as Mozart, Rachmaninoff, Tchaikovsky, and other great composers. He'd always thought it a pity his mother had not been able to have the proper musical education and training, since in his opinion she'd had a voice worthy of the Metropolitan Opera in New York City.

Automatically, his hand reached for one of her favourites, Puccini's *Tosca*, but after looking at the Maria Callas disc for a moment he put it back, pulled out another one, a selection of Puccini and Verdi arias sung by Kiri Te Kanawa, whose voice he loved and who was his preferred opera star. After turning the volume up, he went back to the bathroom, leaving all of the doors open so that he could enjoy the music.

Staring at himself in the bathroom mirror, Jake ran a hand over his chin. No two ways about it, he needed a shave. He lathered himself with soap and scraped the razor over his chin, rinsed his face, combed back his damp black hair and then went back into the bedroom, all the while listening to Te Kanawa singing arias from *Don Carlos*, *Il Trovatore*, and *La Traviata*.

By the time he was dressed in clean blue jeans, a fresh blue-and-white checked shirt and a dark blue sports jacket, she was still singing.

One of the arias he liked the most was 'Vissi d'arte' from *Tosca*, and now he walked through into the living room, touched the track number for *Tosca* on the CD player and sat down. He didn't want to be late for the meeting with Samantha Matthews, but he did want to hear his favourite piece from *Tosca*.

As Te Kanawa's voice filled the room, soared up to the rafters, Jake was engulfed. He felt himself falling down into her wonderful voice, falling into the music, which never failed to touch him with its beauty and sadness.

Te Kanawa *was* Tosca, and she was singing of her sorrow, her tribulation, her hour of need, and Jake leaned his head back against the chair, closed his eyes, gave himself up to the music.

Unexpectedly, he felt choked. Tears welled. His emotions were suddenly laid bare . . . he was filled with yearning . . . for something . . . although he was not exactly sure what he yearned for. Then he knew . . . he wanted to *feel* again. I know there's more, he thought, there's got to be more to life . . .

He let the music wash over him, relaxing his body, and he remained very still even after the aria had finished. In repose, his lean, sharply-sculpted face looked much less troubled.

After a short while Jake roused himself, and went to turn off the CD player. He had to be in Kent in five minutes, and it would take him longer than that to get there.

He left the house through the kitchen, and ran to his pick-up truck.

On the way to Kent he thought about the meeting he was about to have with Samantha Matthews. He had met her a few weeks ago on the big lighting job he was doing at a mansion in nearby Washington. She was a resident of the town who designed and produced unusual, handmade fabrics which the owner, his current client, was using throughout the house.

He and Samantha had started talking over a cup of coffee one day, when they were at the house together, and she had been interested in hearing more about the special lighting effects he was creating inside the house and in the grounds.

Several days later she had phoned him with an offer. It was an invitation to work with her on the stage sets for an amateur dramatic group she was involved with in Kent.

He had agreed to come to one meeting at least. And it was tonight. He had no idea what to expect, and he wasn't sure whether it would be the first and last, or the first of many.

Although he had not told Samantha, he was excited about working in the theatre, if only with an amateur group such as hers. It was a wonderful challenge and a way to learn more, he felt.

As he drove towards Kent, his mind preoccupied with lighting techniques, Jake Cantrell had no idea that he was being propelled towards his destiny. Nor did he have any way of knowing that his life was about to change, and so profoundly it would never be the same again.

Later, when he looked back to this night, he would

do so wonderingly, reminding himself how ordinary it had seemed. He would ask himself why he had not sensed that something momentous was going to happen, why he had not realized that he was about to set out on the journey of his life.

CHAPTER 2

SAMANTHA MATTHEWS LOOKED UP from the script she was making notations on and stared across the table at her friend Maggie Sorrell, frowning. 'Now you tell me you think I've chosen the wrong play! Just when I've got it cast and everyone's madly learning their lines!' she exclaimed, her voice rising slightly.

'I didn't say that!' Maggie protested. 'I asked you *why* you'd chosen it. I was merely thinking out loud. Honestly.'

'Thinking out loud or not, you sounded *critical*.'

'I didn't, Sam!'

'Doubtful, then.'

'Not doubtful either. You know very well I never doubt you, or anything you do. I really was only wondering why this particular play, that's all.'

Samantha nodded. 'Okay, I believe you. I know you're my true blue friend who's stuck by me through thick and thick and thin and thin over the years. My very best friend in the world.'

'Just as you're mine,' Maggie murmured. 'So come on, tell me. Why did you pick *The Crucible*?'

'Because last year, before you'd come to live here, we did *Annie Get Your Gun*, and I didn't want to direct a musical again. I wanted to stage a drama. Preferably one by a great American playwright who was still alive; that's why I chose an Arthur Miller play. But I must admit, there's also another reason –'

'Because we did it at Bennington all those years ago,' Maggie cut in knowingly, smiling. 'That's it, isn't it?'

Samantha sat back in her chair and regarded her friend intently for a moment, then she shook her head slowly. 'No, not at all.'

'And I thought you'd chosen it for sentimental reasons.' Maggie made a face and shrugged. 'Oh silly me.'

'Sentimental reasons?' Samantha echoed.

'Of course. We were nineteen and rapidly becoming fast friends. Best friends, actually. We'd both fallen in love for the first time; also, we were treading the boards for the first time. In *The Crucible*. It was a very special year for us, but you'd forgotten, hadn't you?'

'No, I do remember that year at college. It was 1971. In fact, I thought about it only the other day. And in a way you're correct. When I selected *The Crucible* I *was* playing it a bit safe, because I do know it so well. But when I said I chose it for another reason it was because Arthur Miller lives in Connecticut and we're a Connecticut theatrical group. So, call me sentimental if you like, Mag.'

'You are a sentimentalist at heart, even though you like to pretend you're not,' Maggie answered.

'Maybe I am,' Samantha agreed and laughed. 'Although there are those who call me bossy.'

'Oh you're that all right!' Maggie shot back, laughing.

'Thanks a lot, friend. Anyway, getting back to the play, you know it pretty well too, and that's going to be a decided advantage when you start designing the sets.'

'You do realize I'm very worried about this whole project, don't you, Sam? I can't imagine how I ever let you talk me into it. I've never designed a stage set in my life.'

'But you have designed some beautiful rooms, especially lately, and anyway there's a first time for everything. You'll be okay, you'll do fine.'

'I wish I felt as confident as you sound. To tell you the truth, I'm not sure where to begin. I read the play through again last night and my mind went totally blank. In fact, I balked at the project. Are you certain there's no one else to do the sets for you?'

'There isn't, Maggie. Besides, you're only suffering from a touch of stage fright, and that's quite normal. Look, you'll be fine as soon as you pick up your pencil and start sketching. *Trust me.*'

'I'm not so sure I should do that, Sam. When I've trusted you in the past it's only got me into a heap of trouble.'

'No, it hasn't,' Samantha countered and pushed her

chair away from the card table. She stood up, walked across the stage, gesturing as she did.

'You'll have to create some sort of major scenic backdrop here, Mag, and the furniture must be representative of the period. Early American, obviously. But you're an expert on furniture, so I don't really know why I'm even mentioning it.'

Samantha swung to face her old friend. 'I see something dramatic in my mind's eye, something really unusual for the backdrop. Black and white, maybe even a few greys, something like a painting in grisaille. What do you think?'

Maggie rose and went to join her, nodding as she did. 'Yes!' she exclaimed, sounding excited by the project for the first time. 'I know exactly what you mean. It needs to be stark. Bleak almost. Certainly sombre, very eye-catching as well. I think the set has to be a little offbeat, not the usual thing. Let's take the audience by surprise.' Maggie raised a brow. 'Don't you agree?'

Samantha grinned at her. 'I sure do and I knew you'd catch the bug, once I got that clever little brain of yours working. You're so talented, Maggie, and very imaginative, and I'm certain you'll come up with exactly the right thing.'

'I hope so, I'd hate to let you down – ' She broke off, looking thoughtful, then added, 'You know, I think I'll drive into New York later this week, pick up some books on theatrical design and stage sets.'

'Yes, do that. No, wait a minute, there's no need to go into Manhattan. Try the bookstore in Washington and the one in Kent. I know they're both well stocked. They have everything from soup to nuts.'

Maggie laughed, as always amused by her friend's colourful expressions, as she had been since their college days.

The two women stood centre stage, discussing ideas for the backdrop and the sets for a few minutes longer. At one moment Maggie went and got her notebook, began to sketch rapidly, all the time listening to Samantha and nodding.

Both women were forty-three and good-looking, but they were strikingly different in appearance and personality.

Samantha Matthews was of medium height and slim, with prematurely silver hair cut short with a fringe. The silver colour did not seem at all ageing since she had a youthfully pretty face and a fresh complexion. Her large eyes, set widely apart, were dark brown and full of soul.

Energetic, enthusiastic and gregarious, she had an outgoing personality and a friendly nature. Somewhat given to taking control, she liked to be in charge. Nonetheless, she was kind, good hearted and easy to get along with.

In contrast, Maggie Sorrell was tall, willowy, with the brightest of light blue eyes that were, at times, highly appraising. Her thick mane of chestnut hair was shot through with auburn lights and she wore it brushed back and falling to her shoulders. Although her face was a little angular and arresting rather than pretty, she was attractive and appealing in her looks.

Maggie had a fluidity and a gracefulness when she moved and she appeared to take things at a more leisurely pace. But she had as much energy and vitality as Samantha. Very simply, her style was slightly different. It was calm, controlled, and she was the quieter and more reserved of the two. And yet she was a vibrant woman, full of life and optimism.

Even in their style of dressing they were true to themselves. Tonight Samantha wore what she termed her uniform: well-tailored blue jeans, a white cotton shirt, a black gabardine blazer with brass buttons, and highly polished black oxfords with white socks.

Maggie, who tended to be less tailored, was dressed in a full, three-quarter length skirt made of brown suede, matching suede boots, a cream silk shirt and a brown cashmere stole flung over her shoulders.

Both women had a casual style about them which reflected an understanding of clothes and what suited them; it also bespoke their privileged backgrounds.

Best friends since college days, they had remained close even though they had been separated by thousands of miles for many years. They had managed to meet quite frequently, at least twice a year, and they had spoken to each other on the phone every week for as long as they could remember. Maggie had moved to Connecticut eight months ago, after a dreadful upheaval in her life, and they had become inseparable again.

The banging of a door at the back of the theatre startled both women, made them jump. Automatically they swung around, peering into the dimly lit auditorium.

'Oh, it's only Tom Cruise,' Samantha said immediately, a look of pleasure settling on her face. She waved with a certain eagerness to the man walking down the aisle towards the proscenium.

'Tom Cruise,' Maggie hissed, grasping Samantha's

arm, following the direction of her gaze. 'Why didn't you tell me, for God's sake! Has he moved here? Is he taking an interest in the theatre group? Oh my God, I hope he's not slumming, doing a part in the play just for kicks. I'll never be able to design the sets! Not with a real pro around.'

Samantha burst out laughing. She said, in a low voice, 'As far as I know, Mr Cruise is still living in Westport. The guy walking towards us could be him though, and that's why I call him Tom Cruise.'

Maggie let go of Samantha's arm as the young man walked across the stage to join them.

'Sorry I'm late,' he said to Samantha, stretching out his hand, shaking hers.

'No problem,' Samantha answered. 'Come and meet my friend. Maggie, this is Jake Cantrell. Jake, this is Margaret Anne Sorrell, usually known as Maggie. She's an interior designer and will be designing our sets. Maggie, Jake's a genius with lighting and special effects. I hope he's going to become part of our little group and work with us. We certainly need a lighting expert of his calibre.'

Jake gave Samantha a small smile that hinted of shyness and then turned to Maggie. 'I'm very pleased to meet you,' he said politely and offered her his hand.

Maggie took it. His hand was cool, his grasp firm. 'I'm happy to meet you too,' she murmured.

They stood staring at each other.

Maggie thought how extremely good-looking he was, realizing at once that he was completely unaware that he was. He's a troubled man, she thought, recognizing the sadness in his eyes.

Jake was thinking that he'd never met a woman like

this in his life, so beautifully groomed and well put together. He was suddenly awed by this woman who was looking at him so thoughtfully through her cool, intelligent eyes.

CHAPTER 3

THE THREE OF THEM sat down at the table on the stage and Samantha handed Jake a copy of the play.

'Thanks,' he said, glancing at it, then looking up at her as she continued, 'As you can see we're doing *The Crucible*, and I think you should read it as soon as possible.' She flashed him a vivid smile, and added, 'Basically, the meeting tonight is for us to become acquainted. I was hoping the three of us could get together again later this week, maybe on Friday or Saturday, to have our first detailed discussion about the scenery and the lighting. By then you'll have a better understanding of what's required.'

'I know the play,' Jake replied, giving her a pointed look. 'And very well. From high school. I also saw a revival of it a few years ago. I've always liked Arthur Miller.'

If Samantha was surprised to hear this she certainly disguised it. Merely nodding, she murmured, 'That's great. Obviously I'm delighted you know the play; it'll save us a lot of time in the long run.'

'I've never done any stage work before, as I told you when you phoned,' Jake said. 'But what's required for this play in particular is real mood, that I *do* know. All stage lighting should underscore the meaning of the drama, the scenes being acted, and create an atmosphere. In *The Crucible* it should be one of ... mystery. Deep mystery, I think. And revelation ... impending revelation. It's important to introduce a sense of time as well as place. In this instance, Salem, Massachusetts in the seventeenth century. Candles are going to be important, as are special effects. It's necessary to simulate dawn and night-time. I remember a night-time scene in the wood. You'll need interesting combinations of light and shadow –' He stopped, wondering if he'd said too much – even worse, made a fool of himself.

Jake sat back in his chair and looked at the women. They were both staring at him intently. He felt himself flush and experienced a surge of acute embarrassment.

Maggie, who had been observing him closely and giving him her entire attention, sensed that he was suddenly feeling uncomfortable, although she wasn't sure why. But wishing to put him at ease, she said swiftly, 'You've hit it right on the mark, Jake. I'm fairly familiar with the play myself, but I know the scenery is going to be tough for me to do. This is *my* first stab at theatrical design. Like you I'm a bit of a novice.

Maybe we'll be able to help each other as we go along.'

Smiling, Maggie finished, 'Samantha has a good point about meeting again later in the week, once we've both had a chance to refresh our memories about the play. I'm available either Friday or Saturday.' She glanced at Samantha and then back at him. 'Which day do you both prefer?'

'Saturday,' Samantha answered.

Jake was silent. An unfamiliar discomfort had settled over him. They were taking it for granted he was going to get involved with their drama group, but he still wasn't sure that he would. Or whether he even wanted to. He wondered if he'd said too much a moment ago, if he had led them to believe he intended to participate.

'Would Friday be better for you, Jake?' Maggie asked.

He shook his head. 'No, I don't think so. I – ' He cut himself off abruptly, suddenly wary of making any kind of commitment to them. It might take up too much of his time; after all, he did have a business to run these days. Also, he was beginning to feel a bit out of his depth with these two women. They were so sure of themselves, were from another world, one he didn't know at all. And there was another thing: it seemed to him that they took their amateur theatrical group very seriously. Certainly they were determined to put on a good production, he could tell that. He knew Samantha Matthews was a perfectionist, his client in Washington had indicated that only the other day. It was apparent to him that she would be a hard taskmaster, very demanding. Better to skip it, he thought.

Clearing his throat, he looked across at Samantha and said, 'I agreed to come tonight because I'm always interested in extending my knowledge, so the idea of designing stage lighting appealed to me. But I have the feeling you want a real commitment from me, Samantha, and I can't give you that. What I mean is, I'm very busy with my electrical business. I work late most nights –'

'Oh, Jake, don't be so hasty,' Samantha interrupted. 'Maggie and I are also up to our necks with work. We've all got to earn a living, you know.'

Once again she offered him that vivid smile of hers, and added, 'Whatever you might think, you wouldn't be making such a huge commitment. Not really. Once you'd created the lighting effects you wouldn't have anything else to do. I'd take it from there. I've got several good stagehands to help me and an electrician as well.'

'Lighting isn't easy,' he answered. 'In fact, it's very complicated and especially so for *this* play.'

'You're absolutely correct,' Maggie interjected. 'But I do wish you'd reconsider. From what Sam's told me about your work at the Bruce house, you really do know what you're doing. Look, I know how you feel, I just started a new business myself a few months ago, and I'm totally committed to it. Nonetheless, I think I'll learn a lot from this little theatrical venture.' She smiled at him winningly.

He looked at her, looked right into her eyes, and he felt the hairs on the back of his neck bristling. Maggie Sorrell was not pretty in the given sense. But there was something about her that went beyond mere prettiness. She was arresting, intriguing, the kind of woman a man would look at twice. She had an elegance that had nothing to do with her clothes, but with herself. He felt oddly drawn to her. Instantly, he pulled back. He had never known a woman like this; he was not sure he wanted to.

Since he had remained mute, Maggie continued talking. 'You did say yourself that initially you thought you'd learn something. Actually, Jake, we'll both benefit, and in innumerable ways. For instance, there's the publicity. We'll get quite a lot, and that can't be bad for your business or mine. Anyway, I've come to realize that whatever I'm doing I'm usually meeting a potential client somewhere along the line.'

'Bravo! Said like a true professional!' Samantha exclaimed. 'And Maggie's correct, Jake, you can profit from this in a variety of different ways.'

When he still said nothing, she pressed, 'What do you have to lose?'

Hesitating for a moment longer, he finally said in a quiet voice, 'It's the time that's involved, I can't let my business suffer.'

'None of us can,' Maggie pointed out. 'Come on, Jake, give it a try. I am. The whole project is challenging and I love a challenge, don't you?' Not waiting for his answer, she said, 'In any case, I think we'll have a lot of fun together.'

Before he could stop himself he agreed. He wondered what he was doing, making such a commitment. To cover himself, he added swiftly, 'If it gets to be too much, gets in the way of my work, I'll have to quit. You do understand that, don't you?'

'Of course,' Samantha replied.

'What about the next meeting, Jake? Do you prefer Friday or Saturday?' Maggie asked.

'Saturday's definitely better,' Jake told her. 'I'm working late on Friday, and on Saturday morning. Can we make it Saturday afternoon? Late afternoon?'

'Fine by me,' Maggie murmured.

'You've got a deal!' Samantha cried, her voice suddenly full of excitement. 'We're going to make a great team! And you'll enjoy it, Jake, you'll see. It's going to be a gratifying experience. Incidentally, I was impressed with what you said earlier, about the lighting for the play. Your ideas are brilliant. Personally, I think you've already got the lighting licked.'

'I hope so,' he replied, trying not to look pleased at her compliment. 'I've always found that play very powerful.'

'Yes, it is, and frightening in a sense, when you think it all hinges on lies – the terrible lies people tell,' Maggie remarked.

It was a few minutes before nine when Jake walked back into his kitchen, and he realized how hungry he was as he opened the fridge door and took out a cold beer.

After swallowing a few gulps, he went through into the living room, draped his sports jacket over a chair back and returned to the kitchen. Within a few minutes he had opened a can of corned beef and a jar of pickles and made himself a sandwich.

Carrying the plate and the beer back into the living room, he put them on the small glass coffee table, sat down, picked up the remote control and flicked on the television. He ate his sandwich and drank his beer, staring at the set. It was a sitcom on one of the networks and he wasn't paying much attention.

Jake was preoccupied with the drama group, *The Crucible* and the two women he had left a short while before. They were opposites, but they were both very nice and he liked them. And so he had let himself be persuaded to do the lighting for the play. Now he wished he hadn't agreed. He had done so against his better judgement and instinctively he knew it was going to be more trouble than it was worth. Why did I let myself get swept up into this? he asked himself yet again.

Suddenly impatient with the television and with himself, he flicked off the set and leaned back in the chair, taking an occasional swallow of beer.

After a moment Jake got up, walked over to the window, stood looking out at the night sky. He wondered what she was really like, Maggie Sorrell, but he figured he would never get to know her well enough to find out.

CHAPTER 4

MAGGIE SORRELL AWAKENED with a start. Reaching out, she turned on the bedside lamp and looked at the alarm clock. It was three-thirty.

Groaning to herself, she doused the light, slid down under the covers and attempted to go back to sleep. But her mind raced when she began to think about the living room and library of the house in Roxbury she was redecorating for a client. Fabric patterns, carpet swatches, paint colours and wood finishes swirled around in her head.

She finally gave up trying to envision a scheme. Jake Cantrell kept intruding into her thoughts. There was something about him that was appealing, very engaging, and of course he was stunning looking. But he doesn't know it, not really, she thought again, as she had a few hours ago. And then remembering the sadness she had detected in his light green eyes, she wondered what had gone awry in *his* life.

Obviously someone had hurt Jake Cantrell and very badly. She recognized that look only too well. The shell-shocked look she called it.

A woman did him in, Maggie thought, still focusing on Jake. She sighed to herself. Women. Men. What they did to each other in the name of love was diabolical. It bordered on the criminal. She ought to know, it had been done to her.

Mike Sorrell had destroyed her just as surely as if he had stuck a knife in her. But then he'd been killing her soul for years, hadn't he?

The big upheaval had happened two years ago, but the memory of it was still there. Although most of the pain had receded, there were moments when it came rushing back, took her by surprise with its intensity. She tried to squash the bad memories but they seemed determined to linger.

I'll be forty-four next month, she thought. *Forty-four*. It didn't seem possible. Time had rushed by with the speed of light. Where had all the years gone? Well, she knew the answer to that. Mike Sorrell had devoured them. She had devoted most of her life to Michael William Sorrell, attorney-at-law by profession, and to their twins, Hannah and Peter, college students both, soon to be twenty-one years old.

The three of them were gone from her life and she had learned to live without them. But it still pained her when she thought of the twins. They had sided with their father, even though she had done nothing wrong. He was the guilty party. But then he was Mr Money Bags and that apparently carried weight with them.

How terrible it was to know your children were greedy, avaricious and selfish, when you'd tried so hard to bring them up right, to instil proper values in them. But there it was. They had proved to her that she had failed with them.

In taking his side they had destroyed something fundamental deep within her. She had borne them, brought them up, looked after them when they were sick. She had always been there for them and guided them all of their lives. What they had done to her was rotten, in her opinion. They had flung all that caring back in her face. Flung her love for them back at her, as if it were meaningless.

In a sense, their cold-hearted defection had stunned her more than Mike's ugly betrayal of her. He'd dumped her when she was nearly forty-two for a younger woman, a woman of twenty-seven who was a lawyer in another Chicago law firm.

But I survived, Maggie reminded herself, thanks mainly to Samantha. And myself, of course.

It was Samantha who had reached out to her two years ago, that awful day in May, the day of her birthday when she had finally admitted to herself that she would be spending it alone.

Hannah and Peter were both attending Northwestern, but were far too busy with their own lives to make time for their mother's birthday celebration. And their father had left that morning on a business trip without wishing her a happy birthday. Apparently he hadn't even remembered it.

That May morning, sitting alone in the kitchen of their apartment on Lake Shore Drive, she had felt totally, completely alone. And without her husband

and children she was. Her parents were dead and she had been an only child. That special morning she had felt something else – abandoned, cast aside, of no use to anyone anymore. Even now, so long after, she was unable to pinpoint her exact feelings, but she had been disturbed, she knew that.

When the phone had rung and she had answered, had heard Samantha singing 'Happy birthday', she had burst into tears. Between sobs she had explained that she was spending her birthday alone because the kids didn't have time for her and Mike had gone away on a business trip.

'Pack a bag, get out to O'Hare and take a plane to New York! *Immediately*!' Samantha had exclaimed. 'I'll book us into the Carlyle. I have some pull there, I can usually get rooms. I'm taking you out on the town tonight. Somewhere posh and smart. So pack your fanciest gear.'

When she had tried to protest, Samantha had said, 'I'm not listening to your excuses. And I won't take no for an answer. There's a plane leaving every hour on the hour. Just get on one and get yourself to New York. *Pronto, pronto, pronto*, honey. I'll meet you at the hotel.'

True to her word, Samantha had been there when she arrived, full of warmth and love, sympathy and support. They had enjoyed their two days together in Manhattan, doing a little shopping and eating at nice restaurants. A Broadway play and a trip to the Metropolitan Museum had been mandatory; they had also found time to talk endlessly, reminiscing about their days at Bennington College, when they first met, and their lives thereafter.

Samantha had married several years after Maggie. Her husband had been a British journalist based in New York. She and Angus McAllister had tied the knot when she was twenty-five and he was thirty-one. It had been a very happy marriage, but Angus had been tragically killed in a plane crash five years later, en route to the Far East on an assignment.

It was only a few months after this that Samantha, who was childless, moved back to Washington, Connecticut, where her parents had long owned a country house they used at weekends. Heartbroken though she had been, she had managed eventually to get her grief under control. But she had never remarried, although there had been several men in her life in the intervening years.

At one moment, during the birthday visit, Maggie had asked Samantha why this was so. Samantha had shaken her head and said, in her colourful way, 'Ain't found the right man, honey chile. I'm looking to fall head over heels in love, the way I did with Angus. I want my stomach to lurch and my knees to wobble.' She had laughed, and finished, 'I want to be swept off my feet, into his arms, into his bed and his life forever. It *must* be like that for me or it won't work. And I'm still waiting to meet him.'

Later, on the plane going back to Chicago, Maggie had admitted to herself that her marriage to Mike was growing more and more unsatisfactory with the passing of every day. She did not know what to do about it. He did. A day later he returned from his trip. He walked into the apartment, announced he was leaving her for another woman, and walked right out again.

Once the shock had subsided and she had recovered

her equilibrium to a degree, she had set about cleaning up the mess his unexpected departure had created.

Divorce proceedings were started, the apartment went on the market, and once it was sold she moved back east, back to her home town. New York.

She had lived there for six months in a small, rented studio. Her parents were already dead, she had no family, and she'd lost touch with all of her old friends from her youth. It was a lonely life for her.

It didn't take much persuasion on Samantha's part to get her to start looking at houses in the northwestern part of Connecticut.

Samantha also talked her into working as an interior designer again. Some years ago, she had been the junior member of a successful Chicago decorating firm and had loved every moment working there. She had finally given up her job because of pressure from Mike.

But she did what her best friend suggested and hung out her shingle, once she was installed in her small Connecticut colonial in Kent. The house, a little gem in her opinion, was only a few miles from Washington, where Samantha lived.

Thanks to Samantha's many contacts, design work had started to come Maggie's way quickly. They were small jobs. However, they had helped to pull her back into the swing of decorating, and the money she earned paid part of the mortgage.

Samantha, the eternal optimist, kept telling her a really big job would come her way one day soon. Maggie believed her because she was also an optimist.

Soon Maggie began to accept that sleep would be evasive for the rest of the night. Putting on the light, she peered at the alarm clock again and decided to get up. It was just turning four o'clock and she often rose at this hour. She accomplished a lot before eight whenever she did.

An hour later Maggie sat at her desk, sipping a mug of coffee. She was dressed and made up and ready for the day ahead. Later in the morning she would be driving over to Samantha's studio in Washington to look at her latest handpainted fabrics for a bedroom she was doing in New Preston. Then she would be presenting the scheme for the library to the owner of the house in Roxbury. Pulling the swatches and samples together for this room was the order of the day and of vital importance.

Maggie began to assemble the small samples from various canvas bags at her feet. There was a variety of different greens and reds, colours the owner wanted, but not one of them was pleasing to her. Most of the reds were too bright, the greens too pale. Something sombre, she muttered under her breath. And then for a reason she couldn't explain she thought of *The Crucible,* and of the meeting last night.

Again Jake Cantrell insinuated himself into her thoughts. If she were honest with herself, she'd have to admit she felt rather foolish, believing as she had, if only for a few moments, that he was Tom Cruise. But Samantha had sounded so convincing when she'd spotted him coming down the aisle of the auditorium. He'd taken them both by surprise when he started to talk about his ideas for the lighting. It was obvious to her from that moment on that he was knowledgeable about his work, and most likely as brilliant as Samantha said. Of course, you never knew with Sam. She had always liked a pretty face, Maggie thought, as she shuffled the samples on the desk, and then she stopped and sat back in her chair, staring into space. 'But he's too young for her,' she muttered aloud. And for you too, she added to herself silently.

CHAPTER 5

JAKE HEARD THE PHONE ringing as he stepped out of the shower. He reached for a towel, partially dried himself and pulled on his terry-cloth robe.

Walking into the bedroom he heard Maggie Sorrell's voice saying goodbye. The answering machine clicked off; he depressed the button and played the message back.

Her voice filled the room. 'Jake, this is Maggie Sorrell. I've just been hired to do a big job in Kent. A farm. It's a beautiful old place but it needs a lot of work. The grounds are superb. I was wondering if you would be interested in doing the electrical work? Interiors and exteriors. Please call me. I'm here at home.' She then repeated the number she'd given him last Saturday at the drama group meeting.

Jake sat down on the bed and played the message again. He loved her voice. It was light, musical, cultured. It suited her. He had met her three times now at meetings about *The Crucible,* and he realized that his attraction to her was powerful. He thought about her a lot. But he had no intention of doing anything about her. She'd never be interested in him.

He would like to do the electrical work, though. The major job he had been doing in Washington was just about completed, and he and his crew would finish in the next couple of days. With four men on the payroll he had to pull in as many jobs as possible to keep them busy. Two were married and had families to support, and he felt a great sense of responsibility.

He picked up the phone to call Maggie back, and then he dropped the receiver in the cradle. He did not want to seem too anxious. Then again, he always felt a bit nervous around her.

Returning to the bathroom, he combed his wet hair and finished his ablutions, then went to get dressed, pulled on blue jeans and a sweater.

Fifteen minutes later he sat down at the desk in the small room at the back of the house, which he used as an office. Pulling the phone towards him, he dialled Maggie's number.

She answered immediately. 'Hello?'

'It's Jake, Maggie.'

'Hello, Jake, you got my message?'

'Yes, I did. I was in the shower when you called.' He wondered why he'd told her that. Rushing on, he continued quickly, 'The farm job sounds interesting. Where is it exactly?'

'It's not too far from Kent, near Bull's Bridge Corner,

actually. It's a pretty property and the house has great charm.'

'Is it really a big job?'

'I think so. To be honest with you, Jake, the entire farmhouse needs rewiring, and it needs remodelling and restoring. It hasn't been touched in thirty years, in my opinion anyway. The woman who's bought it, my client, wants air conditioning and central heating systems put in, all new appliances in the kitchen, and she wants to build a laundry. Then there are the grounds. The exterior lighting will be extensive. She wants to build a pool and patio, oh, and there's an old cottage to be remodelled for guests, as well as a caretaker's apartment over the cottage.' She laughed. 'So I guess it is a huge job.'

'It sounds like it to me, Maggie. What are we looking at? About six or seven months' work?'

'Probably. Maybe a bit longer. Can you handle it?'

'Yes, I'm pretty sure I can. And thanks for thinking of me.'

'Samantha's always said you're the best, and yesterday I saw the work you've done in the Washington house, and on the grounds there. I was very impressed.'

'Thanks. When can I see the farm? I'd like to, before I commit to it.'

'We could go over there later this week.'

'Okay.'

'How does Friday sound? That's the fourteenth of April.'

'Great. What time?'

'Could you do it around eight?'

'Sure thing. Whereabouts is it?'

'It's hard for me to give you the right directions . . . it's up a lot of twisting roads. I think we should meet at my house, since you know where it is, and we can go from here. It's easier and it'll save time.'

'I'll be there at eight sharp. And Maggie?'

'Yes, Jake?'

'Thanks for thinking of me.'

After hanging up, Jake wrote the appointment in the small pocket diary he carried around with him, and also put it in the agenda on the desk. Then he got up and left the house.

As he walked out to the pick-up truck it struck him that perhaps he hadn't been so foolish after all, getting involved with the drama group. It looked as if he was getting a job because of it. But he knew the real reason he had become involved with the theatre group. It was because of her, of course. He had done it because of Maggie Sorrell.

He sat at the steering wheel without moving for a few seconds, bracing himself. He was on his way to an appointment, and he wasn't looking forward to it.

Amy Cantrell stood in the centre of the living room of her apartment, looking around slowly, all of a sudden noticing the untidiness of the place. Dismay swamped her.

She had managed to talk Jake into coming over tonight, for the first time in months, and she knew he would be furious. He loathed mess and disorder. He was as neat as a pin himself, and had been as long as she had known him, which was forever. Her lack of organization and her untidiness had been a bone of contention between them. She never understood how she could create chaos in a room within seconds. She never meant to, it just happened.

Shaking her head and frowning, she began quickly to pick up the newspapers and magazines scattered all over the coffee table and on the floor underneath. She put them on a chair, plumped up the cushions on the sofa, and took the newspapers out to the kitchen.

When she saw the dirty dishes in the sink she groaned. She had forgotten about them. Flinging down the papers angrily, she opened the dishwasher; it was stacked to the brim and had not been turned on. Everything was dirty. Trying to stack more items into it and moving quickly, she dropped a mug. It shattered.

The phone rang shrilly. She grabbed it. 'Hello?'

'Amy, it's me. Has he arrived yet?'

'No, Mom, he's not coming until after eight.'

'Why so late, Amy?'

'I don't know. He works, Mom.'

'Tell him about the alimony. That you want alimony.'

'Mom, I gotta go. Honestly I do. I'm trying to tidy up here. Jake hates mess.'

'So what do you care? He left you.'

'I gotta go, Mom. 'Bye.' She hung up before her mother could say another word.

Moving across the kitchen floor in the direction of the dishwasher, she crushed the shards of pottery from the broken mug under her feet. Amy looked down, bit her lip. She went to find the brush and dustpan; she was on the verge of tears.

For the next few minutes she attempted to bring order to the kitchen before going through into the bedroom. The bed was unmade, as it usually was these days. The mere thought of making it overwhelmed her, and defeated by the domestic chores which needed doing, she scurried into the bathroom.

After washing her face and cleaning her teeth, she combed her pale blonde hair. It hung listlessly around her face.

Amy Cantrell sighed as she regarded herself in the mirror. She wondered how she could make herself look better, and reached for the Cover Girl foundation, patted some of it on her face and added powder. Once she had highlighted her cheekbones with the blush-on, she outlined her mouth with pale pink lipstick.

The image of herself in the mirror infuriated her. She didn't look any better than she had a few seconds ago. Tears flooded her eyes. She was a mess. The apartment was a mess. She had never known what to do about either.

Her friend Mandy had once offered to show her how to use cosmetics, but she had never taken her up on it. She wondered why. As for the state of the house, there was never any time, and the more she did to clean it up, the more chaotic it became. Reaching for a tissue, she blew her nose and wiped her eyes. It just wasn't fair. Other people seemed to get through life so easily, so flawlessly. All she could do was stumble along, dragging mess in her wake.

The doorbell rang, making her jump.

My God, was he here already! She hurried out into the little entrance foyer, realizing, as she went to open the door, that she was still wearing the cotton housecoat she had donned earlier when she had started the housework.

'Who is it?' she asked through the door.

'It's Jake.'

Glancing down at her grubby housecoat, she made a face and then opened the door.

'Hi, Amy,' he said, coming in.

'Hi, Jake,' she echoed, closing the door, trailing after him lethargically.

'How've you been? All right, I guess.'

'I guess. And you?'

'Busy. With the business.'

'Oh.'

Jake glanced around and then sat down on one of the chairs.

Amy could not help but notice the distaste on his face. She winced inside. He had always been particular about the apartment, and his appearance. She glanced at him obliquely. He looked impeccable tonight. As he always had. Always did. He was wearing a beige turtleneck sweater and dark blue jeans with a navy blazer. His boots shone, his hair shone, so did his teeth and his face. He looked brand spanking new, like a freshly minted coin.

More conscious than ever that she looked awful, if not worse than awful, Amy simply sat down on the chair opposite and smiled at him.

Jake cleared his throat. 'You said you had to see me. You were very insistent. What do you want to talk about, Amy?'

'The divorce.'

'We've discussed it so much we've worn the subject out,' he answered in an even tone.

'I just want to be sure you're sure, Jake.'

'I am, Amy. I'm sorry, but there's no going back.'

Her pale blue eyes filled. She blinked the tears away, pushed her hair out of her face. Trying to get a grip on her emotions, she took several deep breaths. 'Well, I have been to see the lawyer. Finally. I'm sure you're pleased about that.'

'When did you go?' he asked.

'Yesterday.'

'I see. I'm glad you did. We should get this over, Amy, so that we can settle everything.'

'He asked me if we'd tried to solve our problems. I told him yes, but that it wasn't any good, that it wouldn't work. Are you really sure, Jake? Maybe we should try again.'

'I can't, Amy. Honestly, honey, I can't. It's finished.'

The tears rolled down her cheeks.

'Oh, Amy, please don't cry.'

'I still love you, Jake.'

He said nothing.

'All the years,' she said, staring hard at him. 'We've known each other since we were twelve. It's a long, long time.'

'I know. And maybe that's the problem. Perhaps we know each other too well. We've become like brother and sister. Listen to me, Amy, you've got to face up to the fact that our marriage is over, and it's been over for years and years.' He cleared his throat and finished gently, 'You just never noticed.'

'I don't know what I'm going to do without you,' she wept.

'You're going to be fine. I know you are.'

'I don't think I am, Jake. Would you get me a glass of water, please? Do you want a beer?'

'No, thanks. I'll get the water for you.' Jake

manoeuvred himself through the living room into the kitchen, and he could not help noticing how dirty the apartment was. He bent down, picked up the broken mug and put it on the counter top. His eyes fell on the dishwasher jammed with dirty dishes and the sink piled even higher, and he grimaced. Once he had found a relatively clean glass in the cupboard, he rinsed it, filled it with cold water and took it to her.

Amy thanked him, sat sipping it for a few moments, staring at him over the rim of the glass. She was trying to think of something to say to him, but no words would come, and her head was empty of thoughts. All she really wanted was for him to come back to her. Then she wouldn't feel so lonely.

Jake said, 'I'll have to be going, Amy, I've work to do tonight.'

'You're not dressed like you're going to work!' she exclaimed, giving him a furious look, suddenly filled with jealousy.

'Paperwork, Amy, I've loads of it.'

'Do you want me to come and help you?'

'No, no,' he said hurriedly, standing up. 'But thanks for the offer.' He began to edge his way to the hall.

Amy put the glass down and stood up. She followed him to the front door. 'The lawyer says I'm entitled to alimony,' she announced.

'That's no problem, Amy, and it never was. I always told you I would look after you.'

'Then stay with me.'

'I can't. What I meant was I'd look after you financially. Tell the lawyer to go ahead and talk to my lawyer. Serve me with papers, Amy. Let's get this over with.'

She did not answer him.

'So long,' he said. 'I'll talk to you soon.' When she chose not to answer him he simply closed the door behind him quietly and left. Poor Amy.

CHAPTER 6

On friday morning Jake set out for Maggie Sorrell's house in Kent.

He knew where it was. He had gone there with Samantha Matthews the previous week to have another meeting about the lighting for *The Crucible*. It was not too far from where he lived, on the other side of town, half way down Route 7.

As he pulled out of his yard and headed up Route 341 in the direction of the town centre in Kent, Jake thought what a glorious morning it was, the way you always hoped an April day would be. It was crisp and dry, with bright sunlight and a vivid blue sky filled with puffed white clouds, the kind of day that made him feel good to be alive. Opening the window of the pick-up, he took a few deep breaths of the pure clean air.

Jake was finally feeling better in spirits. After his meeting with Amy on Tuesday night, he had been depressed for almost two days. She always managed to drag him down, to drain the energy out of him with her negative personality and her total lack of direction and purpose.

Sometimes Jake wondered how Amy managed to keep her job in the store, where she had worked for a number of years; it baffled him. It was a bath speciality store, selling everything for the bathroom from towels to accessories. Seemingly the owner liked her enough to keep her on, despite the constant mistakes she made.

Jake glanced out of the pick-up's window, noted that the light was crystalline today. Perfect. He wished he had time to get out his paints this weekend, but he knew it was not possible. He had paperwork to finish; also, if he was lucky, and Maggie hired him, he would have to start analysing the electrical work required at the farm.

He had allowed himself half an hour to get to Maggie's house, but since there was no traffic he arrived there fifteen minutes early. He parked in the back yard and walked towards the kitchen door, noting how pristine and well-cared-for the traditional Connecticut colonial looked. The clapboard walls were painted white and all of the shutters were dark green.

Before he reached the kitchen door, Maggie opened it. She stood there on the step, smiling at him.

The minute he saw her his chest tightened and he felt himself grow hot. To cover his nervousness, his sudden confusion, he coughed several times, then murmured, 'Good morning, I'm afraid I'm early.'

She stretched out her hand. He took it in his. She said, 'Good morning, Jake. That's no problem – I've been up since dawn. Come on in and have a cup of coffee before we leave.' She smiled at him once more and extracted her hand.

He didn't want to let go of it, but he did. 'Thanks, coffee would be good.' He followed her into the immaculate kitchen, stood there glancing around, feeling slightly awkward.

Maggie said, 'Sit down, Jake. You take your coffee black, if I remember correctly, with one sugar.' One of her dark brows lifted questioningly.

'That's right, thanks,' he answered, and took a seat at the old pine table at one end of the kitchen, noticing that it had been set for breakfast for two.

She moved past him, and he caught a faint whiff of shampoo in her thick, luxuriant hair, the scent of her perfume on her skin, something light and floral; he heard the gentle swish of her skirt against her boots, the tinkle of the gold bracelets she always seemed to wear on one of her slender wrists.

Maggie moved around the kitchen quickly, but with the gracefulness he had noticed before. She was tall and slender, full of life and energy; he could not take his eyes off her. Eventually he did so, realizing he was staring.

Jake looked away quickly, let his eyes roam around the kitchen. He was struck by its singular charm, as he had been last week. It was decorated to make a statement, but it was certainly not overdone. Everything was in the best of taste, from the white walls and cabinets and the terracotta tile floor, to the sparkle of copper.

Delicious smells were suddenly wafting on the air . . . freshly baked bread, cooked apples and the hint of cinnamon mingled with the smell of coffee. He inhaled, then sniffed.

Maggie, who had turned around at this moment, said, 'I baked the bread earlier this morning and it's still warm. Would you like a slice? It's delicious, even though I say so myself.'

'I would, thanks very much. Can I do anything to help?' He started to rise.

'No, no, I can manage. The coffee's coming up, and then I'll bring the bread and honey.' As she spoke she glided across the kitchen floor, carrying the mugs of coffee, and a second later she was back again with the homemade bread, a honeycomb and a bowl of baked apples on a tray. She placed this in the centre of the table and sat down opposite him.

'I love baked apples,' she confided. 'Try one. They're great with a slice of warm bread and honey.'

'I will,' he said, as tongue-tied as ever, then thought to say thank you to her.

Maggie sipped her coffee and regarded him surreptitiously. He had helped himself to a baked apple and was eating it with relish, then he took a slice of the warm bread, spread it with butter and honey, took a bite.

He said, a second later, 'I haven't had homemade bread since I was a kid. It's nectar.'

'I know what you mean,' she answered, laughing, glad he was enjoying the breakfast. She had prepared it especially for him. It had struck her the other day that he probably didn't have very many proper meals. She knew from Samantha that he was single and lived alone in a charming white clapboard house on Route 341.

Maggie wondered if he had a girlfriend. Obviously he did. Looking the way *he* looked, and being as nice as he was, it was more than likely that women chased after him. She felt a little twinge of something, of what she was not sure. Envy? Jealousy? Or a bit of both? Of course he'd never be interested in her, so why daydream about him? Which is exactly what she had been doing since their first meeting. Actually, she couldn't get him out of her mind. The other night she had even had fantasies about making love with him, and now, as she remembered those images, she felt herself flushing.

Maggie stood up swiftly and hurried over to the counter, convinced that her face had turned scarlet. She was extremely conscious of Jake's presence in her kitchen. He seemed to fill it with his masculinity and strength. And his sexuality. She had not felt like this for years and years.

Pouring herself another cup of coffee, Maggie Sorrell cautioned herself to put Jake Cantrell out of her mind. At once. He was, after all, much younger than she. Beyond her reach in so many ways.

From the other side of the kitchen, Jake's eyes were riveted on her. She was half turned away from him, so he was seeing her partly in profile, and he was struck yet again by her unusual beauty. There was a great deal of strength there, and yet she was the most feminine woman he had ever met, and vulnerable. He wanted to protect and cherish her. And love her. He already did. He had fallen for her the first night they met.

And he wanted to make love to her. He had done this so many times in his mind he was beginning to think it had really happened. But of course it hadn't; he fervently wished it had. Jake wanted to make love to her right now, had a terrible urge to get up and walk across the floor, take her in his arms and kiss her passionately. And he wanted to tell her exactly how he felt about her, but he didn't dare. It took all of his self-constraint to remain seated.

Jake picked up his coffee cup and discovered, to his dismay, that his hand shook slightly. Whenever he was near her she had the most extraordinary effect on him. I want her in every possible way, he thought, yet I know I can't have her. Oh God, I don't know what to do. What to do about her.

Maggie turned around.

Taken by surprise, he gaped at her.

She exclaimed, 'Are you all right, Jake?'

'Yes. Why?'

'You're looking a bit pale. And a bit odd.'

'I'm fine, thanks.'

'Would you like another cup of coffee?'

He shook his head. 'No, thanks. I'll finish this and then perhaps we'd better be on our way,' he answered, and was surprised his voice sounded so normal.

'I'll just go and get my things,' she said. 'I won't be a minute. Excuse me.'

Left alone he leaned back against the chair and exhaled. He wondered how he would be able to work with her on a continuing basis, and experienced a sudden surge of panic. For a split second he considered turning the job down if she offered it to him. Instantly he dismissed this idea. He needed another big job if his business was to grow and flourish. Not only that, he needed to be with her on a daily basis, needed to be near her however painful that might prove to be.

Jake Cantrell knew deep within himself that his wild imaginings about Maggie Sorrell would never come to pass. They were from wholly different worlds. She had never shown the remotest interest in him since the day they first met, other than to offer him this chance to bid on the electrical job at the farm she was decorating. It was obvious to him that his work and his knowledge about lighting impressed her. That would have to suffice.

Jake drove them to the farm in his pick-up truck, following Maggie's directions once they had left the centre of Kent.

Because he was so drawn to her, so smitten, and therefore needed her to think well of him, he was reluctant to say a word. He was afraid he might say the wrong thing. And so he sped to their destination in total silence.

For her part, Maggie believed he was naturally shy, a little withdrawn. Days ago she had decided he was a troubled man, one who had been badly hurt; he needed to be handled with gentleness, in her opinion.

Because of her own painful experiences, Maggie empathized with him and felt that she understood him without really knowing him. After two years of struggling with her own pain, she had finally managed to regain her self-confidence, but she was only too well aware that emotional damage could take a long time to heal. After Mike's rejection of her, and the break-up of their marriage, she had felt nothing for so long.

And so she began to talk to Jake quietly, discussing the play they were involved with and their designs for the scenery and lighting. She was able to draw him out a little; he became enthusiastic and articulate as he began to speak about the lighting techniques he was planning to use.

She listened attentively, making an occasional comment. But mostly she let him do the talking, recognizing that as he opened up to her he became more sure of himself. He was gaining confidence as he spoke fluently about his work.

In no time at all they were turning through white gates and heading up the driveway of Havers Hill, the farm Maggie had been hired to remodel, restore and decorate.

Jake parked near a big red barn and then walked around to help her get out of the pick-up. He gave her his hands and she took them. As she jumped down she lost her balance and stumbled against him. He caught her, held her in his arms for a brief moment, and she clung to him. They drew apart quickly, staring at each other self-consciously.

Maggie turned away, straightened her jacket to cover her sudden confusion, and then reached into the truck for her briefcase and handbag.

After she had moved away, Jake, swallowing hard, closed the door of the pick-up and swung around, glancing about him as he did.

The property was magnificent.

Well-kept green lawns sloped away from the drive,

rolled as far as the eye could see. Beyond were pastures, and even farther beyond mountains partially encircled the property. Nearby, an old stone wall bordered a smaller lawn where a gazebo sat in the shade of an ancient gnarled maple, and the wall itself made a fitting backdrop for an English-style border of perennials.

He shaded his eyes with his hand. In the distance he could see an apple orchard. 'What a place!' he exclaimed. 'It's beautiful. I'd like to own something like this one day.'

'Then I'm sure you will,' she replied, smiling at him. 'If you want something badly enough you can usually get it, if you work hard at it, of course.'

Gesturing to a series of buildings just ahead of them, she went on, 'That's the caretaker's house over there, Jake, and the farmhouse is the bigger building to the right. Come on, I want to show you around.'

She began to walk rapidly towards the house, continuing, 'I told the caretaker, Mrs Briggs, that we'd be coming over, so the front door's open.' She glanced over her shoulder at him as she spoke.

Jake caught up with her and they went into the house together, their shoulders brushing in the narrow entrance.

Even though the lights were on, the hallway was dark and Jake blinked, adjusting his eyes to the murkiness of the interior.

'It's very old,' he said to Maggie, peering about, moving forward, looking inside several rooms that opened off the entrance hall.

'Yes, it is. About 1740 or 1750, somewhere thereabouts,' she told him. 'And it was furnished in Early

American style; most authentically, in fact. Most of the furniture's been sold though. My client only wanted to keep a few choice pieces.'

'Think about it, Maggie, this house was built before the American Revolution. My God, what these walls could tell us if they could talk!'

Maggie laughed. 'I know exactly what you mean. I've often thought that myself. About other places I mean, especially in England and France.'

'Who owned the farm?' he asked, turning to her.

'A Mrs Stead. It had been in the Stead family for several hundred years. The last Mrs Stead died about a year and a half ago. No, two years ago, to be exact. She was very old, ninety-five when she died. Her English granddaughter inherited the property, but since she's a married woman with children and lives in London, obviously her life is on the other side of the Atlantic. So she put the property, the farmhouse and its contents on the market two years ago. She thought she'd sell Havers Hill immediately, because it is such an idyllic place. But the asking price was in the millions and it's no longer the 1980s. So naturally she didn't have any takers. She finally had to drop the price.'

Jake said, 'A lot of people who want to sell their weekend homes up here are beginning to realize the prices of the eighties are finished. Anyway, who finally bought it? Who's your client?'

'A married couple. Anne and Philip Lowden. They own an advertising agency on Madison Avenue. They live in Manhattan during the week, and wanted a retreat in the country. Anne fell in love with this place, especially the grounds. She came to me through a client in New Preston, whom I've done work for. Anne told me she liked my understated style. "No *nouveau riche* folderol for me," she said when we met. She didn't even bother to interview any other designers, just hired me to do it all. Anne wants me to modernize the farmhouse and the guest cottage.'

'The farmhouse certainly needs it,' Jake remarked, and turned to look at Maggie. 'Okay, where shall we start?'

'Let's go into the kitchen first. We can put our things there: it's the only place with any furniture in it anyway.'

Maggie led the way down a short corridor and into the kitchen. This was a medium-sized room with two adjoining pantries, a couple of small windows, and a beamed ceiling. It overlooked a vegetable garden, an old stone well and, to the right, a flower garden.

'A decent-sized room,' Jake commented as they surveyed the kitchen together. 'But it's too dark, not much natural light coming in; you'll have to supplement it with really good artificial lighting.'

'I know,' Maggie murmured. 'And that's the problem with the whole house, Jake. It's so . . . so gloomy. Personally, I find it quite depressing. I like airiness, pale colours, a sense of space. My aim is to get rid of the sombre feeling without having to put in too many additional windows. I don't want to kill the period look of the place. After all, it's one of the reasons my clients bought it. For its rustic charm and antiquity.'

'I understand.' Jake's eyes scanned the kitchen once more. He looked up at the ceiling and then walked around the room a few times, a thoughtful expression settling on his face.

Maggie placed her briefcase and handbag on the kitchen table, took out a notebook and made a few notations.

Jake said, after a moment, 'I don't think this room presents too many problems. We could use several large-sized ceiling fixtures, such as old lanterns, something like that, plus wall sconces, in order to introduce proper artificial light. And you might want to think about putting in a new kitchen door, one that has panes of glass in the upper portion.'

'Yes, I had thought of that . . . it would let in additional natural daylight.'

'What about high hats? Would you or the clients object to a few in the ceiling?'

'No, since they're fairly unobtrusive. But can you do it?'

'I think so. I'll have to cut into the ceiling first, to investigate what's going on up there. But it shouldn't present any real problems. If I get the job, that is.'

Maggie stared at him, frowning slightly. 'Jake, surely you know you're going to get the job.'

'You might not like my estimate, it might not fit into your budget.'

'We'll make it fit into my budget, won't we, Jake?'

He gave her a long look and was silent for a few seconds. Then he said, 'I guess so. Have you found a contractor yet?'

'I'm thinking of hiring Ralph Sloane. He's done a bit of work for me, and I've seen some of his really huge jobs in the last few days. I like the way he operates, I like his style. Do you know him?'

'Yes, I've worked with him before. He's a good guy. Are you going to hire an architect? Or don't you plan on making structural changes?'

'The answer is yes to both of those questions, Jake. I met with Mark Payne the other day –'

'He's the best!' Jake cut in, sounding enthusiastic.

'That's what I thought. I've seen a lot of his work now, and he seems to be an expert when it comes to Colonial architecture. He'd like the job, I know that, and I was impressed with his ideas.' There was a small pause and then she finished, 'I think I'm putting together a good team, don't you?'

He glanced at her and nodded, gave her half a smile and then headed out of the kitchen. 'Shall we go through the rest of the house?'

'Yes, let's look at the rooms on this floor first.'

Three hours later they came out of the farmhouse together, blinking in the sunlight. Slowly they walked back to the pick-up truck.

Jake leaned against the hood, and said, 'It's a huge job, Maggie, bigger than I initially thought. The whole place needs rewiring. It obviously hasn't been touched in years. And there's so much else to do. We haven't even thought about the exterior lighting for the grounds.'

'I know.' She threw him a worried glance. 'You're not saying you don't want to tackle it, are you?'

'No. I want the job. I need it. As you know, I'm building a new business. Anyway, I like a challenge. And I want to work with you, Maggie.' He paused and stared into her face. Suddenly making a decision, taking control of the situation, he said in a firm voice,

'Let's go. I'll take you to lunch. I know a good place for a hamburger or a salad, whichever you prefer.'

'Good idea,' she responded. 'I'm starving.'

CHAPTER 7

WHEN JAKE KNOCKED on Maggie's kitchen door and there was no answer, he opened it and went inside.

She was nowhere in sight, so he wandered through the kitchen and into the small back hall, heading for her office. But he stopped at once, stood perfectly still, listening.

In the few weeks he had known Maggie Sorrell he had never seen her ruffled. Nor had he ever heard her raise her voice. But she was doing so now, obviously speaking on the phone in her office.

'He did it on purpose!' she exclaimed. 'Nothing you say will convince me otherwise. And he did it to hurt me. He simply doesn't want me there to celebrate with you.'

There was a sudden silence.

Jake guessed she was now listening to whoever it was on the other end of the line. Wanting to be polite, to make sure she was aware of his presence, he walked across the hall, knocked on the open door, poked his head around it and raised his hand in greeting.

Maggie stared at him so blankly he realized at once how preoccupied she was. But then she nodded quickly, acknowledging him.

He half smiled in return and ducked out. Swinging around, he headed towards the small sitting room opposite. After placing the envelope he was carrying on the coffee table, he walked over to the window and stood looking out of it at her garden, lost for a moment in his thoughts of her.

It was apparent to him that Maggie was not only angry but upset as well, and this disturbed him. He had become very protective of her.

Jake glanced at his watch. They had agreed to meet at six o'clock tonight, and as usual he was far too early. It seemed to him that he was continually ahead of himself whenever they had an appointment. He just couldn't help it. He wanted to be with her all the time; he hated it when they finished their work and he had to leave her.

They had known each other only five weeks yet it seemed so much longer to him. He had discovered that they were compatible, liked the same things. She loved music as much as he did and she was impressed with his knowledge of it. He enjoyed talking to her because she was so well informed; she was a news buff and, as he was, a great fan of CNN.

There were other things that he liked about her. She had a good sense of humour, laughed a lot, and she was a truly feminine woman. For all her ability and talent, strength and independence she was not hard. Just the opposite. He forever felt the urge to look after her.

Since his first visit to the farmhouse, two weeks ago now, Jake had begun to relax with her and, at the same time, he had acquired more self-confidence. In fact, ever since that Friday morning, when he had taken her for a hamburger in Kent, he had considered himself to be in command of the situation.

Lately she had seemed to defer to him, and frequently she used him as a sounding board about the work to be done at the farmhouse. It had struck him only the other day, quite forcibly, that she depended on him, and he was pleased about this. They had become good friends; he wished it could be more.

Tonight he had come over to discuss the detailed estimate for the electrical work at the farmhouse. He had given her a ballpark figure a week ago; then he had had to spend endless hours over at the farm, studying every aspect of the property inside and out. Now he was anxious to talk to her, get her approval of the figures.

From the doorway, Maggie said, 'Hello, Jake.'

He spun around, looked across at her. She was very pale. When she remained standing in the doorway, looking hesitant, he hurried across the room.

'Are you all right?' he asked quietly, drawing to a standstill in front of her, his black eyebrows puckering together in a frown.

'I'll be fine in a minute,' Maggie answered. 'I'm afraid I became angry –' She broke off, biting her lip.

'Anything I can do to help?'

'No, thanks anyway.' Her voice was trembling and she paused again. Suddenly tears welled in her blue eyes and she looked at him helplessly.

'Maggie, what's wrong?' He could not bear to see the pain settling on her face. Concerned, he took a step towards her.

And as he did she moved towards him.

He reached for her, drew her to him, enfolded her in his arms.

'Maggie, Maggie, what is it? Please tell me what's bothering you?'

'I don't want to talk about it . . . I'll be all right in a . . . minute . . . really I will . . .'

But she wept on his shoulder, clinging to him fiercely.

He stroked her hair and kissed the top of her head, murmured gently, 'I'm here, I'll look after you. Please don't cry. I'm here for you.'

Turning suddenly, she twisted her face to stare up into his. Their eyes locked. He felt her trembling in his arms, and he tightened his grip on her.

Maggie's lips parted slightly, almost expectantly, and before he could stop himself he bent down and kissed her fully on the mouth.

She kissed him back, pressing her body against his. Because she was tall, almost as tall as he was, their bodies fitted together.

We're a perfect fit, Jake thought, his heart racing.

After a few moments of intense kissing, they stopped, drew apart, and stared at each other breathlessly, wonderingly.

Jake said softly, 'I've been wanting to do that for a long time.'

'I've been wanting you to do it,' Maggie whispered.

Emboldened, still staring hard at her, he went on, 'I've wanted to make love to you since that first night we met.'

'And I . . .'

'Oh Maggie, Maggie.'

'Jake.'

He drew her towards the sofa; they sank down onto it. Pushing her gently against the cushions, he leaned over her, looking deeply into her eyes. Bending closer, he kissed her eyelids, her nose, her face and lips, moved his mouth down into the hollow of her neck, then he began to unbutton her blouse. His hand slipped inside, cupped her breast; somehow he managed to release it from her bra.

When his mouth found her nipple, Maggie sighed deeply and moaned. And then she gave herself up to her feelings entirely, her hurt and pain of a short while ago forgotten for the moment.

She had thought of Jake constantly, had envisioned making love to him so often, she could scarcely believe it was happening now.

His mouth was soft if insistent, his touch gentle but firm, and when he stopped with suddenness she held herself perfectly still, wondering why he had stopped. She wanted him to continue.

A moment later his face was resting against her hair, and he said softly, 'Please, Maggie, let's go upstairs.'

'Yes,' she answered and he straightened, pulled her off the sofa; together they went up the wide staircase, their arms wrapped around each other.

Maggie pushed open her bedroom door, led him inside, and walked to the centre of the room.

Jake closed the door behind them and followed her.

The light outside was changing. The sky had turned a warm golden colour and it was flooding the room with a soft radiance.

He took hold of her shoulders and stared into her face. 'Be sure of this, Maggie.'

'I am, Jake.'

'Once this happens there's no going back. Not for me.'

'Nor me.'

He brought her into his arms.

They stood there for a long time, kissing, touching, familiarizing themselves with each other. They pulled apart, gazed at each other, started kissing again, their ardour growing.

Eventually, Jake began to undress her, taking off her blouse, unfastening her bra, then her skirt. Everything fell on the floor around her feet.

She stepped over the heap of clothes and stood gazing up at him intently, her emotions written all over her face: She wanted him.

Jake returned her gaze, recognized the need in her eyes and nodded slightly. He pulled his sweater over his head; Maggie stepped closer to him, began to unbutton his shirt, then took it off. He struggled out of his boots and jeans, and she took off her stockings and they came together totally naked.

They held each other tightly. Jake ran his strong hands over her shoulders, across her back and down onto her buttocks; she smoothed her hands over his shoulders, pushed them up into his thick hair.

Finally he led her over to the bed. After he had

pressed her down onto it, he bent forward, kissed her, then said, 'I'll only be a minute.'

Maggie lay waiting for him, her heart beating rapidly. It was years and years since she had felt like this, had wanted a man so much. She wished he would hurry, come back. She could hardly wait.

Jake walked across the room towards the bed.

She thought he looked magnificent.

He stood next to the bed, staring down at her. He noticed that her eyes had turned the darkest of blues, so dark they were almost purple, the dark bluish-purple of pansies. They were full of urgent desire for him, he recognized that once more and he felt heat rising in him, his excitement growing as he stood looking at her.

How beautiful she was in her nakedness, in the soft golden radiance of the fading light, he thought. He had not realized what a lovely body she had, covered as it always was with her bulky sweaters and heavy jackets and long, flowing skirts.

But she was very slim, he noted, with curving hips, and long, long legs. She had perfect breasts, softly rounded, and her skin was smooth and pale.

As Maggie returned his long, contemplative gaze she thought that a man's body could be beautiful. His was. Jake was tall and slim; he had a broad chest and wide shoulders above slender hips and long legs. He was splendid to look at. She could hardly tear her eyes away.

Jake joined her on the bed at last.

He took her in his arms and held her close to him, kissing her hair and her neck, smoothing his hands over her marvellous breasts. He began to kiss her mouth.

Maggie kissed him back ardently. Their kisses grew hot, harder and hotter still, more passionate than before.

Jake propped himself up on one elbow, looked into her face and traced his finger along the line of her mouth. 'I want you so much,' he murmured. 'But I don't want us to hurry. I want to prolong this, savour it.' He bent into her. 'You really excite me, Maggie; if we're not careful it'll be over all too quickly.'

She half smiled, said nothing.

He went on quietly, 'I've wanted this for so long, ached to be with you.'

'I felt the same.' She paused, eyed him carefully. 'But I thought you weren't interested in me.'

'I thought the same . . . of you.'

Reaching up, she touched his face lightly with her fingertips. 'We're a couple of fools.' She ran a finger around his mouth, thinking how sensual it was.

He took hold of her hand, put her finger in his mouth and began sucking it, curling his tongue around it. Maggie felt the heat surging through her, settling in her loins. He was exciting her . . . there was something so erotic about the way he was sucking. She felt herself growing moist.

After a moment he stopped and said, in a voice thickened by emotion, 'I love you, Maggie. I want you to hear this now. Not in the heat of it all, when I might well say it. I want you to know it's true, not just the sex talking.'

Startled, she simply nodded.

Putting her arms around his neck, she drew his face down to hers. She kissed him deeply, as he did her. Their mouths locked together, their tongues entwining. Maggie felt as though he were sucking the breath out of her, and she grew more excited than ever. Desire flooded her, blinded her to everything except him.

Abruptly Jake moved his head, began to kiss her breasts, cupping them together in both of his hands, moving his mouth from one nipple to the other, brushing his lips over them until they stood erect in the centre of their dark, plum-coloured aureoles.

Moving on, thrilling to her, tremendously aroused now, Jake trailed his mouth down over her stomach, and his hands followed, smoothing and stroking.

Jake lifted his head, looked at her face. Her eyes were closed. 'Maggie,' he said softly.

'Yes?'

'Am I pleasing you? Can I love you this way?'

'Oh yes.'

He began to make love to her tenderly, wanting to give her pleasure. He touched the core of her lightly at first, but as his supple fingers began to know her they became more insistent. He explored and massaged the flower of her womanhood, did so expertly, tantalizingly, enjoying touching her in this most intimate way, feeling her coming alive under his hands.

Maggie lay very still, hardly breathing. Her longing for him was rampant; her body ached to be joined to his. She felt herself opening up to him more and more as his mouth followed where his fingers had been. He lavished her with kisses and his tongue was a darting arrow hitting its mark. She began to pulse under his kisses.

And then suddenly she was spiralling up into ecstasy as wave after wave of pleasure rolled over her. She convulsed, her body arching slightly as he brought her to a climax; and she cried out his name harshly.

Jake moved his body onto hers, parting her legs wider with his own. He had an enormous erection but she was ready for him, and he slid right into her, thrusting deeply.

Maggie was panting, moving against him, matching his rhythm, floating with him somewhere she had never been before.

Higher and higher she rose as he moved deeper and deeper into her, and once again the waves of ecstasy started, began to engulf her.

Jake knew he was touching the core of her with the core of himself. He was strong and hard inside her, riding the crest of her second climax with her. This was the way it was meant to be. The way it should always be and never had been for him. Until her.

She was cresting higher and higher, flying into the unknown, saying his name over and over.

He let himself go, crested with her, gave himself up to her, flowed with her and into her. And he shouted out, 'Oh Maggie! Oh my love!'

The colours of the sky had changed again, the bright golden radiance laced through with crimson, magenta and violet. It was that magic hour, twilight, just before darkness falls, when everything looks soft and rosy and at peace.

Jake lay on top of Maggie, his head between her breasts. Her hands rested lightly on his shoulders. After a while she began to stroke his back and then his hair.

His voice was muffled when he said, 'I don't ever want to move. I want to stay right here forever.'

Maggie said nothing. She bent over him and kissed the top of his head, thinking of his words earlier, before their passionate lovemaking. He had told her he loved her, startling her with this declaration. But she believed him. Jake always meant what he said and he was very sincere. She felt the same way about him, but for days now she had been suppressing her feelings, convinced he had no interest in her. How wrong she had been. But nothing could ever come of this, there was too big a difference in their ages.

Before she could stop herself, Maggie said, 'I'm a lot older than you, Jake.'

'I like older women,' he laughed. 'They're more interesting.' He chuckled again. 'Anyway, you don't look it.'

'But I am. I'm almost forty-four.'

'Numbers don't mean anything. And I told you, you don't look much older than thirty-two, thirty-three. But who cares?'

'I do. How old are you?'

'How old do you think I am?' he asked in a teasing voice.

'Thirty, thirty-one.'

'Wrong. Guess again.'

'I can't. Please tell me.'

'I'll be sixteen in June.'

'Be serious, Jake!'

He laughed. 'Okay, okay. I'm twenty-eight until June the twelfth. Then I'll be twenty-nine.'

'That makes me fifteen years –'

'Who's counting!' he exclaimed peremptorily, cutting her off. He lifted himself up, lay next to her, taking her in his arms.

Jake started kissing her, quietly at first and then more passionately, and soon he was moving on top of her. He was fully aroused and he entered her quickly, without preamble, possessing her more forcibly than before.

'Oh God, how I want you,' he groaned against her hair. 'I've never wanted a woman the way I want you, Maggie. I want all of you, every bit of you. Come to me, please come to me.'

'Oh Jake,' she cried, 'I want you too, you must know that.'

He pushed his hands under her buttocks, brought her even closer to him. They moved together with rhythmic grace, rising and falling as one. They soared, crested on the heat of their passion for each other.

Finally they lay still, their breathing rapid and harsh.

When Jake regained his breath he said against her neck, 'And you think age matters . . . this is what counts. This . . . this . . . chemistry between us, Maggie. It doesn't often happen, at least not like this, with such intensity. It's very rare . . .'

When she was silent, he said, 'You do know that, don't you?'

'Yes.'

'What we have together is something very powerful, and believe me, age has nothing to do with it.'

They ate supper together in the kitchen. It was a simple meal which Maggie had prepared quickly: scrambled eggs, English muffins and coffee.

'More like breakfast, I'm afraid,' Maggie said, smiling across the table at him. 'I haven't had a chance to do much shopping this week.'

'I don't mind. I was starving.' Jake smiled back at her and added, 'Can I have it again for breakfast, please? You are going to let me spend the night, aren't you?'

'If you want to,' she replied, and felt suddenly shy with him.

'I want.' He reached out and took hold of her hand and squeezed it. Then he lifted it to his lips and kissed her fingers. 'You have beautiful hands, Maggie, such long, supple fingers. And *you're* beautiful.' He shook his head. 'Oh God, you do have a terrible effect on me . . . I could take you back to bed right now and do it all over again.'

As he finished speaking he began to kiss the tips of her fingers, her knuckles and the spaces in between. Then he turned her hand over and kissed the palm. After a second he lifted his eyes and looked at her. 'Don't ever doubt this, Maggie. It's real and it's the best.'

She stared back. His face was serious, his light green eyes intense, and there was so much yearning for her in them she was touched. She felt herself choking up for a reason she couldn't fathom. 'Oh Jake,' was all she could say, and for a split second she thought she was going to weep.

As if sensing this, and wishing to avert it, Jake rose and said, 'How about some more coffee?'

She shook her head. 'No, thanks.'

He went and filled his own cup, returned to the table, and sat down opposite her once more.

There was a small silence between them. It was broken by Jake, who said in a low voice, 'You were very upset earlier, Maggie.'

'Yes, I was,' she agreed. Giving him a candid look, she continued, 'I think I should explain something.'

'If you like, but it's up to you. I don't want to pry.'

'A few weeks ago Samantha made a reference to my divorce. So I know you know I was married once. You do, don't you?'

'Yes, I'd gathered that.'

'What you don't know is that I have two children. Twins. A boy and a girl. They'll be twenty-one in a couple of weeks. They live in Chicago. They're attending Northwestern. Anyway, I had hoped we could all be together for their birthday, but their father is taking them away for a long weekend in California. Without me. When you arrived earlier this evening I was talking to my daughter Hannah, who was explaining this to me. Naturally, I was very upset to be excluded.'

'I don't blame you. That's kind of a lousy thing to do, isn't it?' He raised a brow quizzically, then rushed to add, 'In my opinion it is.'

'I agree.' Maggie shook her head. 'But it's par for the course.'

'What do you mean?'

She sighed. 'You've never been married, never had children, Jake, so it would be hard for you to understand all the ramifications. In any case, I prefer not to talk about it anymore. I just wanted you to know I was upset about something personal and not business.'

He nodded and changed the subject.

CHAPTER 8

THE JANGLING TELEPHONE brought Maggie out of the shower swiftly. Grabbing a large bath towel, she wrapped it around herself and raced through into her bedroom.

Reaching for the phone, she said, 'Hello?'

'It's me.'

'Hello, Jake!' she exclaimed, as always delighted to hear his voice. 'We're still on for ten o'clock, aren't we?'

'You bet,' he answered quickly. 'The only thing is, I'd like to meet you a bit earlier. Is that possible?'

'Of course, Jake, but is there something wrong?'

There was the merest hesitation before he said in a rather tentative voice, 'No, not really, Maggie. I just want to talk to you about something, that's all.'

'What? You sound odd. Tell me now, Jake, tell me on the phone.'

'I prefer to talk to you in person, Maggie, face to face. Really I do.'

There was something in his voice that alarmed her, but knowing him the way she did she knew he would not succumb to pressure from her. She said, 'All right then. What time do you want to meet?'

'Nine-thirty. If that's okay with you?'

'It's fine. Do you want to come here?'

'No. I'll meet you at the site,' he answered swiftly.

'All right.'

'See you then.'

''Bye, Jake.'

Maggie stood with her hand resting on the phone, a puzzled look on her face. His voice had been peculiar and so had his words and his delivery. He had been almost, but not quite, abrupt with her. This was unlike him. Also, she had detected a nervousness in him, and she could not help thinking he was about to break off with her. What else could it be?

She sat down heavily on the bed, shivering suddenly, even though it was a lovely May morning, warm and sunny outside. Her heart sank. Yes, that was it. He was going to end their relationship. Sighing, she lay back on the pillows and closed her eyes, thinking of Jake Cantrell. It was exactly a week ago today that they had first made love here in this bed.

Crazy, exciting, passionate love. He had been insatiable, unable to get enough of her, bringing her back to bed after they had eaten her potluck supper of scrambled eggs. And she had felt the same way; desire had overwhelmed her.

It seemed to Maggie that they hadn't stopped making love since then, although this was not strictly true. They had managed to do an enormous amount of work together at the farmhouse, or the site, as he called it.

But, now that she looked back, he had been odd for the last couple of days, withdrawn and shy with her. It suddenly struck her that his demeanour had been the same as it had on the first night they had met with Samantha to discuss *The Crucible.*

Opening her eyes, Maggie resolutely pushed herself up and left the bed. She went back to the bathroom, finished her toilet, and then returned to the bedroom to dress for the working day ahead.

Since it was warm and sunny, she chose a pair of lightweight navy blue gabardine trousers with a matching jacket and took out a white cotton T-shirt. Once she was dressed, she hurried downstairs to her office and put her papers in her briefcase.

A few minutes later, just before nine, she left the house, knowing it would take her a good half hour to drive to the farm near Bull's Bridge Corner in South Kent.

Jake's pick-up truck was already parked outside the old red barn when she arrived. Bringing her Jeep to a standstill, Maggie alighted, picked up her briefcase and slammed the door.

As she went into the farmhouse, heading for the kitchen, she braced herself, not knowing what he was going to say to her, not knowing what to expect.

He stood up when he saw her and smiled faintly, almost apologetically, but he made no move in her direction, as he would normally have done.

Maggie thought he looked drawn, on edge, and his light green eyes, usually so full of vitality and life, were dull and anxious.

'Hi,' Maggie said from the doorway.

He nodded. 'Thanks for coming early. I wanted a chance to talk to you before the other guys arrived. Come and sit here at the table, Maggie. I brought a Thermos of iced tea. Would you like some?'

She shrugged, then walked into the room briskly. 'Why not?' Sitting down at the table she waited for him to pour the tea, thanked him and said, 'Why didn't you want to talk to me on the phone, Jake? What's this all about?' Maggie heard the strain and anxiety in her voice and she was annoyed with herself.

Jake cleared his throat several times, and explained, 'I've been feeling terrible this past week, Maggie, really awful. Ever since we made love last Wednesday.' He cleared his throat again. 'I . . . I . . . look, I just haven't been fair to you.'

Staring hard at him, she asked, 'What do you mean, Jake?'

He shook his head, and looked embarrassed when he said in a sudden rush of words, 'I haven't been exactly honest with you. It's not that I've lied to you, because I haven't, but there's something I should have told you. And I guess I've had a very guilty conscience. I just couldn't stand it any longer. That's why I wanted to see you this morning. *Explain.*'

'What is it, Jake?' Maggie asked, sounding slightly perplexed. 'What are you trying to say to me?'

'Last Wednesday night you made a remark about me not understanding why you were upset because I'd never been married, never had children. But I have been married, Maggie, and I should have told you so then. I didn't though, and I lied by omission. It's been troubling me.'

Maggie sat back in the chair, her large blue eyes riveted on him. 'Are you a married man cheating on his wife? Is that what you're trying to tell me?'

Colour suffused his face and he exclaimed vehemently, 'No! I'm not! I've been separated for over a year. I'm in the middle of a divorce. I live alone and I rarely ever see Amy. And I hope to be single again soon. But look, I should have told you before. I'm sorry,' he finished quietly.

She heard the misery in his voice, saw the contrite expression on his handsome face, and reached out and took hold of his hand. 'It's all right, Jake, really it is.'

'You're not mad at me?'

Maggie shook her head and smiled at him. 'Of course not. Anyway, I don't get mad that easily. It has to be something really important to get me going . . . like my children's defection, for example.'

Jake said, 'You didn't explain that to me . . . I'm not sure I understand what's going on.'

Taking a deep breath, Maggie said, 'We've never had a proper talk, you and I, Jake. We were friends involved in a drama group, and then we started to work together professionally, when suddenly, unexpectedly, we became lovers. We don't know very much about each other. Let me tell you about me. Okay?'

'Yes, I want to know all about you, Maggie.'

She chuckled. 'I'm not so sure I'm going to tell you *everything*. I think I should remain a little mysterious, don't you?'

He laughed with her and nodded.

'Two years ago my husband left me for a younger woman. Mike Sorrell's a very successful lawyer in Chicago, and he dumped me for a twenty-seven-year-old lawyer he'd met and was working with on a case. I ought to have known something like that was going to happen, things hadn't been right between us for a very long time. But what threw me, truly hurt me, was my children's defection. I've never really been able to understand why they took Mike's side when he was the guilty party.' Maggie gave Jake a long, thoughtful look, and added softly, 'Except that he's the one with all the money, of course.'

'Little shits,' Jake said, and then flushing slightly, he murmured, 'Sorry, I shouldn't be making remarks like that.'

'It's okay, Jake, I understand, and I've often thought the same thing. Anyway, I wanted them to celebrate their twenty-first birthday with me, and I had written to Hannah, some weeks ago actually. When I didn't hear from her, I phoned her. You came in on the tail end of my conversation. The upshot is that she and her twin brother Peter are going to spend their birthday with their father. He's taking them to some beautiful inn in Sonoma for the weekend.'

'And you're not invited.'

'No.'

'I'm sorry, Maggie, really sorry they're hurting you in this way. I wish I could make it up to you.'

'Thanks, Jake,' she said, squeezing his hand. 'But I'm better now, I'm over it. Well, more or less.' Maggie sighed and said in a low voice, 'In a way, I think I'd written them off ... they haven't shown much interest in me ever since all this happened.' Forcing a laugh, she added, 'I guess I wasn't a very good mother.'

'Knowing what I know about you, I bet you were a hell of a mother!' Jake exclaimed. 'And kids in this kind of situation can be very . . . treacherous. I think that's the best word. I know my sister Patty is going through something similar. She got married a couple of years ago. Her husband was a divorced man, and his children have been behaving very badly lately. Not only towards him but Patty as well. And she had nothing to do with their parents' divorce. Bill had been single for four years when she met him. Things were apparently relatively okay between him and his kids until he married Patty. Then they turned nasty and adopted a very hostile stance.' Jake shook his head. 'God knows why.'

'You said you were separated, Jake. Do you have children?'

'No, I don't. Sadly. Well, perhaps I shouldn't say that now that we're getting divorced. I wanted children, though. Amy didn't.'

'I see,' Maggie murmured, looking at him through thoughtful eyes, then she said, 'You must have been married very young.'

'Nineteen. We were both nineteen. We'd been friends since we were twelve, sort of childhood sweethearts in high school.'

'I married young, too, just after I left Bennington College, when I was twenty-two. I had the twins a year later.'

'And you were living in Chicago all those years?'

'Yes, that's Mike's home town. I come from New

York, I grew up in Manhattan. Where are you from, Jake? Kent?'

'No, Hartford. I was born there. After Amy and I were married we lived there for a while, then we moved to New Milford. Once we separated last year I lived in a studio apartment on Bank Street. Until I found the house on Route 341, that is.'

'Where does Amy live now?'

'She's still in New Milford.' Jake took a long swallow of his iced tea and went on, 'Do you know Samantha from New York? From when you were growing up, I mean?'

'No, we met at Bennington. And we became instant friends. Best friends.' Maggie smiled as she thought of Samantha with affection. 'I don't know what I would have done without her. Especially in the last couple of years. I don't think I would have managed to survive without her.'

'Oh yes you would,' Jake remarked in a knowing voice. 'You're a born survivor. That's one of the things I admire about you, Maggie. Your strength of character, your resilience. You're a very special woman. I've never met anyone like you.'

'Thank you. I've never met anyone quite like you, Jake.'

He stared at her.

She stared back.

Jake said softly, 'You do care about me then?'

'Oh yes, I do,' she answered.

'Is everything all right between us?'

She nodded, smiled.

He also smiled, relief flooding his eyes. 'I couldn't stand it if you were angry with me.'

Suddenly Maggie laughed, feeling relieved herself. 'I feel the same way.'

'Can I see you tonight?'

'I'd love it.'

'Would you like to come to my house? I could make pasta and a salad. I'd like to go over the final lighting designs for *The Crucible* with you.'

'That's a good idea! I'd like to show you my drawings for the sets and finalize everything with you. There's not much time left, especially since Samantha and I are going away.'

'Oh. When is that?' he asked swiftly, sounding surprised.

'In about six weeks. In July.'

'Where are you going?'

'To Scotland. And then we're stopping off in London for a few days, on our way home. The trip's been planned for a long time. It's partly business.'

'I'll miss you,' Jake said. But he didn't really know how much until she had gone.

CHAPTER 9

IN HIS WHOLE LIFE Jake had never missed anyone the way he missed Maggie Sorrell. She had only been gone five days, but to him it seemed like five months.

It would be another ten days before she returned to Kent, and he knew he was going to be miserable until then. He was glad they were involved professionally as well as personally, working on the remodelling of Havers Hill. It made him feel closer to her, especially when he went to the old farmhouse. Her presence was everywhere.

For the same reason, he'd been up to the Little Theatre in Kent twice, to tinker around with the lighting for the play, and he planned to go there again before she returned.

The woman designing the costumes, Alice Ferrier,

was a friend of Samantha's and Maggie's, and he enjoyed chatting to her, and to the stagehands working on Maggie's sets. It gave him a sense of belonging to Maggie's group, was like being part of a large family, and he enjoyed the camaraderie. Also, it helped to deflect the loneliness he was feeling in her absence.

Until he met Maggie, Jake had been self-sufficient, going about his business, doing his own thing, occasionally seeing the odd male friend, and he'd had a couple of short-lived affairs. But he had never relied on anyone for anything.

Now he felt that Maggie was necessary to his well-being, his very existence, and this bothered him. He disliked being dependent on another human being; it made him feel vulnerable.

At the outset of their relationship, the night they had slept together for the first time, Jake had come right out and said it – told Maggie that he loved her. It was true, he did.

But Maggie had not declared herself. He was not really worried, although he would like to hear her say it, because he knew she cared about him. Cared a lot. She gave herself away constantly.

Thoughts of Maggie continued to swirl in his head as he went out of the kitchen and crossed the yard, heading for the old red barn in the field at the back of the house. He had turned it into a studio and workshop, and he wanted to complete the plans he was drawing up for the exterior lighting at Havers Hill Farm. He wished Maggie had been with him at the farm today; finally he had come up with solutions for some of the more intricate lighting problems and he would have enjoyed explaining them to her.

Jake paused as he walked down the path, staring at an unusual brown-coloured bird with an orange breast that had just flown out of the giant oak which shaded the lawn. As the bird hopped along at the edge of the grass he wondered what species it was. He had never seen this kind of bird before. The garden and fields surrounding his house were full of wildlife, as were the wetlands that stretched beyond. Canada geese and ducks made the wetlands their habitat.

Wandering on towards the barn, he stopped again as a chipmunk skittered across his path and disappeared into the innards of an old stone wall; the entire place was a haven for these funny little creatures and squirrels and rabbits. A fleeting thought crossed his mind – that this place would be a natural wonderland for a child.

As Jake struggled with the lock on the door, which was stuck, he could hear the phone ringing inside, but by the time he managed to get the door opened it had stopped.

Could it have been Maggie phoning from Scotland? he wondered. He hoped so; she had said she would give him a call this week. He depressed the button on the answering machine.

'It's me, Jake,' he heard Amy's voice saying. 'I've got to talk to you. It's urgent. Please call me.'

Immediately he dialled her apartment. The phone rang and rang. There was no answer. Just as there had been no answer yesterday, even though he had received the same kind of message on his machine last night. Obviously she wanted to talk to him about something, but when he returned her calls she was not there.

Walking over to the long table which served as a desk for him, he resolved to buy her an answering machine. Since she hadn't bothered to get one, as he had suggested months ago, he was going to have to do it for her.

Jake sighed under his breath. That was the story of his life with Amy. For as long as he could remember, ever since they were twelve, he had always been the one to take care of everything, and he had always had to look after her. She was like a baby. She couldn't manage to do the simplest task. Eventually it had begun to irritate him.

The odd thing was he *wanted* to take care of Maggie, to look after *her*, even though there was no need. She was such a competent woman and well able to take care of herself. Over the last few months he had come to know her well, and he was aware that she was clever and practical, but he still felt the need to protect her. Certainly he saw a vulnerability in her, a softness he found most appealing.

Pushing aside thoughts of Maggie and Amy, Jake turned on the architect's lamp he used on the old oak table, pulled a drawing pad towards him and began making sketches for the exterior lighting systems at Havers Hill Farm.

The red barn where he was working had become a refuge for him since he had moved into the house. He found the big open space conducive to work, whether it was designing lighting effects, tinkering with lamps and other electrical equipment at the bench, or painting at the easel under the big window situated at the far end of the barn. These three areas were quite separate and self-contained, and he had furnished the barn sparsely. It was austere, painted white, and only the things required for his work had been used. His one luxury was a CD player, so that he could listen to music whenever he felt like it.

Jake concentrated on the plans for lighting the trees at Havers Hill for an hour, and then he tried Amy's number again. There was still no answer, and immediately he turned his attention back to the plans in front of him. He had always had tunnel vision, and this had served him well.

At nine he stopped working, shut off the lights, left the barn and went back to the house. He found a cold beer in the refrigerator, made himself a cheese-and-tomato sandwich and took his evening snack into the living room. After turning on the television, he sat down in the chair, ate his sandwich, drank his beer and absentmindedly channel surfed. He was preoccupied with thoughts of Maggie, missing her, wanting her, longing to see her.

When the phone rang again Jake jumped up, grabbed it and exclaimed, 'Hello?' hoping it was she.

'It's me,' Amy said. 'I've been trying to get you for two days. Why haven't you called me back, Jake?'

'I have, Amy,' he answered, striving not to sound impatient. 'I got your message when I came home from work last night. I phoned you. No answer. I tried you at the store this morning and was told it was your day off. I just missed your call by a few seconds tonight. You must have gone out immediately, because there was no answer and I dialled you within minutes.'

'I went to the movies with Mavis.'

'I see.' He cleared his throat. 'You said you wanted to talk to me urgently. What about?'

'Something important.'

'Then tell me, Amy, I'm listening,' he said, sitting down on the arm of the sofa. When there was no response from her, he said in an even tone, 'Come on, Amy, tell me what this is about.'

'Not on the phone. I need to talk to you in person. Can't you come over?'

'*Now?*'

'Yes, Jake.'

'Amy, I can't! It's too late! It's turned ten, and I have to be up very early. Let's talk now if it's so important to you.'

'*No!* I have to *see* you.'

'Well, I'm not driving over to New Milford at this hour, so you can forget that!'

'Can I see you tomorrow? It's really urgent that we meet.'

'All right,' he agreed, although he did so reluctantly.

'Tomorrow night, Jake? I could make you supper.'

'No, no, that's not necessary,' he replied and, thinking swiftly, he improvised, 'I have to go to New Milford tomorrow morning to pick up some equipment. I need it for the job I'm doing in South Kent. How about if I come to the store around noon? I'll take you to lunch.'

'I guess so . . . I wish you could come over now . . .'

'I'll see you tomorrow,' he said firmly. 'Good night, Amy.'

''Bye, Jake,' she muttered and hung up.

Later, as he undressed, Jake asked himself if he had made a mistake, agreeing to see Amy. There was no question in his mind that she was going to grumble about the divorce, try to talk him out of it. She was already procrastinating; there had been no word from her lawyer. He wasn't even sure she had been to see him again. He was going to have to do something about it himself, take matters into his own hands, he decided, if he ever wanted to be free. As usual, Amy was incapable of handling it.

When they met the following day, the first thing Jake noticed about Amy was that she had made an effort with her appearance. Her wispy blonde hair was pulled back in a ponytail and tied with a blue ribbon, and she had applied a little make-up.

Nevertheless, as he sat looking at her across the table in the Wayfarers Cafe in New Milford, where he had brought her for lunch, he thought she looked tired. She was only twenty-eight, but it struck him now that she appeared older, a little worn down. But this was nothing new, really; there had been something lack-lustre about her for the past few years. Amy had faded quickly. It saddened him really, and he couldn't help feeling a little bit sorry for her. She wasn't a bad person, just unfocused, disorganized and isolated.

They chatted about inconsequential things, looked at the menus, discussed what they would like to eat. In the end they both settled on the Cobb salad and iced tea.

Once the waitress had taken their order and they were alone, Amy said, 'So what's the job you're doing in Kent?'

'A farmhouse,' he explained. 'A very old place, actually. It's picturesque and has beautiful grounds. It's a challenge, especially the interiors. I'm also doing the outside, creating lighting for the landscaped areas and the pool. It's a big job for me and I'm pretty excited about it.'

She nodded. 'I know you like doing intricate work, the fancy stuff, and you're good at it, Jake.'

'Thanks.' He gave her an appraising glance and said, 'What is it you want to talk to me about, Amy?'

'Let's wait until after lunch.'

'*Why?* You've been calling me for two days, asking me to meet you, saying it's urgent, and now you want to wait.'

She nodded. Her mouth settled in a stubborn line.

Jake let out a small sigh. 'Whatever you say, Amy, but I do have to go back to work you know. In a couple of hours.'

'My mother doesn't think we should get a divorce,' she blurted out, and then took a quick sip of water, eyeing him over the rim of the glass.

'I know that,' he replied, his eyes narrowing slightly. 'Is that why you wanted to see me? To discuss the divorce? Has your mother been going on at you?'

She shook her head. 'Not really.'

Jake leaned forward over the table and pinned her with his eyes. 'Look, Amy, I'm sorry it didn't work out, really sorry. But there it is . . . these things happen, you know that.'

Before she could answer the waitress was back, placing the salads in front of them, returning a second later with the glasses of iced tea.

They ate in silence for a while. Or rather Jake ate; Amy picked at her food.

Finally she put down her fork and leaned back in the chair.

Jake glanced at her, frowning slightly. Suddenly she

looked pale, paler than usual, he thought, and she seemed to be on the verge of tears.

'What is it, Amy? What's wrong?' he asked, putting his fork on the plate. When she didn't answer, but gaped at him oddly, looking scared, he pressed, 'What's the matter, honey?'

'I'm sick,' she began and stopped with abruptness.

His frown intensified. 'I'm not following you. Do you mean you feel nauseous at this moment? Or are you saying you have an illness?'

'Yes. I went to the doctor, Jake. I haven't been feeling well.' Her eyes brimmed. 'It's cancer. He told me I've got ovarian cancer.'

'Oh my God! Amy! No! Is he sure?' Jake leaned forward and took her hand, holding it tightly in his. 'Is the doctor certain?'

'Oh yes,' she whispered.

For a moment Jake was at a loss for words. A compassionate man by nature, he filled with sympathy for her. He wondered how he could comfort her, and then realized there was no way. His words, if he could find the right ones, would be cold comfort. Far better to leave them unsaid. And so he sat there, holding her hand, patting it from time to time, hoping he was making her feel less alone.

CHAPTER 10

IT HAD RAINED EARLIER, and as Maggie walked down the path that led through the garden of Sunlaws House Hotel she paused for a moment and lifted her eyes to the sky. The sun was coming out again, penetrating the light clouds, and quite suddenly a rainbow trembled up there above the trees, a perfect arc of pink and blue, violet and yellow.

Maggie smiled inwardly, thinking it was a good omen. Her mother had been the most positive person she had ever known, one who had always believed in the pot of gold at the end of the rainbow, silver linings and bluebirds bringing happiness.

Mom was an eternal optimist, she thought, still smiling to herself, filled with the fondest of memories. I'm glad I inherited that trait from her. If I hadn't I don't think I would have survived the debacle with Mike

Sorrell. They would have taken me away in a strait-jacket. But she had indeed survived and life had never been better for her, she decided. And then she thought: how many people get a second chance at life?

When she reached the end of the path, Maggie turned around and headed back to the hotel. She and Samantha were staying here overnight, en route to London by rented car. They had driven down from Edinburgh and Glasgow, and had arrived at Sunlaws in time for lunch.

The manor was in Kelso, in the area known as The Borders, in the heart of Roxburghshire. The gracious old house, which belonged to the Duke and Duchess of Roxburghe, had been turned into the most charming of country hotels.

Sunlaws was handsomely furnished, full of mellow antiques and fine paintings, and it was imbued with the comfort and welcoming warmth that Maggie loved. It was a look and an environment that she strove hard to create in her own decorating schemes for her clients.

The landscape around the hotel was equally captivating, and it reminded her of the northwestern highlands of Connecticut. The moment she had set eyes on it she had begun to feel homesick.

Maggie now realized that she couldn't wait to get back to her house in Kent. And to Jake. He was constantly on her mind; she rarely stopped thinking about him, wishing he were here, wishing he could be sharing this trip with her. And she wished he had been with her when she bought the antiques in Edinburgh and Glasgow. They were for the farmhouse and were good pieces made of dark, ripe wood, some of them handcarved, and all were very old and beautifully made. They would sit perfectly in the rooms at Havers Hill Farm, would underscore the mood of the house and its overall feeling of antiquity.

Maggie was glad she had come to Scotland with Samantha. The trip had been highly successful for both of them. Apart from the antique furniture she had purchased, she had found other interesting things: antique lamps, porcelains and all sorts of unique accessories.

Samantha had invested in a variety of fabrics which she planned to sell in the studio shop she was opening in three months' time. Maggie's favourites were the Scottish wools, mohairs and tartans, which had taken her fancy as well as Samantha's.

All in all they had done well, and Maggie made up her mind to come back next year. With Jake. He had never travelled abroad and had recently confided that he would enjoy making a trip to England one day.

She had missed him, missed his warmth and affection, his sense of fun, his dry humour, his passion, and his constant cosseting of her. He made her feel so wanted, so loved, in a way which Mike Sorrell never had.

She heard her name and glanced up, peering ahead, shading her eyes against the bright light with her hand. She waved when she saw Samantha coming down the path towards her.

'I've been looking all over for you!' Samantha exclaimed, tucking her arm through Maggie's, falling into step. The two of them continued on to the hotel together.

Maggie said, 'I love this time of day, just before dark. It's magic.'

Samantha nodded. 'So do I. And that's what they call it in the movie business . . . *the magic hour*. Apparently cinematographers think it's the most wonderful light for filming.' Samantha shivered. 'Let's go inside, Maggie, it's turned coolish. There's a breeze blowing up for one thing, and it smells of rain.'

'I'm a bit cold myself,' Maggie admitted.

They increased their pace, and once they were inside the hotel Samantha looked at her watch. She said, 'It's nearly seven. Let's go and have a drink in the lounge. There's a huge fire blazing in there. It might be July, but they know something about these cool Scottish nights, the locals do.'

A short while later the two friends sat in the comfortable lounge. It was furnished with deep leather chairs and sofas, and there were wonderful old paintings on the walls. Vases of flowers were everywhere and their mingled scents filled the air. The only sounds were the ticking of a clock somewhere at the other end of the room and the hiss and crackle of the logs burning in the huge marble fireplace. Silk-shaded lamps had been turned on and the lounge had a soft glow to it.

Samantha looked around and said, 'It's so intimate and cosy in here, and the room has a real country-house feeling to it, don't you think?'

'It's a look that's hard to reproduce properly,' Maggie said. 'The British do it so well, maybe because it's endemic to their way of life.'

Samantha merely smiled and took a sip of her white

wine. Then she glanced across at Maggie. 'I've really enjoyed the trip, haven't you?'

'Yes, I have.'

Now Samantha eyed her carefully and murmured, 'But you've missed Jake, haven't you?'

Maggie smiled. 'A bit . . .' She laughed, added, 'A lot actually. How did you guess?'

'You've seemed distracted sometimes, and sort of . . . well, *faraway* is the best way of describing it.'

Maggie was silent. She averted her face for a brief moment, sat gazing into the fire, a quiet, reflective expression settling in her eyes. After a moment she glanced at her best friend and said, 'There's something I want to tell you.'

Samantha nodded. 'And oddly enough, I've got something to tell you. But you go first.'

There was a fractional silence. Maggie then said, 'I'm pregnant, Sam.'

'Good God! You can't be! Surely not! Not in this day and age! Don't tell me you didn't use anything, for God's sake!'

'Yes. I missed my period for the second time last week, when we first got here. And no, we didn't use anything.'

Samantha sat back, gaping at her askance. 'There's something out there called AIDS, Maggie.'

'I know. But . . . well . . . I trust Jake, I know he's not promiscuous.'

'When you slept with Jake you slept with everybody else he's ever been with . . . you don't know anything about *them*.'

Maggie did not respond. She leaned back against the tapestry cushions in the leather chair and stared into space. Then finally rousing herself, she muttered, 'You said you had something to tell me. What is it?'

Samantha hesitated, cleared her throat, and leaning closer to Maggie, she said quietly, 'You'd better know this, even though it might hurt more than ever. Jake's a married man, Mag. I found out just before we left, but I didn't want to tell you then and upset you. However, I thought you should know, now that we're heading back home. I purposely waited so as not to spoil your trip.'

Maggie said quickly, 'But I already know that! He told me himself, weeks ago. Actually, it was a few days after we became lovers. He was very honest with me, Sam. He said he had been separated for a year, living alone for that time, and was in the middle of a divorce. Are you suggesting he's still living with his wife?'

Samantha shook her head and said swiftly, 'No, no, I'm not.'

'Who told you he was married?'

'A client. She bought me a present from the bath and body shop in New Milford. When she gave the basket of goodies to me, all kinds of aromatherapy products, she said they'd been recommended by Amy Cantrell. I suppose I must have reacted to the name, and my client said something about Amy being the wife of Jake Cantrell, the lighting expert. But if you say he's separated, then I'm sure he is.'

'And he does live alone,' Maggie asserted. 'I've been to his house several times.'

'Why didn't you tell me he was in the middle of a divorce?'

Maggie shrugged. 'I didn't think it was particularly important, Sam.'

'What are you going to do about the baby, Maggie?'

'I'm going to have it, of course.'

Samantha gave her a questioning stare. 'What about Jake? I mean, what do you think he'll say? Do?'

'I'm sure he'll be pleased. I hope so. But in any case it's my choice, and only mine. I'm certainly not going to have an abortion.'

Maggie leaned forward, and her face was suddenly bright with happiness and hope, when she added, 'While I was walking in the garden earlier, I couldn't help thinking that not many people get a second chance in life. I *did*. The baby's my second chance, and Jake of course. I think I'm very lucky.'

'Do you think he'll want to marry you?'

'I don't know . . . I don't really care . . . about making it legal. I can bring up a baby myself and support a child. I'm very competent, Sam.'

'You don't have to tell me! I know that only too well,' Samantha remarked pithily.

'Maybe you think I'm crazy,' Maggie ventured. 'Here I am, forty-four years old, pregnant by my much younger lover of twenty-nine, who's not even divorced yet, whom I'm not sure even wants to marry me.' She began to laugh and lifted her hands in a helpless gesture. 'And do I want to marry him?' Maggie shrugged and lifted a dark brow.

Samantha shook her head wonderingly. 'There's nobody like you, Maggie, when it comes to coping. Let's not forget that you came through a pretty rotten situation with your husband of twenty-odd years who decided to take a walk. A situation which might have felled many another woman.'

'Don't spoil my day! Don't mention Mike Sorrell. Anyway, getting back to Jake, he does love me.'

'He told you?'

'Yes, he did.'

'Do you love him, Mag?'

'Yes. Very much.'

'You're very brave, Maggie.'

'Oh, Sam, I'm very lucky . . .'

Samantha Matthews was glad she had insisted that they stay at Brown's Hotel. It was handy to Piccadilly, Bond Street and just about everywhere else, being in the centre of the West End. It was easy to walk to all the shops, and cabs were readily available.

Now as she hurried down Albermarle Street, making her way back to the hotel, she could not help wondering what Maggie had been doing this afternoon. Her friend had insisted on going off alone, and had behaved in the most secretive way. But she would soon know; Maggie would eventually tell her.

It was hot and muggy this afternoon and a storm threatened. Samantha decided to ask the head porter to order a car and driver for the evening ahead. They were going to the theatre and then on to dinner at The Ivy and the last thing they needed was to be caught in the rain.

When she entered the lobby Samantha made straight for the porter's desk. After ordering a car, she took the lift up to the suite she and Maggie were sharing. It was her treat, her birthday present to Maggie. 'But you've already given me that gorgeous bag!'

Maggie had protested when she had made the announcement in Scotland. Samantha had merely smiled at the time and refused to listen.

Maggie was still out.

Samantha dropped her bag and packages on the sofa in the sitting room and went through into the bedroom. Taking off her dress and stepping out of her high-heeled shoes, she put on a silk robe and lay down on her bed. She was tired from rushing around all day and wanted to relax before dressing for the evening.

After a moment her thoughts settled on Maggie. She loved her like the sister she had never had, and there was no one she felt closer to, or cared more about. Not unnaturally, given the circumstances, she was worried about Maggie. It was she who had introduced Maggie to Jake Cantrell, and she felt responsible for the current situation. On the other hand, Maggie was a forty-four-year-old woman who was highly intelligent and extremely smart. If she didn't know what she was doing, then Samantha didn't know who did.

Samantha sighed under her breath. There were no doubts in her mind about Maggie's capabilities, and in many ways she admired the attitude she was taking about the baby. But what about Jake? Would he come through for Maggie? And what if he didn't? Could Maggie really manage to bring the baby up on her own? That took guts, which Maggie had, of course. She'll be all right, no matter what, Samantha decided. And I'm there to help her. Samantha smiled to herself. Their motto had always been: through thick and thick and thin and thin.

The telephone on the nightstand between the two

beds began to ring. Reaching for it, Samantha said, 'Hello?'

'Is that you, Samantha?'

'Yes, it is. Who's this?' she asked, failing to recognize the somewhat gruff male voice at the other end of the line.

'It's Mike Sorrell, Sam.'

Samantha was so surprised she almost dropped the receiver. 'Oh!' she exclaimed and then added in an icy tone, 'What can I do for you, Mike?'

'I'm looking for Maggie.'

'She's not here.'

'When do you expect her, Sam?'

'I don't know,' Samantha replied, as cold as ever, ignoring his attempt at friendliness.

'Have her call me, please.'

'Where?'

'I'm staying at the Connaught.'

'You're in London!'

'I'm here on business.'

'How did you know where we're staying?'

'I tracked you down, via your assistant in Connecticut. When all I could get was Maggie's answerphone, I phoned your studio.'

'I see. I'll give her the message.'

'Thanks,' he said.

'Goodbye,' Samantha muttered and slammed the phone down. She glared at it. *Son of a bitch*, she thought and angrily zapped on the television set. She got the BBC and the evening news, but watched it somewhat absentmindedly, wondering what Maggie's ex-husband wanted with her.

Half an hour later Maggie walked into the suite

laden with shopping bags. 'Hi, Sam,' she said, walking through into the bedroom, putting the packages on a chair and kicking off her shoes. 'It's just started to rain. Perhaps we'd better get a car for tonight.'

'I already did,' Samantha replied and pushed herself into a sitting position on the bed. 'Sit down, Maggie darling. And brace yourself.'

Maggie stared at her. 'Why? What's wrong?' She frowned, then continued, 'There *is* something wrong. I can tell from the dour expression on your face.'

'Guess who's in London? No, you'll never guess. Don't even try. It's Mike Sorrell. He just called you, about half an hour ago. He wants you to phone him. He's staying at the Connaught.'

'Good God!' Maggie flopped into the nearest chair and stared at Samantha, shaking her head in disbelief. 'How did he find us? Not that it's a secret where we are.'

'Through Angela. When he couldn't raise you he called my studio.'

Maggie bit her lip, suddenly thoughtful. 'Out of the blue he wants to talk to me. I wonder why.'

'As do I, Mag. Are you going to call him?'

'I don't know. What for? It can't be anything to do with Peter or Hannah, he would have told you if there was some sort of problem or emergency.'

'I think he would. He sounded calm enough and controlled.'

Maggie thought for a moment and then made a decision. Pushing herself to her feet, she looked at Samantha and said, 'I'm going to talk to him now, get this out of the way.' She walked into the sitting room looking brisk and businesslike.

Samantha slid off the bed and followed her.

Maggie lifted the phone on the desk, asked the operator to connect her to the Connaught Hotel and a few seconds later she was talking to Mike Sorrell.

'It's Maggie. I hear you want to talk to me.'

'Hi, Maggie! Yes, I do. I was hoping we could get together.'

'Oh. Why?'

'I need to go over something with you. How about tonight? I thought we could meet for a drink. Or dinner.'

'Certainly not.'

'Not even a drink?'

'No. I'm busy this evening.'

'Tomorrow?' he suggested.

'Why can't we talk now, on the phone? That's what we've been doing, off and on, for the last two-and-a-half years.'

'I need to see you in person, Maggie.'

'Are the twins okay?'

'Oh yes, they're fine. Look, I think we have some unfinished business to discuss.'

Startled to hear this, Maggie was silent for a moment. Then she made another decision. 'Nine o'clock tomorrow morning. Here at Brown's Hotel. I'll meet you in the lounge.'

'Okay! Great. 'Bye, honey.'

Maggie put the receiver in its cradle and turned around, stood leaning against the desk, staring at Samantha. 'You're not going to believe it, but that snake in the grass just had the temerity to call me honey.'

'Something's not kosher in the House of Denmark, to paraphrase Hamlet!' Samantha exclaimed indignantly. 'Since you've seen fit to meet with him, I'm glad you made your venue here. I'll be ready and waiting in case you need me . . . to kill that son of a bitch.'

Maggie couldn't help laughing. 'Oh Sam darling, I do love you. No matter what, you can always bring a smile to my face.'

Grinning, Samantha leapt to her feet and went over to the small bar. 'Let's have a vodka on the rocks before we get ready for the theatre.'

'Good idea. You fix it. I want to get something from the bedroom.'

Maggie returned a moment later, carrying a small package. 'This is for you, Sam. It's just to say thank you for all this –' She glanced around the sitting room. 'But mostly it's because you're always there for me, and always have been.'

Samantha took the package, tore off the wrapping paper and opened the red velvet box. It contained a pair of delicate chandelier earrings made of gold and malachite.

'Oh Maggie, how sweet of you! The earrings I admired in that shop in the Burlington Arcade. Thank you so much, they're gorgeous. But you shouldn't have.' She went over and hugged Maggie, and added, 'Your friendship is the most important thing in the world to me.'

Maggie drew away from her, and smiled lovingly. 'Through thick and thick and thin and thin . . .'

The following morning when Maggie got up she wondered, for a moment, why she was feeling so tense. Instantly she remembered. Mike Sorrell was coming over to the hotel to see her, and she was not looking forward to it at all.

Very simply, she had nothing to say to him, and she didn't particularly want to hear what he had to say to her. As far as she was concerned they had no unfinished business, as he termed it. Their business was well and truly finished and had been for a very long time.

'You look fantastic!' Samantha exclaimed, when Maggie walked into the sitting room of the suite a few minutes before nine. 'The bloom is on the rose, and then some, Maggie. You look so well and so happy he's going to be gnashing his teeth.'

'I doubt it,' Maggie said, and grinned. 'I'm sure he's very happy with his lady love, his new wife. He's probably in the midst of starting a brand new family. That's what these second, trophy wives want, isn't it? Kids galore and an insurance policy for the future?'

Samantha laughed. 'Who knows? And who cares? Listen, Mag, I've been thinking about your situation with Jake, and I'm really glad. I know it's going to work out.'

Maggie patted her stomach. 'And the baby?'

'I think you're doing the right thing. Having it, I mean. Just make sure I'm godmother.'

'Who else but you?' Maggie looked at herself in the mirror, straightened the lapels of her navy blue gabardine suit, adjusting the collar of her white silk shirt as she did. 'Give me twenty minutes with him and then come downstairs and get me.'

'I will. Our appointment at Keith Skeel's antiques place is set for ten o'clock anyway.'

'See you in a few minutes,' Maggie murmured and left the suite.

Mike Sorrell was already waiting for her in the lounge when she arrived a few seconds later. He rose to greet her, seemed at a sudden loss, as if he didn't know whether to kiss her or shake her hand. He opted for the latter, and thrust his hand at her.

Maggie shook it quickly and sat down opposite him. She could not help thinking that he looked weary, worn and sad. His face was lined and jowled, his hair very grey, and in general there was a tired air about him. He wasn't wearing well, she decided, and looked much older than forty-nine. An image of Jake, twenty years his junior, flashed before her eyes. She blinked and averted her face, not wanting him to see the sudden smile of pleasure that had settled there. He might misunderstand that smile.

She said, 'Let's order coffee, shall we?'

'Thanks. I could use another cup.' As he spoke he signalled to a waiter. Turning to Maggie he asked, 'Do you want anything to eat?'

She shook her head.

Once he had given the order for coffee, Mike turned back to her, again looking uncertain.

Maggie seized the moment and said, 'Why did you want to see me?'

Mike cleared his throat nervously. 'I was in New York at the end of last week, en route to London for a client. I thought we could get together there. I'm sure Samantha told you I called her studio when I couldn't reach you.'

'Yes, she did. But *why* do you want to see me at all? You dumped me unceremoniously almost three years ago now, and have hardly been in touch since then. Why the unexpected change of heart?'

When he remained totally silent, Maggie added, 'I don't think we have any unfinished business. Quite the contrary, our business is well and truly finished.' She laughed a little acidly. 'You made that quite clear to me when you left me for your legal colleague.'

'Don't be bitter, Maggie,' he murmured. 'I realize now that –'

'Bitter!' she exclaimed, cutting him off. 'I'm not bitter. I've better things to do with my time than waste it feeling bitter about you, or mourning your loss, Mike. I have a life to live, and believe me I'm living it. To the hilt.'

'You look very well . . . glowing,' he said, eyeing her thoughtfully.

Maggie decided he sounded slightly regretful and wondered what was happening in his new life. But she really didn't care, and she didn't want to know. She said, 'Look, Mike, I have an appointment with an antiques dealer this morning, so my time is limited. What's this unfinished business you mentioned on the phone? Let's get to the point.'

He took a deep breath and said, '*Us*, Maggie. We're the unfinished business. We were together for so long, we had a good life, and we have the kids . . .' His voice trailed off as he became aware of her icy demeanour, the disdainful expression on her face.

Maggie's voice was frosty when she said, 'Are you trying to tell me you made a mistake? Is that it, Mike?'

'Yes, for my sins, I did. I should never have left you, honey. We were the best, so good together. As I said, we had a great life –'

'*You* did,' Maggie interrupted. 'I didn't, now that I look back. You were pretty selfish and self-involved, you never really thought about my needs, and the one time I was happy, doing so well at the design firm, you made me leave my job. You just couldn't stand the fact that I had an interest other than you.'

'Don't be like this, Maggie. *Please*.'

She laughed in his face. 'You bastard! You dump me in the most cold-hearted way, barely talk to me for nearly three years and now come around making nice talk. What's all this about? Don't tell me your new wife's left you?'

When he sat back in his chair and glared at her, Maggie knew she had hit the mark. 'Well, well, well,' she said, biting back an amused smile. 'And more than likely for a younger man. Right?'

Mike Sorrell flushed deeply, but still he said nothing.

Maggie said, 'Ironic reversal.'

'I suppose it is,' Mike agreed at last. 'And yes, Jennifer has left me. She took up with a guy about six months ago, unbeknown to me, of course. Anyway, she's gone off with him. Permanently. To Los Angeles. She wants a divorce.'

'Never mind, Mike, you'll manage to cope somehow. I did.'

'Can't we try again, Maggie?' he pleaded. 'Let's give it a shot. The kids are all for it, too. And I need you.'

'Oh, really? Well, it might surprise you to know that I don't give a damn that you need me. Also, what Peter and Hannah think doesn't concern me very much. They have behaved in the most unconscionable way with me. So, my attitude is exactly the same as theirs has been towards me since you dumped me for a younger woman. Let's not forget what you did.'

'Don't be so resentful and bitter!' Mike exclaimed, glaring at her. 'I'm offering you this chance to start all over again, to put the family back together again, and you're behaving as if I'm asking you to commit suicide or murder.'

'Apt words, very apt words indeed!' Maggie exclaimed. 'To come back to you *would* be suicide. And you murdered my soul for years, all the years I knew you, Mike. You never let me be me, be myself.'

'You don't want to end up a lonely old woman, all by yourself, do you?' he asked and then paused as the waiter arrived with the coffee.

Once he had left, Maggie said in an icy tone, 'You egotistical idiot. What on earth makes you think I'm alone? As a matter of fact, I'm very involved with someone.'

'Is it serious?' he asked, and he was unable to keep the angry look off his face.

'Yes, very serious. I expect to be married soon.'

'Who is he?'

'I don't think that's any of your business. We're divorced, remember.' Maggie pushed back her chair, stood up and stepped away from the table. Then she paused and murmured, 'Goodbye.'

As she walked through the lounge she saw Samantha hovering in the doorway. She raised her hand in greeting and smiled. She felt freer and happier than she had in years. In a few days she would be back with Jake. Her future.

CHAPTER 11

JAKE HAD TO KEEP reminding himself that the speed limit was forty-five miles an hour, to resist the temptation to press his foot down hard on the pedal. He was on his way to Maggie's, and he couldn't wait to get there.

She had called him on his bleeper the minute she had arrived at her house in Kent from Kennedy Airport, and when he had asked her if he could come over she had agreed at once. He thought she had sounded glad to hear his voice, excited even, and this pleased him. He had missed her; he wondered if she had missed him.

Ten minutes later he was driving into her yard.

Before he had even turned off the ignition she was coming out of the kitchen door and running down the back steps. Her face was wreathed in smiles.

'Hi, sweetheart!' he cried, slamming the truck's door behind him and almost running towards her.

They met in the middle of the back yard, and he swept her into his arms and swung her around. They were both laughing when he finally set her down on the ground.

Jake held her away from him, looking into her face, smiling widely.

Maggie smiled back at him and exclaimed, 'I've missed you so much, Jake! I can't begin to tell you how much!'

'I know, I've missed you too,' he said and brought her into his arms, kissing her deeply on the mouth. Once he started kissing her he couldn't stop. He showered her with kisses. Her forehead, her eyes, her face and her neck. 'I'm happy you're home, Maggie.'

'Yes, so am I. Let's go inside, Jake.' She cocked her head on one side and gave him a flirtatious look. 'I have something for you.'

'You do?' He looked at her questioningly.

She nodded, took hold of his hand and led him into the house. Her suitcases were still in the kitchen, along with her raincoat and a shopping bag; she reached into the latter and pulled out a package.

Turning, she offered it to him, feeling suddenly rather shy and girlish. 'This is for you, Jake. It's from Scotland.'

Grinning, and just a bit flustered, he took the gift from her and stared at it for a moment. 'What is it?' he asked finally.

'Open it and see,' she answered, gazing up at him.

He did so, pulled out a heavy fisherman's sweater made of thick cream wool and then looked at her. 'Maggie, this is great. But you're spoiling me.'

'I just hope it fits. I had to guess your size. Large, right?'

He nodded and then held it against himself. 'I'm sure it's perfect. Thanks, Maggie.' Putting the sweater down on a chair he moved forward, pulled her into his arms and kissed her on the cheek. 'Thanks . . . for thinking of me when you were away . . .'

'I never stopped, Jake.'

The adoration reflected in her eyes told him what he wanted and needed to know. He bent into her, placed his mouth on hers and kissed her passionately.

Maggie held onto him tightly, returning his kisses, matching his ardour, pressing herself against him, needing to feel his warmth and his love.

Finally, he slackened his hold on her and stared down into her face. 'Can we go upstairs?'

Maggie nodded.

Together they climbed the stairs holding hands.

It occurred to Jake that their lovemaking was more frantic and passionate than ever. They shed their clothes and came into each other's arms with a rush of excitement and urgency; they seemed to grasp at each other, their faces full of intensity and longing.

Jake found himself taking her to him at once, on her urging, and she was hot and yielding and ready for him, as he was for her. They soared together, clutching each other tightly, calling each other's name as they rose higher and higher, lost in the wonder of each other.

When he finally fell against her he felt drained, almost exhausted from their passion. 'Oh God, Maggie,' he gasped. 'It's never been like that. Not ever. Not any time. Not anywhere. Not even with you. Until now.' He raised himself onto one elbow and looked down at her. 'That was a first.'

She smiled and touched his face. 'Jake . . .'

'Yes, sweetheart?'

'I love you . . . I love you so much . . . more than I've ever loved anyone.'

'Oh Maggie, Maggie.' He wrapped his arms around her, held her close to him. 'I've wanted to hear you say that for ages. I love you too. But then you know this . . . I told you the first night.'

'I felt the same way, but I just wanted to be sure. About my own feelings, I mean.'

'And are you sure now?'

'*Absolutely*.'

'I'm glad.'

Maggie lay next to him, her arms wrapped around him, drifting with her thoughts. Finally rousing herself, she said, 'Jake, I have a surprise for you.'

'Mmmmmm,' he murmured lazily without moving.

Maggie tried to sit up. He held her tightly in his arms, would not release her. Struggling slightly, she said softly, 'Let me get up, Jake. I have something to tell you.'

'Tell me then.'

'I'd like to be looking at you when I do.'

'Oh.' Intrigued, he let go of her and sat up himself.

Maggie crawled in front of him, then sat curled up in a ball, staring into his face.

'So go on, tell me, sweetheart,' he said, eyeing her curiously.

Maggie smiled. 'I'm pregnant, Jake. I'm expecting a baby. Our baby.'

A beatific smile spread across his face and his eyes lit up. 'That's wonderful! *A baby*. That's great, Maggie! It really is.'

'You *are* pleased then?' she asked.

'Sure I am. I always wanted a child. I told you that. When did you realize? When is it due? I wonder if it's a boy or a girl?' For a few moments he was full of questions.

Maggie answered each one, enjoying his excitement and happiness, relieved that he had reacted in this way.

Later they made love again. 'To celebrate the baby,' Jake whispered in her ear and then they fell asleep in each other's arms.

It was Jake who awakened first, about half an hour later. He slid out of bed and went into the bathroom where he took a shower.

When he returned to the bedroom wrapped in a towel, Maggie was putting on a loose silk caftan. She turned around as he came in; as always she felt the impact of him . . . his dark good looks, the soulful green eyes, the black hair slicked back after his shower never failed to surprise her. There were moments when he took her breath away.

'You're staring,' he said.

'I know. Sorry. It's just good to see you that's all.' For a moment she was tempted to tell him about the night they first met at the Little Theatre in Kent, when

Samantha had called him Tom Cruise. But she refrained, knowing that the story would not sit well with him. He disliked references to his good looks and his physique.

Maggie moved across the room swiftly, the caftan flaring out behind her. 'I picked up some groceries on the way in from the airport. Steaks and salad for dinner. How does that sound?'

'Great. I'll be down in a minute. If you open a bottle of wine we can have a drink outside, while I grill the steaks on the barbecue.'

'It's a deal,' she said and went out.

After he had buttoned his white shirt, pulled on his blue jeans and boots, Jake went downstairs. He found Maggie outside on the back terrace, sitting at the table, the bottle of wine in an ice bucket. She poured two glasses as he sat down next to her.

'Cheers,' they said together, clinking glasses.

After taking a long swallow, Jake remarked, 'Things are going great at Havers Hill, Maggie. And I know Mark and Ralph have been giving you progress reports. But I can't wait for you to come out to the site tomorrow. You'll be very surprised, pleasantly surprised.'

She grinned. 'I know I will. I guess I'll have to make two trips tomorrow. One in the morning and one at night. I do want to see the outside lighting after dark. You said some of it was in place already.'

'But only temporarily. For you to see. I've rigged it up in such a way that if you don't approve we can change it. My guys haven't done the channelling in the ground for the wires. We'll do that once you've made your final decision.'

'I wish you'd been with me in Scotland, Jake. I found some wonderful antiques.'

They sat talking about the work at Havers Hill for a while, and then they went into the kitchen. Maggie made a green salad and put it on a tray, along with plates, knives, forks and napkins. Jake insisted on carrying this outside for her; Maggie followed him with the plate of steaks.

'I've rarely seen fireflies,' Maggie said, clutching Jake's arm. 'Look! Over there! The little lights dancing among the bushes.'

'You're right!' he exclaimed. 'I haven't seen them since I was a kid myself. When I was about fourteen. Amy and I would go to her aunt's –' Jake broke off, sat back in his chair, sipped a little coffee, suddenly silent and tense.

Maggie said, 'Why did you stop?'

'It's not a very interesting story,' he mumbled and got up. He walked along the terrace and stepped down onto the lawn which stretched in front of it.

Aware of the sudden change in his mood, sensing that something was troubling him, Maggie rose and went after him. She caught up with him on the lawn, took hold of his arm and pulled him around to face her.

'What is it, darling?' she asked, filling with apprehension.

He stood staring down at her and shook his head. A deep sigh escaped him. 'I really didn't want to tell you this tonight. Not on your first evening back. I just wanted us to enjoy being together. But I guess I have to tell you . . .' He sighed again, then put his hand on her shoulder, peered into her face. 'I've got some really bad news, Maggie.'

She stared at him. 'What kind of bad news?'

'It's about Amy . . .'

'The divorce has stalled, is that it?'

He shook his head. 'No, not in the way you mean. But it is stalled.'

'You always said she was very reluctant to divorce you, and I can't say I blame her,' Maggie murmured, feeling deflated after the excitement of earlier and their intimate dinner.

'It's not really her,' Jake began, and stopped. He coughed, and said in a low voice, 'While you were away I found out that Amy has cancer. Ovarian cancer.'

'Oh no, Jake, how terrible! I'm so sorry. Is she getting treatment?'

'Chemotherapy. She started at the beginning of this week. Maybe the treatment will arrest the cancer.'

'Let's hope so,' Maggie said, and moving away she trailed across the lawn, knowing what he was going to say before he said it. She knew because she knew him. He was a decent man, and he was sensitive, compassionate.

Jake caught up with her and put his arm around her shoulders. 'I have to help her as much as I can, do what I can for her, Maggie. You do understand that, don't you?'

'Yes. Of course.'

'I just can't pressure her about the divorce right now.'

'I understand . . .' Maggie paused, took a deep breath and went on quietly, 'Are you moving back to

New Milford? Are you going to live with Amy again?'

'No, I'm not! How could you think that?' he cried and turned her to face him. 'I love you, Maggie. I don't want to lose you. I just want you to understand that I'll have to do what I can for her, especially financially. She's on my medical insurance, I can't pull that away from her. If we got divorced she'd lose her benefits. She needs me to be there for her right now. She's like a child, she's always been dependent on me. As soon as the cancer's arrested I'll talk to her again about seeing her lawyer.'

Maggie compressed her lips and nodded. She was afraid to speak. She didn't want to say the wrong thing. She didn't want to lose him either. Her eyes filled with tears.

In the dim evening light he saw them glittering on her dark lashes, and he brought her into his arms, pressed her head against his shoulder. 'Don't cry. I know what you're thinking. You're thinking about the baby.'

'Yes,' she whispered against his shirt which was soaked with her tears.

'Will you marry me, Maggie? When we can?'

'I will, Jake. I love you.'

'I love you. I want you and I want our baby. But I have to stand by Amy. Until she's better. You do understand that?'

Maggie nodded. 'If you weren't the kind of man you are, I don't believe I would love you as much as I do. I'll wait for you, Jake. I'll wait.'

CHAPTER 12

'IT'S ME, AMY,' Jake called out as he opened the door of her apartment. Bending, he picked up the bags of groceries he had deposited on the floor and went into the hall. Walking across the living room, he stood in the doorway. 'Hello, honey,' he said, smiling at her.

Amy was sitting on the sofa in the dim-lit room, watching television. 'Hi, Jake,' she said in a low voice and gave him a wan smile.

'I'll be with you in a minute, Amy. After I put all of this stuff in the kitchen.'

Amy nodded and leaned back against the sofa. She was so happy to see Jake but she didn't seem to have the strength to show it.

Jake thought she looked excessively pale today and weaker than usual, but he made no reference to her health. Turning, he hurried into the kitchen; after placing the groceries on the table he glanced around. For the past few weeks Mary Ellis, the wife of one of his electricians, had been keeping the apartment clean. She was doing it more as a favour to him and out of the goodness of her heart rather than for the money, and he was pleased with the results. The kitchen was not only neat and clean, it sparkled.

Once he had put everything away, Jake went back to the living room and sat down opposite Amy. 'How're you feeling today?' he asked, inspecting her face closely, thinking she was thinner than ever.

'Tired, Jake, a bit done in,' she answered.

'Do you want me to make you something to eat before I go back to work?'

She shook her head. 'I'm not hungry . . . I'm never hungry these days. But you eat something.'

'No, thanks anyway. I can't stay too long. I have to get back to the site as quickly as possible, we're doing some special wiring. When do you have to go to the hospital again?'

'Tomorrow. My mother's going to take me.'

'What does the doctor say? Are you in remission yet?'

'I think so. But that doesn't mean I'm not going to die, Jake. Not many people survive cancer. We all know that,' she murmured in a low voice.

'You mustn't be negative, Amy,' he replied gently but firmly. 'And you must keep your strength up. Not eating is the worst thing you can do. You need nourishment, some good food in you. Why don't you let me make you something? I did a lot of shopping at the supermarket. I bought all sorts of things, special things you've always liked.'

'I'm not hungry, Jake,' she began and stopped, her voice quavering. Amy took a deep breath, opened her mouth to say something and stopped again. The tears came then, welling in her eyes. Slowly they trickled down her pale cheeks.

Jake got up immediately and went and sat next to her on the sofa. He put his arms around her and held her close. 'Don't cry, Amy. I said I'd look after you, and I will. It's going to be all right, you're going to get better. This is the hard part, you know, undergoing the treatment, suffering through it. I know it's making you weak, but you'll get your strength back eventually. And when you do I'm going to send you and your mother to Florida for that vacation I promised you.'

'You'll come won't you, Jake?' Amy asked, looking at him wistfully.

'You know I can't. I've got to work, I must make sure things keep running smoothly. I can't let anything slip, not now.'

'I wish you *could* come though.'

'I know you do. Listen to me, Amy, you and your mother are going to enjoy getting away. It'll do you both good.'

'Jake . . .'

'Yes, honey?'

'I don't want to die.' She began to cry again, sobbing against his shoulder. 'I'm frightened. I think I'm going to die. I don't want to. I'm afraid, Jake.'

'Hush. Hush. Don't upset yourself like this. Remember what I've said to you before, it's the worst thing you can do, getting yourself so overwrought in this way. You've got to stay calm, be positive. Everything's going to be all right, Amy. Hush now.'

Eventually she stopped weeping, and as soon as she was composed Jake got up and went to the kitchen where he boiled a kettle and made a cup of tea. He brought it to her on a tray and sat talking to her for a while, wanting to allay her worries and fears, hoping to help her reach a better frame of mind.

Jake was preoccupied with thoughts of Amy as he drove to South Kent. He was doing everything he could to help her, but she had to help herself. Her doctor had told him that a positive attitude could work wonders, and that many people had licked cancer because of this. Jake knew only too well how negative Amy was; he wished he could make her understand how important it was for her to look on the bright side, to vow to get better and to do everything she could to achieve this goal. But she was more negative than ever, apathetic, and gloomy. He was doing everything he could, from providing financial support and doing the shopping to coming over whenever he could to sit with her, to cheer her up.

By the time he arrived at Havers Hill Farm Jake had decided to have a talk with Amy's mother. Maybe she could make more of an impression than he had been able to with Amy.

After parking the pick-up, he made directly for the kitchen before going to check up on Kenny and Larry, who were working on the exterior wiring.

Maggie's briefcase was on the floor and her papers were spread out on the old kitchen table, as they usually were, but she was nowhere in sight. He ran up the stairs and found her in the master bedroom, measuring one of the walls.

Hearing his footsteps, she swung around and her face lit up at the sight of him. 'Good morning!' she cried, coming towards him.

His smile was wide, and he was so intent on sweeping her into his arms he did not notice the frown of concern, the worry lurking at the back of her eyes. She knew how much he was juggling – the business, his own work, Amy's illness, and herself. That he was exhausted was apparent.

Hugging her to him, Jake said, 'How're you feeling, Maggie? How's the baby doing?'

She smiled up into his face, pushing her worry to one side. 'We're both terrific and all the better for seeing you. Were you at Amy's?'

'Yes. I got her some groceries.'

'How is she, Jake?' she asked, her brows puckering in a frown.

He shook his head. 'Not too good. Down. Depressed, I think.'

'Who can blame her? How awful for her to be so ill. She's so young. It's very sad.'

'I just wish she had your kind of spirit, your positive nature, Maggie; that would help a lot, I think.'

Maggie nodded and slid out of his arms. 'Come on, I'd like to show you something.' She was purposely changing the subject, wanting to distract him, to cheer him up, since he seemed to have been infected by Amy's dourness this morning.

Taking him by the hand she led him downstairs and into the dining room. 'Yesterday the table arrived from the antiques dealer in New York. Take a look.' As she spoke she whipped off the dustcloth, and stood back, admiring it yet again.

'What beautiful wood!' Jake exclaimed. 'And it's an old piece, I can see that.'

'Fairly old, nineteenth century. And it's yew.'

Jake glanced around. 'This room's really taking shape,' he remarked and walked over to a wall where Maggie had glued on swatches of fabric and carpet, plus a paint chip. 'Tomato red?' he said, raising a brow eloquently.

Maggie laughed. 'That's right. Heinz tomato soup with a dash of cream. Avocado-green carpet . . . that's as far as I've got with possible colours.'

He laughed with her, much to her relief. At least she had managed to take his mind off Amy's illness for a moment or two.

Jake said, 'I've noticed something lately. Whenever you speak about colours you do so in terms of food.'

'I'm pregnant remember. I've got all sorts of cravings.'

'You don't have to remind me, I could never forget.' He leaned into her, kissed her on the cheek. 'I'm going outside to see the guys. How about supper tonight? I'll feed you.'

'You're on,' she answered, grinning at him.

CHAPTER 13

'ARE YOU LISTENING TO ME, AMY?' her mother said, quickly glancing at her daughter out of the corner of her eye, not wishing to take her eyes off the road ahead.

'Yes, Mom, I am. You said Jake thinks I'm too negative about my cancer.'

'That's correct,' Jane Lang murmured. 'He says it would be better for you if you got out more, *did* things when you're well enough, when you're not in pain. Are you in pain now, Amy?'

'No, Mom, I'm not. I don't know what he means by *do* things. We didn't do much when we were married. He was always working, working, working, a real workaholic that guy is for sure.'

'What do you mean *were* married. You're still married to him, Amy, and let's not forget that. If you would only concentrate on Jake I'm sure you and he could get back together. He loves you, honey, and I know you love him. It was ridiculous of you to split up. He's so nice, I've always liked him since you were kids.'

'I don't think he wants to come back, Mom.'

'But just consider the way he's looking after you right now, Amy, taking care of you financially, doing so many things, like getting you this woman to help you in the apartment, and paying for it. And going to the supermarket for you. He loves you, I'm certain.'

'Oh, I don't know, maybe he's just being nice. He's like that.'

'Like what, honey?'

'*Nice*, Mom. Jake's always been kind to me, ever since we were kids in high school,' Amy responded, sounding slightly impatient.

'You never did tell me exactly *why* you and Jake broke up, *why* you decided to get a divorce. What was the reason?' Mrs Lang asked.

'I don't really know, to be truthful, Mom. I guess we just sort of drifted apart, you know . . .' Amy's voice trailed off. She wasn't really sure how the whole mess *had* come about.

'You can win him *back*! It will give you a goal . . . you must try very hard, Amy, put all your heart and soul into it. You and Jake were always right for each other, it's such a shame all this came to pass.' Mrs Lang sighed and then applied pressure to the brake as she turned a difficult corner on the slippery road. 'And it's such a shame you didn't have children. I don't know why you never planned a family. Amy –'

'It's a good thing I didn't!' Amy exclaimed, cutting

her mother off, 'now that I'm dying. Where would they have been? Practically orphans with their mother dead of cancer at the age of twenty-nine and their father working night and day, never home.'

'Don't talk like that, Amy, it's very upsetting to me. And you're *not* dying. Dr Stansfield told me you're doing well.'

'He did?'

'Certainly he did.'

'When, Mom?'

'This afternoon. When you were getting dressed. He thinks you're making wonderful progress.'

'I don't feel that I am,' Amy mumbled. 'I'm not really in pain but I feel crummy, Mom. Really crummy. I told Aunt Violet that when I was in the kitchen tonight, you know, when she was cooking the hamburgers. She offered me a vodka, said it would make me feel better.'

'That woman is incorrigible at times!' Mrs Lang exclaimed.

'She's your sister, Mom.'

'And we're as different as chalk and cheese.'

'I guess so.'

'I know so. Anyway, honey, we're going to take that trip to Florida next month. You'll enjoy it very much. Jake mentioned it to me again this morning when he called. Do you remember when your Daddy took us to Florida? You were six. You loved it so much.'

'Perhaps I'll get to see Mickey Mouse before I die,' Amy murmured.

'Don't, Amy, *don't*,' her mother whispered.

'Sorry, Mom. But I do hope I get to meet Mickey.'

'You will, you will, when we go to Disney World,'

Mrs Lang said, peering ahead. Although it was a wet night the rain had stopped; knowing Amy was tired, wanting to get her home, Mrs Lang pulled out, impatient with the slow-moving Toyota in front of her.

She did not see the vehicle coming directly at her down the other lane on the two-lane road. Blinded by glaring headlights, Jane Lang took one hand off the wheel to shade her eyes and in so doing relinquished a degree of control of her car. But she didn't have a chance. The oncoming truck, moving at an even greater speed, smashed into them head on.

Amy heard her mother screaming and the sound of glass shattering. She felt the impact most forcibly, was thrown forward and then back like a helpless rag doll.

'Mom,' she said before she blacked out.

Amy was suddenly and inexplicably outside the car, floating above it in the air, just in front of the windscreen. She could see her mother inside, pinioned by the steering wheel against the front seat. And she was there, too, sitting next to her mother in the other seat. At least her body was there. Amy realized that she and her mother were both unconscious in the car.

Below her, there were other people milling around now. The driver of the truck which had struck their car, who was himself unscathed; other drivers whose cars were backed up behind because of the crash. Then she heard the sound of sirens and saw two state troopers arriving on their motorbikes.

I'm dying, Amy thought; no, I'm actually dead. I've already died and left my body. She could see that body. She was floating over herself, looking down at the empty shell.

Amy was not afraid. Nor did it matter to her that she was dead. In fact, she felt extremely happy, free of all pain and sadness, and without a care in the world.

Unexpectedly, Amy was being sucked forward as if by a giant vacuum hose. She was in that hose. It was not a hose, she discovered, but a long tunnel. She was being pulled up it by some great force. But she still felt good, not in the least upset, even though she was dead.

At the very end of the long tunnel she could see a tiny pinpoint of light. As she continued on her way, rushing towards the light, it grew bigger and bigger, and so much brighter. Soon she emerged from the tunnel, blinking, adjusting her eyes to the light. It was the most magnificent light. She was surrounded by it, enveloped in its warmth and brilliance. The light embraced her, made her feel lighthearted, and so happy. She had never experienced feelings like this ever in her life before. They were feelings of tranquillity and peace and unconditional love, and they came from the all-embracing light. She basked in it.

Amy was floating in the light, totally weightless; she had shed her cumbersome human body. And she realized she had entered another world, a different dimension, and that she was pure spirit.

Soon she became aware of other spirits, floating in the brilliant light. They were sending her love and warmth and they did so without speaking. But somehow they were communicating. She reciprocated their love, beaming it to them, and she knew they welcomed it.

The light changed, its white brilliance picking up

prisms of colour, all of them rainbow hues. Another spirit drew closer to her, accompanied her, and Amy understood that she was being guided now, gently wafted towards a destination by this spirit. She knew without being told that this spirit was an old soul, that her name was Marika. It was Marika who was moving her along, but tenderly so, and with great love.

The light was growing softer and softer, losing its sharpness. Amy was moving out of it and into the most beautiful landscape she had ever seen. It was a place without a blemish, perfection, paradise. And it was a place without pain, one that was filled with purity and goodness.

The landscape where Amy floated was one composed of green pastures, flower-filled glades, wooded hillsides above a shimmering blue lake. Surrounding this pastoral setting were mountains capped with glittering white snow, and everything was bathed in golden sunlight.

Floating over the glades were many spirits like herself. Somehow Amy knew that there were old spirits mingling with younger souls. And then she saw him. Her father. The sight of him took her breath away. She knew it was him. Even though he was in spirit form, pure essence, as she was, Amy felt that special love flowing from him to her, and it was the self-same love she remembered from her childhood.

At this moment she felt her mother's spirit floating towards her father. Her mother's aura was radiant and serene, not the crushed human body which Amy had left behind the wheel of the wrecked car. Her parents joined each other and came over to her. They spoke to her. Although no actual words were used, she understood everything. They told her how much they loved her. They said they were waiting for her, but that she must go back for a while. *It is not time,* her mother was saying to her. *It was my time, Amy, but not yours. Not yet.* Their great love for her was enveloping her, and she was not afraid; she was happy.

Marika, the old soul guiding her, explained that she must move on. Soon they were floating through the bright light once more, entering a crystal cave that shimmered and radiated an intense and most powerful light.

Amy was immediately aware that she was in the presence of two women, that they were ancient spirits of great wisdom, and that some of their wisdom was going to be imparted to her. She was told by Marika that she would understand it all, understand the universe, the meaning of everything.

The cave was beyond imagining, made entirely of crystal rock formations and giant stalactites which glittered in the white light, sent out hundreds of thousands of prisms of coloured light, ranging from pale yellow to pink and blue.

Amy was momentarily blinded by the clarity of light in the crystal cave, and she blinked several times.

A moment later she saw more clearly than she had ever seen before. She saw her past life, saw herself, and she understood at once why she had failed in her earthly life. It was because of her negative approach, her apathy; and she was made to understand that she had wasted much, had thrown away the special gifts she had been given. The two women spirits explained this, and Amy felt contrite and sorry.

Then she saw Jake. She saw him at this very moment

in time, as if he were right here with her. But he was not. He was in a room somewhere, and he was with a woman, a woman he cared about. A woman he loved. Deeply loved. She recognized the fulfilment and warmth between them. Instantly Amy understood his life. She saw him in the past, in the present, in the future. His whole life was there for her to view, as if she were seeing it on film.

Now Marika was conveying something, saying that she must leave, must move on, but Amy did not want to go. She fought going. She wanted to stay here. Suddenly she was spinning out of the cave, pushed along by Marika.

Marika was urging her in a gentle way to go back to the tunnel. She did not want to and she fought it. She yearned to stay here in this paradise where there was only peace and happiness and unconditional love. But Marika would not permit it. She said she must return.

Amy was hurtling down the tunnel, moving through the darkness, leaving that shimmering dimension behind, leaving the light.

She felt a sudden push and there she was back on an earthly plane, floating again above her mother's wrecked car with their bodies trapped within.

Amy saw the truck-driver and the other drivers and state troopers still hovering near the car. And then an ambulance slowed to a stop. She continued to watch as her mother was removed from the car, and then her own body was lifted out and put on a stretcher.

With a sudden, awful jolt Amy went back into her body.

Eventually she opened her eyes. And then she

closed them again. She felt so tired, so exhausted. There was a pain in her head, a terrible pain as if someone had been hammering on her forehead. She fell into unconsciousness immediately.

Amy's aunt, Violet Parkinson and her daughter Mavis rarely, if ever, left Amy's side at the New Milford Hospital. Jake had to come and go because he had to attend to his business, had to work, but he was genuinely concerned about her, apprehensive about her reaction when she finally regained consciousness to learn that her mother had been killed in the terrible car crash.

Jake was also worried about Amy's own injuries. She was badly cut and bruised, and whilst the doctors believed she had no internal injuries, she *was* in a coma.

Now, on the third evening after the accident, Jake sat by the bed in the hospital, holding Amy's hand. They were alone for the time being. He had sent Mavis and Aunt Violet downstairs to have coffee and sandwiches, since they had apparently been sitting with Amy throughout the day.

His thoughts drifted for a while. He worked out some complicated wiring systems for Havers Hill in his head, and thought for a moment or two about Maggie, and then he looked up, startled, when Amy said: 'I'm thirsty.'

Immediately bringing his attention to her, he exclaimed, 'Amy, honey! Thank God! You're awake!'

'I've been in another place, Jake,' she began in a whispery voice. 'I want to tell you about it.'

He nodded. 'I'll say you have, Amy. Unconscious

for three days. Did you say you were thirsty? Let me get you some water.'

'Jake!'

'Yes, Amy?'

'My mother's dead.'

He was so startled he gaped at her, and for a moment he was unable to say a word.

'Don't tell me she isn't, trying to protect me, because I know she's dead.'

Jake, who had stood up, now bent closer to her, gave her a puzzled look. 'Let me go and fetch the water, and tell the doctor you've regained consciousness, honey.'

'I died too, Jake, but I came back. That's how I know my mother's dead. I saw her spirit with my father's spirit.'

Sitting down on the chair again, he asked gently, 'Where, Amy?'

'In Paradise, Jake. It's such a beautiful place. Full of light. A place you'd like, you've always been fascinated by light.'

Jake was speechless. He simply sat there holding her hand, not knowing what to say, truly startled by her words.

Amy sighed lightly. 'My mother's safe there. And she's happy now. She's with my father. She always missed him, you know.'

'Yes,' he answered, still at a loss. He wondered whether it was the drugs talking. Certainly the doctors had given her a number of injections, although he was not sure what these were. She was so calm, so in control, and this was mind-boggling to him. He had known Amy most of his life, and he would never have expected her to act like this after her mother's death. They had always been close, and why Amy wasn't hysterical he would never know. Yes, perhaps it was the drugs talking when she had said, a moment ago, that she had just died herself but had come back.

As if reading his mind, Amy remarked quietly, 'I did die, Jake. Believe me.'

He stared at her, a small frown knotting his brow.

Amy sighed. 'I'm tired. I want to go to sleep.'

'I'll get the doctor, Amy.' He extracted his hand from hers, and rose, moved to the door. 'I'll bring the nurse so that she can give you a drink of water.'

'Thanks, Jake.'

He nodded and left the room.

'It was the weirdest thing, Maggie,' Jake said quietly, looking across at her intently. 'When Amy finally came out of her coma tonight she told me her mother was dead. She wasn't hysterical like I thought she would be, but calm. In control.'

Jake shook his head, took a swallow of his beer. 'She also said something else that was strange.' He hesitated.

'What was that?' Maggie asked.

'She said her mother was with her father. In another place. A place she'd been to . . . she called it Paradise. I thought about her words all the way here from the hospital. How did Amy *know* her mother had died in the crash, Maggie? She's been unconscious since it happened.' He exhaled. 'That's what mystifies me.'

Maggie sat back in her chair and regarded him for a long moment, then she said, 'Maybe Amy knew her mother had died because she did see her in another place, just as she claims.'

'I'm not following you,' he answered, giving her an odd look.

'It's possible that Amy had an NDE.'

'What's an NDE?' Jake asked, lifting a brow.

'Near-Death Experience. There's been a lot written about them in the last few years. Doctor Elisabeth Kubler-Ross, the social scientist, who used to practise in Chicago, wrote an article on the terminally ill during her tenure at Billings Hospital at the University of Chicago. This eventually became the basis for her book, *On Death and Dying*, which I found fascinating. She wrote a number of other books, and appears to believe in Near-Death Experiences. As do many people actually, Jake. And doctors as well. Doctor Raymond Moody did the first anecdotal study of the phenomenon. Another expert is Doctor Melvin Morse who has also written several books about Near-Death Experiences.'

'So you're saying that Amy told me the truth?'

'Very possibly . . . most probably, actually.'

'How do you explain an NDE, Maggie?'

'I don't know, I don't think I can . . . because I don't really know enough, Jake,' Maggie murmured. 'There are a few good books available, as I just mentioned. Perhaps you should read one.' Leaning forward slightly, pinning him with her eyes, Maggie went on, 'Did Amy describe this place she went to?'

'No. She just said it was very beautiful.'

'Did she mention anything about light?'

'Well, yes, she did. How did you know that?'

'Because light, very bright light, always figures in

Near-Death Experiences. People feel as if they are embraced by the light. Some even think they are transformed by it.'

'Amy did say it was a place I'd like because it was full of light.'

'Anything else?'

'No, I don't think so.'

'And when exactly did she tell you this?'

'The moment she woke up – when she first came out of the coma.'

'Then perhaps she did have a Near-Death Experience. She certainly didn't have enough time to invent such a thing, invent that kind of story. Anyway, deep unconsciousness, or coma, is supposed to wipe the slate clean, wipe the mind clean,' Maggie pointed out.

'Okay, so let's say Amy did have an NDE, what exactly does that mean? To her?'

'It's an experience that she's not likely to forget, for one thing. Apparently people who have them never do, the experience stays with them always, for the rest of their lives. Of course they are as baffled by them as everyone else, and they generally look for meanings, special meanings behind them. An NDE does make people change . . . that brush with death and a glimpse of the afterlife does have an effect.'

'You seem to know a lot about Near-Death Experiences, Maggie,' Jake murmured, eyeing her speculatively.

'Well, I haven't had one myself, but I have talked with several people who have. I did quite a lot of charity work when I lived in Chicago, and I worked at a hospice for terminally ill people several afternoons a week for over four years. That's when I first heard about NDEs. People recounted their experiences to me, and the thing is, they drew such enormous comfort from them.'

'So you do believe there is such a thing then?'

'I guess so, Jake. I don't *disbelieve.* I'm not that arrogant. One would be a fool to dismiss these things out of hand. How can anyone debunk Near-Death Experiences? Or life after death? Or even the idea of reincarnation, for instance? None of us knows anything. Not really. There are far too many unexplained things in this world. I'd be the last person to say that the paranormal doesn't exist. Or couldn't happen. I've got an open mind.'

'Amy doesn't read a lot,' Jake volunteered. 'So I'm sure she doesn't know anything at all about Near-Death Experiences from books, Maggie.'

She nodded. 'There has been quite a lot on television about them, over the past few years, but I'm quite positive Amy did have some sort of experience. I don't think she's inventing this, not for one moment.'

'Why do you say that?'

'From what you've told me about her, Jake, Amy doesn't have the imagination to invent such a thing.'

'You're correct there,' he agreed. Jake leaned back in the chair, stifling a yawn.

Maggie exclaimed, 'Oh Jake, you're so tired after your vigil at the hospital. I think you'd better go to bed. You need your rest, you've got to be up so early tomorrow. We've got the meeting at the farm.'

He nodded. 'I am pretty bushed. But thank God we've finally finished the last design plans for the farm. Lately they seem to have been endless.'

She laughed. 'Only too true. But isn't Havers Hill now looking perfectly wonderful?'

'It sure is, thanks to you, Maggie of mine.'

CHAPTER 14

It was a golden, shimmering October day. The foliage had already changed, and the trees were a mass of copper and gold, russet and pink, brilliant in the bright sunshine.

Amy feasted her eyes on the landscape at the back of Jake's little house on Route 341, thinking how magnificent everything looked. Such breathtaking colours, such fire in the trees. And the sky was a perfect blue, without a single cloud. It was a mild day, mild enough for her to sit here without a jacket, which she had shed earlier when she and Jake were having lunch.

She rested her head against the chair and closed her eyes, enjoying the warmth of the sun on her face. She felt relaxed, at peace.

Earlier in the week Jake had asked her what he

could do to make her feel better, and she had said she wanted to have a picnic out in the country. It had been his idea to bring her here to his new house, and she was glad he had. It was nice to see where he lived, now that they were no longer together. Also, she liked his yard with its beautiful trees, pretty garden and the pastures beyond. He had even shown her around his studio-workshop in the red barn, which had pleased her.

Hearing his footsteps on the path, Amy opened her eyes and sat up.

Jake said, 'Here we are, honey. Ice cream and apple pie, just as you requested.'

Amy smiled at him. 'You're spoiling me. And I'm enjoying every minute of it.'

He placed the tray on her lap. 'Tea or coffee later?'

'Tea, please, and thanks for this.' She glanced down at the ice cream. 'Oh Jake, you remembered how much I love pistachio and raspberry mixed together.'

Jake nodded and grinned, pleased that she was happy. She never complained, but he knew she was frequently in pain these days. If bringing her here and having a picnic with her helped to alleviate her suffering then he was all for it.

'Be back in a minute, honey,' he said, and strode down the path to the kitchen. 'And don't wait for me. I'm only having coffee.'

Amy ate some of the ice cream, enjoying it, but she couldn't finish it all. Her appetite was poor, and she was only able to take a few bites of the apple pie. She leaned back in the chair again, waiting for Jake to return to the garden.

Strains of music suddenly filled the air and she

smiled to herself, knowing that he had somehow managed to wire the garden and put speakers outside. Kiri Te Kanawa singing 'Vissi d'arte' filled the air, her magnificent voice soaring into the sky.

'Where's the music coming from, Jake?' Amy asked when he was back, standing over her, offering her the cup of tea.

'The singing rocks, just over there in the flower beds,' he explained.

She laughed in delight and he laughed also. Then he said, 'Don't you want any more dessert, Amy?'

'No, thanks, Jake, but what I ate was delicious.'

He took the plate away, and then sat down next to her with his mug of coffee. 'I hope you've enjoyed the picnic, being out in the country,' he murmured, glancing at her.

'I have, and it was nice of you to give up your one free day. I know how precious Sundays are to you.'

'I've enjoyed it too, Amy. You know I'll do anything to help, to make you feel better.'

Turning slightly in the chair, Amy focused her eyes on him. She loved him very much. He was the only man she had ever loved . . . since she was twelve years old. He had always been so special to her; he had made *her* feel special. And he had been so kind. Always. Amy had considered herself the luckiest of women to have him, to be his wife; her friends had envied her. But she knew they were focusing on his good looks. Only she really knew what a truly nice person he was.

Jake said, 'You're staring at me, Amy. What's wrong? Do I have dirt on my face?'

She shook her head. 'I was just thinking how long we've known each other.' She paused, cleared her throat and then went on carefully, 'Mavis took me to see the lawyer on Friday, Jake, and I – '

'But Amy, you don't have to worry about the divorce right now. Just get yourself better first.'

'I didn't go to see him about the divorce. A divorce is not necessary.'

He sat looking at her, his expression unchanging. He was not sure how to answer her.

She said, 'I'm dying, Jake. I'm not going to see the end of the year . . . I know that.'

'But Amy, the doctor said you were making good progress!' he cut in swiftly.

Amy shook her head. 'He might think so, but *I* know I'm not. Anyway, I went to see the lawyer because I wanted to make a will. It's necessary now that my mother's dead. She left me her house in New Milford, you know, and her furniture and everything else she owned. And a little money. So, I made a will and I've left everything to you.'

Jake stared at her speechlessly. Then he said, 'But what about Aunt Violet and Mavis? They're your next of kin.'

'No, they're not. You are, Jake Cantrell. You're my husband. We're still married, even though we might not be living together. And as your wife I am leaving you all my worldly possessions. Except for a few items for Aunt Violet and Mavis, you know – some bits of my mother's jewellery, china, that kind of thing. I want you to have everything else.'

'I don't know what to say,' he began and stopped abruptly, staring at her.

Amy gave him a small smile. 'You don't have to say anything, Jake.'

'If that's the way you want it, then thank you, Amy,' he murmured, not knowing what else he could say.

'There's something I want to say . . . I want to apologize to you, Jake, tell you how sorry I am that I was a bad wife.'

'Amy, for God's sake, you weren't a bad wife!' he cried. 'You did the best you could, always. I know that.'

'My best wasn't good enough. Not for you, Jake. I was always so negative and apathetic, and I never helped you when you were trying to make a better life for us. I did everything wrong, and I'm truly sorry.'

He stared at her silently, again at a loss for words.

Amy said, 'I really did die the night of the crash. I did leave my body. My soul did, I mean. Or my spirit, if you prefer to call it that. I went to another plane, to another dimension. And I saw my father. Then my mother joined him, and that's how I knew she was dead. There was an old soul there looking after me, and she took me into a crystal cave of wisdom. There were two wise women spirits, and they told me things. And they showed me how wrong I'd been. I saw my whole life, Jake; I saw my past and I saw your past.'

Jake was silent.

Amy said, 'I can't change anything in my life now because I have no time to do so. I have become the person I should have always been, and I must try to make amends.' Amy leaned back in the chair and focused her eyes on Jake. 'You're sceptical, aren't you? I mean about my dying and coming back.'

'No, as a matter of fact, I'm not,' he replied. 'I do

know there are other people who have had similar experiences, and a number of books have been written about them.'

'I didn't know that, although I didn't think it could have happened only to me.'

'What happened to you is called a Near-Death Experience, Amy.'

Amy nodded then closed her eyes. After a moment she opened them. Leaning forward, she fixed them on Jake.

He blinked. They seemed brighter, more full of life than he'd ever seen them, and the smile spreading itself across her face was one of pure radiance.

Amy said, 'I not only saw my past, and your past, Jake. I also saw your future. I didn't see mine because I don't have one. Not on this plane at least.'

'You saw my future,' he repeated.

'Yes, I did. There's a woman in your life, Jake, and you love her very much. She is older than you, but that is of no consequence. You and she are meant to be together. You were always meant to be together, and your whole life has been a journey towards her. As hers has been a journey towards you. Once you were souls who were joined together as one, and then you were split asunder. Your whole lives have been spent trying to get back to each other. When you found each other you became whole. Never doubt her in any way.'

Jake opened his mouth but no words came out.

She said, 'This woman, your soulmate, is carrying your child. She's five months pregnant. The baby is due in February. It's a boy, Jake, you're going to have the son you always wanted. The future is good for you. You will be prosperous; you were always right to start your own business. It will go well, and this woman, who is devoted to you and will be your wife, will also be your partner in your business. You are going to have all the things you always wanted, Jake, and somehow never managed to get with me. But you must not let your success change you, or turn your head. You're such a good person. You must cling to your values always.'

'Amy, I don't know what to say. It's true, I did meet someone. In April. I never mentioned her to you because I didn't want to hurt your feelings –'

'Don't say any more; it's not necessary. I am the one who hurt you. This was shown to me, and I was sent back in order to put things right with you and to help you with your future.'

'Help me how?'

'To show you the way, to set you on the right path. You have already started out on it with your soulmate. She is strong, wise, and you must always listen to her.' Amy nodded. 'You must take her advice. And you must also follow all of your instincts. You are usually right. Trust yourself more.'

'I don't know what to say,' Jake began and stopped. Amy was looking at him intently and he realized how lovely she was. It seemed to him that at this moment she had undergone a startling transformation. Her face was radiant, her pale blue eyes bright and sparkling, and even the curly blonde wig she was wearing looked suddenly right on her.

'Now it's my turn to say you're staring at me,' Amy exclaimed.

'I was thinking how beautiful you looked.'

'I am. *Inside.* I want you to promise me something, Jake.'

'Yes, Amy, I will. Tell me what it is.'

'I want you to promise me you'll get married immediately after I die. I don't want you to have any mourning period. That would be false anyway, since we've been separated for almost two years.' She paused and gave him a very direct look. 'Longer, if you think of the years we lived together without communicating. Do you promise?'

Jake nodded.

Amy went on, 'I think I'll die soon, Jake.'

'Oh Amy . . .'

'There's something else I need to say to you and it's this: love is the most important thing in the whole world.'

'I know you're right,' Jake responded.

Amy smiled her radiant smile and said softly, 'I'm not afraid to die. Not anymore, Jake. You see, I know there is life after death. Not life as we know it here, but life on another plane. I will be glad to shed my body, then my spirit will be free at last . . .'

CHAPTER 15

MAGGIE STOOD STARING out of the kitchen window, wondering what had happened to Jake. It was snowing hard, the tiny crystalline flakes sticking to the panes. She always worried about him in bad weather. The roads could be so treacherous.

Christmas traffic, she decided, that's what was holding him up. He had promised to be here by two, but perhaps he had been delayed at the Little Theatre in Kent. At Samantha's request he had gone up there to look at one of the lighting systems which had blown the night before. None of the stagehands knew how to fix it permanently. Since Jake had designed it, Samantha and Maggie knew he would be able to solve the problem.

Maggie's thoughts drifted to the play for a moment. *The Crucible* had opened in September and, much to everyone's surprise and delight, it was still running. It was a sell-out at weekends; Samantha was in her element as the producer, director and owner of the theatre.

Turning away from the window, Maggie walked across the room, her steps slower these days. She was seven months into her pregnancy. The baby, a boy, was due in two months and she couldn't wait to deliver. The baby was big and she was heavy; and every day she seemed to grow slower and slower.

Sitting down at the kitchen table, she looked at her list of gifts. She had finished almost all of her Christmas shopping, having started it earlier in the year. Today was Saturday the sixteenth of December, and anything else she still needed Jake would have to buy. Maggie knew she did not have enough energy to struggle through the stores, the big stores at any rate.

At least she wouldn't have to do much cooking. She and Jake were going to spend Christmas Day with Samantha. That was the big day, of course; on Christmas Eve Samantha was coming to them along with some of the cast and other members of the theatrical group. Weeks ago Maggie had decided to make the supper a cold buffet, so much simpler for her to handle.

Rising, Maggie lumbered into the small sitting room and walked over to the tree. Jake and she had decorated it slowly, gradually, over the past two weeks, mostly because he was so busy with business. And she was unwieldy, not very much help to him.

Maggie smiled inwardly and put her hands on her stomach. The baby was her treasure. Hers and Jake's. He couldn't wait for the child to be born, and was forever pampering her, treating her like a piece of crystal.

Stepping up to the tree, she eyed it critically, knowing that certain branches were still rather bare. Perhaps today they would have time to stop at The Silo to buy some more gold and silver icicles, gold angels and fruits. She and Jake had created a gold and silver tree, with touches of red and blue here and there; and it was eyecatching, she thought.

Maggie walked slowly back to the kitchen and stood at the window again, waiting for him, wishing he would get home. After a while, she moved away, went to the radio and turned it on.

'Hark! the herald-angels sing, Glory to the new born king. Peace on earth and mercy mild . . .' a female voice was singing on the Christmas record the station was playing.

Maggie was immediately distracted. She heard the pick-up coming into the yard and stood looking at the door expectantly, waiting for him.

As always, she felt the impact of him in the pit of her stomach whenever she saw him, even after a very short absence. What it was to be so in love. Sometimes she worried that she loved him far too much.

'Hi, sweetheart,' Jake said, striding over to her, tracking snow across her clean floor.

But Maggie did not care. 'Hello, darling,' she answered, beaming at him. 'I was beginning to worry, wonder what was taking so long.'

'That stupid system I invented!' he exclaimed, brought her into his arms and kissed her cheek.

'Oh Jake, your face is cold, and your hands. Why didn't you put on your gloves and a scarf?'

He grinned at her boyishly. 'Oh stop worrying about me. I'm fine. Anyway, the system's okay for tonight and tomorrow. But I think I'll have to rig up something else next week. Samantha's going to kill me if I don't get it perfect, and this one's not.'

'Do you want a cup of coffee?'

Jake shook his head. 'I think we'd better get going. It's snowing hard, and the snow's settling. It's going to take us a good half hour to New Milford. Do you have the plant for Amy?'

'It's over there on the counter top.'

Jake walked over and looked at it. 'You've made it look pretty with the blue and silver bow, Maggie.'

She nodded. 'Shall we go, Jake?'

'Yes. Let me get your coat.'

The snow had stopped falling by the time they arrived in New Milford, and the sun was shining in the brilliantly blue sky.

Maggie held onto Jake's arm tightly as they walked down the path. There was a light covering of snow on the paving stones, and she was afraid she might slip.

'Here we are,' Jake said a few seconds later. 'Now, just let me undo this.' As he spoke he pulled the wrapping paper off the plant and shoved it in his pocket. Bending down, he placed the miniature evergreen on the new grave.

Straightening, he turned to Maggie and put his arm around her. 'I'm glad we came,' he murmured. 'I gave her my word we would. "Come and visit my grave as soon as you can after you're married," she said and then she made me promise.'

'She's at peace now,' Maggie said. 'Out of her pain and suffering.'

Jake nodded. 'Her soul is free. She wasn't a bit afraid to die in the end.'

Maggie pulled off her gloves. Leaning over the grave, she straightened the blue and silver bow. Her broad gold wedding ring gleamed brightly in the afternoon sunlight. 'That's because Amy knew where she was going,' Maggie murmured.

Jake merely nodded and put his arm around his wife protectively. Together they stood in silence at the grave for a few moments, lost in their own thoughts. Jake was thinking of Amy, who had died ten days ago. He had known her most of his life, and she had been his high-school sweetheart. Somehow everything had gone awry with them. Still, in the end, they had remained friends. He was glad of that, and happy that he had been able to give her comfort in the end, had helped her through her illness. He had been with her when she died, and her last words had been for him. 'Bless you, Jake,' she had said. 'And your soulmate and the baby.'

A week after her death he and Maggie had married, fulfilling Amy's wish that they do so immediately. He had wanted it that way himself, and he knew that Maggie had too. The wedding had been at Samantha's house in Washington; Sam had insisted. She had also arranged for a local judge, who was a friend of her family, to perform the short ceremony. She and Alice Ferrier, the costume designer from the drama group, had been the witnesses.

Jake knew he would never forget last Saturday morning. Their wedding day. Maggie had looked so beautiful and full of life. She had worn a blue wool maternity dress that reflected the colour of her eyes but did little to conceal the fact that she was seven months pregnant. Neither of them cared. Maggie's eyes had been full of tears when the judge pronounced them husband and wife, as his had been. They had both been very emotional that morning, and for days afterwards.

Sam had given a small lunch and members of the cast of *The Crucible* had come in to toast them and wish them well before going off to the Little Theatre in Kent. It had been the most special day of his life.

Jake said, 'I think we'd better go, Maggie. It's starting to snow again.'

Together the two of them walked along the path that led to the gate of the cemetery. At one moment Maggie glanced up at the sky, and high above them she saw the arc of a rainbow. It was indistinct but it was there. She blinked in the bright sunlight and looked away. When she turned her eyes to the sky again the rainbow had disappeared.

She held Jake's arm as they continued on down the path, and at one moment she said quietly, 'The cycle of life is endless, and it never changes.'

'What do you mean?' he asked, glancing down at her, frowning.

'There has been a death . . . and soon there will be a birth. That's the way it is. *Always*. One soul has gone to her rest, a new soul is about to be born in a few months.'

Jake nodded and was silent as they made their way out of the cemetery and back to the Jeep. Once he had helped Maggie in and settled himself in the driver's seat, he leaned in to her and kissed her cheek. 'I love you, Maggie of mine,' he said. Looking at her huge stomach he placed his hand on it and added, 'And I love our baby. He's going to be born well blessed.'

'Oh I know that,' Maggie said, smiling into his eyes. 'Come on, darling, it's time to go home.'

Home, Jake thought, as he put the key in the ignition and turned it. *Home.*

Where You Belong

Barbara Taylor Bradford

With all the glamour, drama and passion which have made Barbara Taylor Bradford an international bestseller, *Where You Belong* is the captivating story of a young woman finding herself and her place in life, in love, and in the world.

Valentine Denning is a courageous photojournalist on the frontlines in Kosovo: her colleagues, British Tony Hampton and American Jake Newburg, are her comrades-in-arms, men whom she loves and trusts. One is her best friend; one her lover. In a nightmarish ambush all three are shot, Tony fatally, and for Val an even worse nightmare begins.

For there are memories and lies – lies which force Val to find herself again by leaving her past life of heartbreaking war-danger for what seems like the gentler world of celebrity-shoots: but this too brings danger – a famous artist whose reputation as a playboy does not steel against a powerful attraction. Valentine's sense of searching for something leads her to retrace paths which she thought she had left behind.

Barbara Taylor Bradford's new novel captures a woman's search for strength, and her ability to find her way to where she belongs – in life, in love, and within herself.

ISBN: 0 00 225695 9
Publication date: 15 May 2000

The Women in his Life
Barbara Taylor Bradford

At the centre of this stunning novel stands Maximilian West, billionaire tycoon, corporate raider extraordinaire and a man of almost mythical power, glamour and charm. Yet, while Maximilian appears to have everything, in reality he is riven with internal conflict – and torn apart by personal doubts.

Many women have loved Maxim – and many strive to reach his fortress heart: Anastasia, his first wife; Camilla, the beautiful English actress; Adriana, the competitive American career woman; and Blair, the mistress who schemes to become his wife. But only one woman holds the key that will unlock Maximilian's secret – and set his soul free . . .

Sweeping through war-torn Berlin, through the heady atmosphere of Paris, Madrid and Tangier, to contemporary London and New York, *The Women in his Life* is a superb, compelling novel and ranks triumphant alongside Barbara Taylor Bradford's other phenomenal international bestsellers.

'Another surefire bestseller from an ace storyteller' *Annabel*

'Legions of readers will be satisfied by the romantic fortunes of the cultured, wealthy and powerful people she evokes'
Publishers Weekly

ISBN 0 586 07035 4

Everything to Gain

Barbara Taylor Bradford

Mallory Keswick is a woman with the world at her feet. Then out of the blue, that world is shattered by violent tragedy and she loses all that she holds dear.

Torn by grief, Mal knows that she must rebuild her life. She flees to a village on the Yorkshire moors where she learns to draw on the deepest reserves of her spirit, and to look life in the eye once more.

Returning to Connecticut, Mal opens a café and shop selling gourmet food and kitchenware and turns it into a highly successful venture. But there remains in her life an aching void, a grief that no individual, nor her new-found business acumen, can assuage. Then she meets Richard Markson, and once more, Mal's life has come to a crossroads. It is he who shows her that she has everything to gain – but only if she has the courage to take it.

Totally absorbing and heartrendingly real, *Everything to Gain* lays bare Mallory's life to expose powerful feelings that are startlingly familiar, because they are our own.

'Heart-rending stuff . . . *Everything to Gain* is truly uplifting' *Today*

ISBN: 0 586 21740 1

Dangerous to Know

Barbara Taylor Bradford

Sebastian, the fifty-six-year-old patriarch of the Locke clan, is handsome, charismatic, a man of immense charm and intelligence. He heads up the philanthropic Locke Foundation, funded by the vast family fortune built by his forefathers. Committed to relieving the suffering of those in genuine need, Locke travels the globe, personally giving away millions a year to the poor, the sick, and the victims of natural disasters and wars. He is seen as a beacon of light in today's darkly violent world. That is why the police are so baffled when Sebastian is found dead in mysterious circumstances. Has he been murdered, and if so who would want to kill the world's greatest philanthropist? Could such an upstanding man have enemies?

Vivienne Trent, an American journalist, met Locke as a child, married him, divorced him, but stayed close to him. Aware that there was another side to this enigmatic man, she sets out to find the truth about his death and about Locke himself.

'Few novelists are as consummate as Barbara Taylor Bradford at keeping the reader turning the page. She is one of the world's best at spinning yarns.' *Guardian*

ISBN: 0 586 21739 8

Her Own Rules

Barbara Taylor Bradford

Meredith Stratton is forty-four and a successful business-woman.

The owner of six international inns, she is about to celebrate her only daughter's engagement. At this seemingly happy time in her life, Meredith begins to suffer from a strange illness that baffles everyone. Her doctor cannot find a cause for her debilitating symptoms, and, desperate for answers, she seeks the help of a psychiatrist. Through therapy, Meredith peels back the layers of her life to discover the truth behind her most careful creation – herself.

Secrets, survival, redemption and love abound in this compelling story of a woman who uncovers the key to her tormented past, and finds the courage to live by her own rules.

'Barbara Taylor Bradford is a wonderful storyteller who can convey the power of love. The warmth and compassion of her tale brought tears to my jaded old eyes.'

Sunday Express

ISBN: 0 586 21741 X